The Wreck of the Cassandra

SAVED from catastrophe at sea, nine people of different backgrounds are cast ashore on a large and apparently savage island somewhere between Hong Kong and Australia. There, after an orderly and almost idyllic beginning to the co-operative existence that their situation requires, they unexpectedly set about creating their own private catastrophes. What helps to precipitate them all towards chaos is their growing awareness that they are surrounded by unknown forces either actively inimical to their fates or, like nature, sinisterly indifferent to them.

This is an absorbing story of human beings who, in a situation of extremity and danger, are forced to recognise not only their own natures but also the nature of the human condition.

Frederic Prokosch

The Wreck of the Cassandra

W. H. ALLEN
LONDON
1966

© Farrar, Straus and Giroux, Inc.

1966

Printed in Great Britain by photolithography
Unwin Brothers Ltd., Woking and London
for the publishers
W. H. Allen and Company,
Essex Street, London W.C.2
Bound by Webb, Son & Co., Ltd., London E.C.1

Contents

Part 1   *The City*   3

Part 2   *The Ship*   19

Part 3   *The Beach*   57

Part 4   *The Jungle*   115

Part 5   *The Village*   151

Part 6   *The Rocks*   183

Part 7   *The Flames*   213

Part 8   *The Gods*   243

PART I
The City

One day in late summer a blond young woman in a sky-blue smock strode briskly into the lounge of the Repulse Bay Hotel. She was carrying a butterfly net and a flat, misty killing jar; she wore dusty white sneakers and a floppy straw hat. She placed the jar on a tea table and dropped the net on a chair; wiped her brow, glanced about, and stepped cautiously out on the terrace, where a dark, hawk-eyed woman in a diamond necklace sat under an umbrella.

She leaned forward somewhat awkwardly and said to the woman with the necklace, "Do forgive me for bothering you. Are you Mrs. Domingo, by any chance?"

The woman looked up. A dreamlike glaze passed over her eyes. She raised her brows, hesitated a moment, and said hoarsely: "I am Mrs. Domingo."

"I thought so. How pleasant. I'm Miss Eccles. Penelope Eccles. I'm a friend of Mrs. Zafirides. She told me you were staying here."

"Mrs. Zafirides. Oh, of course. That's the girl I was playing bridge with. An extremely clever woman. Has a collection of Chinese vases."

"It was purely by instinct that I sensed you were Mrs. Domingo. I saw you on the terrace and I said to myself, 'It's Mrs. Domingo.' "

"Your instinct didn't betray you. You look warm. Been playing tennis?"

"I've been up by the reservoir. Looking for butterflies," said Miss Eccles rather guiltily.

"Butterflies. I see. What a charming hobby. Do sit down, please, Miss Eccles. Let me order you a drink. You must be weary, chasing these insects." Mrs. Domingo waved to a gold-braided boy who was emptying the ash trays, and said, "What will you have, dear? This is a planter's punch I'm drinking. Perfectly vile. These poor little Chinks haven't the foggiest idea. All the same, I'm having another. Plenty of ice this time, waiter, chopped very fine, and much less sugar. And what about you, Miss Eccles?"

"Just some tea, I think, with lemon."

"In this heat? How heroic of you. Make it iced tea, at any rate."

"Excellent idea," said Miss Eccles. "You are sailing on the *Cassandra*, aren't you?"

Mrs. Domingo said stonily, "Perfectly true. I am sailing on the *Cassandra*."

"So am I. That's how Lola Zafirides happened to speak of you. She said, 'Mrs. Domingo, a friend of mine and a most unusual woman, is also sailing on the *Cassandra*. You must make a point of looking her up.'"

"Well, you've made a point of it, I see. God knows what possessed me. It was Hugo, my secretary, it was dear little Hugo who persuaded me. Australia is the last place on earth that I yearn to investigate, but having exhausted the other continents, I let myself be coaxed into Australia. I am not interested in kangaroos but I hear that the Australians are full of vigor. May I ask what on earth you are planning to do there, Miss Eccles?"

"There are some rather amazing specimens in Australia," said Miss Eccles.

"Male or female?" said Mrs. Domingo, narrowing her eyes a little.

Miss Eccles smiled pallidly. "Merely insects, Mrs. Domingo. It's a shocking thing to say but I much prefer them to people."

The heat hung in a honey-colored haze over the tennis

court. Three young bathers in white kimonos were returning
from the beach. A skeletal Chinese in khaki shorts was sprinkling water on the hydrangeas and in the distance a tiny junk
was floating on the sea, black and motionless.

Mrs. Domingo stroked her neck and lowered her voice
confidentially. Her llamalike eyes grew darkly intimate and
slightly predatory. "It's not shocking. Not in the least. I am
totally in sympathy with you, Miss Eccles. The older I grow
the more distressed I am by the spectacle of humanity. And
here in the East, on the edge of savagery as it were, this feeling
is accentuated. Oh, this city looks thoroughly safe, almost
absurdly so, in fact, with its neat little cricket greens and
nurses and perambulators. But one senses a gaping hollowness
beneath it all, like a crater. It is poised on the brink of the
void. That's my dominant impression. I don't wish to sound
grim, but after all it's a sense of nothingness which lies at the
root of all philosophy, isn't it, Miss Eccles? There is something
black and boglike, a smoldering decay, a desolation—forgive
these flowery phrases, but that's the Orient for you in a
nutshell. All this talk about inner serenity, all this Asiatic
poise and delicacy—well, it's nothing but a veil to hide the
horror underneath. Some of these dewy-eyed idiots see a
Utopia lurking in the future, but I tell you, Miss Eccles, I see
nothing but misery and degradation."

"The climate is rather trying, I'll admit," said Miss
Eccles.

"It is more than the climate. It is spiritual," said Mrs.
Domingo.

"One keeps hoping. It's only human to keep on hoping,"
said Miss Eccles.

"The forces at work are anything but human," said Mrs.
Domingo.

Miss Eccles glanced at her wrist watch. "Goodness me.

Quarter past six." She smiled wanly at Mrs. Domingo. "You'll excuse me? I'll have to paper my specimens."

Mrs. Domingo nodded her head with a playful glitter in her eyes, and Miss Eccles wandered back into the lounge and picked up her net. She strolled across the hall, past the red-haired girl at the reception desk, and came to a halt in front of the showcase next to the elevator. A row of jade animals stood on the shelf, brightly illuminated: a lion, a dragon, and a fierce-eyed little parakeet.

A man in a shantung suit, with a scar in his cheek, stepped out of the elevator and paused for a moment beside the showcase. He glanced casually at Miss Eccles with a look of amusement, then strode quickly across the hall and walked out through the porte-cochere. Miss Eccles lowered her eyes and sighed rather wistfully. Then she gripped her net firmly and stepped quickly into the elevator.

2

"Your backhand is developing beautifully," said the man, "but your service is feeble. Relax, Laura, relax! You stiffen up like an Egyptian mummy."

"There are times," said the woman, "when I almost feel like a mummy."

"Taking it easy, that's what counts. A bit more confidence would do wonders for you."

"I am touched by your solicitude for my moral welfare, my dear Tony."

They picked up the tennis balls and dropped them in a sack and then sauntered across the lawn toward the bar at the end of the terrace. The man was a powerful blond with thinning hair and a thickening waist and an amiable, earnest, slightly embryolike face. The woman was delicate and bony, with wispy bangs and huge brown eyes which wavered between curiosity, accusation, and cunning.

They stepped into the bar and sat down in the leather armchairs.

"What will you have, dear?" said the man.

"Scotch and soda," said the woman.

"You look bushed. It was pretty silly to play in this heat, I guess," said the man.

"Oh, I'm wiry," said the woman. "I am used to the tropics. I can stand it."

The man turned his head and stared intently at one of the sporting prints.

"Something funny about this place."

"Naturally, dear. It's an anachronism."

"Everybody's waiting for something or other, God knows what. That's my feeling."

"Not surprising, with that slitty-eyed colossus across the water."

"Tell me, Laura. Why has this whole goddamn trip been such a disaster? Dysentery in Damascus, rain in Ispahan, cheating in Delhi, insults in Singapore. It's almost like a conspiracy. They just don't like us, these Asiatics."

"There's a streak of paranoia in your make-up, Tony Wagenseller. When your wrist watch was stolen in Hyderabad it was a personal effrontery."

"There you are, explaining it all in terms of my own deplorable complexes. I suppose those bedbugs in Cairo were just a case of dementia praecox. You're too clever, that's the trouble. You can't see the forest because of the trees. I kept hoping that India would humanize you, but no, you still keep analyzing, analyzing."

"I can't tell you how refreshed I feel by these lessons in humanity. Thank you, Tony. Very thoughtful of you. When I look at that big round face of yours I realize what I'm missing, along the line of human insight."

"Laura, for Christ's sake, let's stop squabbling. That scene in Bangkok was quite enough for me. Calm down. Get out your Leica. I hear there's a leper colony in the neighborhood. And when we get to the Solomons you can take some snapshots of the naked savages. There's still time for you to satisfy those proletarian sympathies of yours."

Laura glanced at the ceiling. "I keep wondering," she murmured.

"What about?" said Tony listlessly.

"The continent of Asia has disappointed you cruelly. Is there really much point in going on to Australia? For someone who thought that the Temple of Dawn was a piece of vulgar buffoonery, I just wonder whether those bushmen have much to offer, aesthetically speaking."

"Look," said Tony. He held his highball in the air and gazed at the terrace.

"Yes?" said Laura.

"Do you see that woman in the purple dress? With the diamond necklace?"

"I do indeed," said Laura.

"I've been watching her," said Tony. "There's something curious about that woman. I noticed it at lunchtime. She and her boyfriend, that Austrian gigolo, kept peering about suspiciously. Later on, out in the card room, I saw him writing in a little notebook. I don't wish to sound catty but I have my notions about that pair."

"What notions, precisely?"

"Please, Laura, don't be childish. It's common knowledge that this city is absolutely lousy with political agents."

"Oh, I see. That's Mata Hari out on the terrace, fondling her necklace."

"I am merely trying to stimulate your interest in humanity," said Tony.

"You'll have to think up something quainter than dear old espionage," said Laura. "Or even gigolos, I fear. There is nothing stimulating about gigolos."

"Well," said Tony, "let me make a suggestion. That woman with the necklace is a witch. You were piqued by the total absence of the supernatural in India, weren't you? I hate to think that your peregrinations through the length of Asia were in vain. Take my word for it, Laura. That woman in purple is an ogress."

"Poor old thing. Just a widow from Omaha looking for a bit of excitement."

"Be prosaic if you wish. I've caught a whiff of the caldron."

Laura put down her glass. "There. I think I'll do some packing."

"Excellent idea. Don't forget the Kafka. And that ivory elephant you found this morning."

After Laura had gone Tony kept sitting in the bar alone. He could see his face reflected in the oval mirror above the bar, and far behind him, like a brilliant cameo, the woman in purple out on the terrace. Nothing stirred; the barman had vanished; the gold-braided boy had returned to the lounge. The woman in purple sat by her table, arms folded, gazing at the sea.

As he stared at his face in the mirror he had a queer little feeling that it too, like everything else, had grown hollow, immobilized. Tony Wagenseller, like the half-breed barman, had mysteriously vanished. All that was left was this rather fatuous mask in the mirror: stalwart and sun-tanned, bloated with idealism, tinged with decay.

"God Almighty," he muttered, and crushed his cigarette in the ash tray.

3

A bald, stoutish man in dusty sandals and a green jacket paused in front of the shop window and gazed at the curios. The street was dark and narrow, filled with low wooden stalls. An old woman crouched over a brazier, stirring a thick reddish hash, and beside her two boys were plucking at the rice with their chopsticks. She glanced at the passing foreigner with a cold, indifferent scrutiny, sprinkled salt on the bubbling hash, and waved the flies from a pile of pancakes.

The man in the emerald jacket scratched his chin rather thoughtfully and stepped through the door into the shade of the antique shop. It was a ramshackle room filled with a chaos of dusty bric-a-brac. The shelves were lined with columns of cheap tourist chinaware—azure roosters and bright red dragons, squatting Buddhas and gesticulating goddesses. Rows of pots, bowls, and vases stood on a table near the door and in the corner stood two large painted jars filled with scrolls. A man in horn-rimmed glasses was showing some brightly colored plates to a tall, sinewy visitor in a white shantung suit.

"Do you happen to have some Lowestoft?" said the customer in a German accent.

"What we call export porcelain," said the man with the glasses. "Very rare. Much desirable. Imitations plenty. But not genuine. Have a fine Lowestoft ginger bowl. Ninety dollars. Want to see?"

He walked toward the table and picked up a small drum-shaped vessel which was decorated with a pattern of lions and unicorns.

The customer took the jar in his hands and looked at it scrupulously. He ran his finger slowly along the scar in his cheek.

"Rather high, ninety dollars."

"Cheap at price," said the owner hastily. "Also Lowestoft sugar bowl. Seventy dollars. Beautiful bargain."

As he rummaged among the bowls the customer reached into the ginger jar, extracted a ball of paper, and slipped it furtively into his pocket.

"Look. Lowestoft sugar bowl. Excellent for price," said the shopkeeper. He held out a small oval bowl which was painted with roses.

The customer glanced at it casually and murmured, "Delightful. Looks perfectly genuine. Do you take traveler's checks? Very good. I'll drop by in the morning."

He glanced with sudden curiosity at the man in the green jacket, wiped his brow with a silken handkerchief, hesitated for an instant, and left the shop.

The shopkeeper stared at the stout little man in the emerald jacket.

"Anything of interest to you, sir?"

"I'll just browse a bit," said the other.

"Elegant jades we have," purred the shopkeeper.

"Thanks. No jades, I think," said the other.

He looked rapidly through the door and smiled sheepishly at the shopkeeper. Then he sighed, patted his belly, and walked drowsily into the street again.

The man in the shantung suit was just vanishing around the corner. As he turned he rolled a yellowish scrap of paper into a ball and tossed it into the street, where it lit in an empty flowerpot.

The stout little man looked puzzled, then intrigued, and then rather furtive. He strolled past a bird stall, where the wicker cages were swarming with parakeets. At the corner of the street he glanced back with circumspection. Then he stooped and picked the small yellow ball out of the flowerpot.

He unrolled it and read: *Cavendish Bar. 7 o'clock.*

A mischievous gleam brightened his eyes for a moment. "Very curious," he murmured. And he waddled back toward the seething thoroughfare.

4

The man in the shantung suit was wandering slowly along the waterfront. He paused by a flower stand, chose a carnation, and tucked it in his jacket. He smiled at the sad-eyed flower girl and dropped a coin in her hand. He strolled on. He looked at the Botticelli prints in a bookseller's window and then at an enormous cobra curled in a jar in front of a chemist's shop. Finally he stopped in front of a café with a green-striped awning, glanced casually at his watch, and walked in through the open door.

The place was nearly empty. It was a dingy little room with a bar at one end and a wooden table on each side of it. Over the bar hung some frayed and faded photographs of film stars. A blue paisley curtain was hanging in front of the window.

Two young sailors were drinking at one of the tables. At the other sat an elderly man with a monocle.

The man in the shantung suit walked up to the table and said softly, "Herr Kleist, if I'm not mistaken?"

"Perfectly correct. You are Herr Grillparzer?"

"Exactly. I am charmed to meet you. I was rather apprehensive, to be quite frank about it. I waited for you yesterday at the Savoy Tearoom till half past seven."

"I must apologize, Herr Grillparzer. I was unavoidably delayed. A friend of mine from Tokyo arrived unexpectedly. I was forced to make use of Contact Twenty-seven, as you noticed. I am delighted you got the message. A gin and tonic, perhaps, Herr Grillparzer?"

"A whisky and soda, if I may. Yes, I was growing a little worried. I am sailing on the *Cassandra* tomorrow evening at five o'clock. I was afraid that I'd have to resort to Contact Thirty at the very last moment. Fortunately I don't. Rather a relief. How do you like it here, Herr Kleist?"

The man took off his monocle and slipped it into his pocket. He smiled somewhat puckishly. "I neither like it nor dislike it. I have always enjoyed traveling, even in my student days in Leipzig. I used to take trips down to Venice and Dubrovnik. The sea has always attracted me. It appeals to my sense of spaciousness. As a child I used to suffer from acute claustrophobia. It started when my Uncle Adelbert locked me in a closet when I stole some Lebkuchen. Ever since I have yearned for the bright, airy spaces of the world—the Saharan immensities, the steppes of Siberia!"

The man in the shantung suit grinned politely and lit a cigarette. He was handsome and rather ascetic-looking, with a small black mustache. He glanced at the two young sailors and then at the ceiling somewhat anxiously. "They spoke of you, Herr Kleist, with the greatest admiration in Teheran. Likewise in Colombo and Rangoon. You have an enviable reputation. You have courage. That's the important thing. It isn't easy to keep one's courage nowadays."

"Courage!" said the other, stroking his nostrils. "My good Herr Grillparzer, I wish that I had it. I lost it—well, no matter precisely when, long ago. One doesn't need courage. That's the point. Courage is superfluous, I assure you. The finest dedication is the dedication of a coward. Oh, I have my little consolations, of course—I still love Beethoven, I still read Goethe—but when it comes to a faith in the future, I find it simpler to do without it. When all is said and done, amid this modern elephantiasis, I find venom and disgust more reliable stimulants than a wide-eyed reverence. Mind you, Herr Grill-parzer, I wouldn't be involved in this little business of ours if my outlook on life were anything but deeply misanthropical. What people need nowadays is relief from pain, a flight from reality, and in that sense our precious commodity, though rather costly, is still cheap at the price. I feel there is some-thing apt in our poetical pseudonyms, for we *are* merchants in dreams, aren't we? The financial aspect is subsidiary."

"Beautifully put, I must say. I share your feelings exactly, Herr Kleist. It is hard to feel reverent in the presence of these huge, impersonal forces. Still, I doubt whether I could put my whole enthusiasm into this work if I didn't still feel capable of at least a flickering of exaltation. I feel that I'm bringing visions of unearthly beauty into a world of drabness, rather than merely a relief and a respite to the defeated ones. I am a romanticist and you are a realist, Herr Kleist. It's as simple as that."

"Well," said the other, "I am deeply grateful for this brief but piquant encounter." He glanced at his watch. "It is half past seven. I have a rendezvous at eight at the Glouces-ter." He grinned ironically. "We have a mutual interest in gastronomy, if I'm not mistaken. Here are the recipes." He took a long bulky envelope out of his briefcase and placed it on the table between the two glasses. It was labeled *Selected Menus from a Provençal Kitchen.* "When you arrive in Syd-ney, Herr Grillparzer, you will be so good as to get in touch with Herr Mörike. I suggest that you make use of Contact Twenty-nine on this occasion. He is staying at the Hotel Bristol. He will be gratified to receive these menus, being, like ourselves, a fanatical gourmet. And give him my regards. I haven't had the pleasure of meeting Herr Mörike, but I've heard that he is a man of culture as well as an accomplished clarinetist. Oh, yes. One final point. I almost forgot to men-tion it. We've been having some trouble lately. Nothing serious, but still . . . Our Herr Eichendorff was trapped in Cairo and escaped by the skin of his teeth. Do be careful, Herr Grillparzer. The *Cassandra* sounds like an innocuous vessel, but I've learned to be suspicious in even the most humdrum of atmospheres!" He rose and shook hands with the man in the shantung suit. "*Auf wiedersehen,* Herr Grillparzer! And bon voyage on the *Cassandra!*"

The man in white remained at the table for several minutes to finish his drink. He ran his fingers caressingly over the long manila envelope and then lifted it in his hand appraisingly, as though weighing its contents. Then he tucked it somewhat absently into his left-hand pocket and glanced cautiously at the two young sailors, who were telling jokes in a Yorkshire dialect.

At this moment he grew aware that someone else had entered the room: a moist and rather flabby little man in a green jacket. He sat motionless for several minutes and stared fixedly at his whisky glass. Then he ran his finger dreamily through a little puddle beside the glass. He closed his eyes for a moment; drops of sweat shone on his forehead. Finally he rose and walked softly through the door into the street, where the screams of the rickshaw boys were echoing through the twilight.

He paused for a moment by the window and peeped through the paisley curtains. The Chinese bartender was standing motionless behind the bar with his arms akimbo. The two young sailors were laughing gaily; the fat little man was watching them wistfully.

He bit his lower lip and drew his thumb across his Adam's apple. Then he started to wander in the direction of the quay. Night was falling. The neon lights began to glow in the dusky labyrinth: *Ritz Café, Imperial Bazaar, Ruby's Lounge, Cadbury's Chocolates.* A man without legs rolled slowly past him on a pair of roller skates. An old woman held a naked, urinating baby over the gutter. A cloud of yellow smoke shot up from the funnel of the Kowloon ferryboat and rose into the night, where it hung like a great, glowing question mark.

He stepped quickly into the street and waved his arm at a passing taxi.

PART II

The Ship

1

On the following evening, the twenty-eighth of August, 1938, at five o'clock, the S.S. *Cassandra* moved slowly through the junk-littered waters of Kowloon. She skirted the shores of Victoria, where the tall white towers shone in the sunlight, and headed for the smooth, silent blaze of the China Sea. The wake grew straight and symmetrical; the motors lapsed into monotony, and a mild salty breeze cooled the freshly painted deck. The shore grew frail as a ribbon and finally vanished altogether. And deftly, almost magically, the life on the ship became a separate entity.

Two old ladies in flowered dresses settled in their deck chairs and closed their eyes. A Japanese boy, stripped to the waist, sat on the sundeck with his ukulele. A girl and a freckled boy were playing ping-pong on the promenade deck; and in the cardroom two men and two women sat down at the bridge table.

They drew for partners. The girl with the bangs drew the seven of diamonds. The man in the dark blue blazer drew the seven of hearts. The man with the black mustache drew the eight of spades, and the woman with the enormous golden bracelet drew the ace of clubs.

"As we are," said the girl with the bangs. "Any special conventions?"

"We play Blackwood, don't we, Hugo? And a two-club opening in the French style."

A sad, thyroidic steward passed the table with a tea tray.

"None for me," said Mrs. Domingo. "What about you, Mrs. Wagenseller?"

"I think not. Would it be rude if I ordered a whisky, Mrs. Domingo?"

"Not in the least. I have similar intentions. And how about you, Mr. Wagenseller? That makes three. The Baron never touches a drop at the bridge table. Will you bring us three whiskies and a bottle of soda, please, steward?"

Tony Wagenseller flicked a handerchief out of his pocket and said, "A spade."

"Double," said the man with the mustache, stroking the scar in his cheek.

"Redouble," said Laura Wagenseller, looking carefully at her partner.

"I can't pretend," said Mrs. Domingo, "that I'm pleased with the *Cassandra*. There's a smell in the lower passages. Cabbage, drains, and a hint of vomit."

"She is badly in need of a facelift," murmured Laura. "Just look at the carpeting."

"There is a most peculiar creak in my cabin," hinted the Baron.

"Well, it's not exactly a trip for the luxury-minded," said Tony Wagenseller.

"We were warned. We've both been steeling ourselves for the worst," said Laura, doe-eyed.

"Well, where were we?" said Mrs. Domingo, staring at her cards with dejection.

"One spade doubled and redoubled, dear."

"Yes. Exactly. I'll say two diamonds."

Wagenseller passed, the Baron passed, and Mrs. Wagenseller said, "Double."

Mrs. Domingo looked harassed. She glanced at the ceiling for inspiration. Then she carelessly shrugged her shoulders and said defiantly, "Two hearts."

Wagenseller passed, the Baron passed, and Laura Wagenseller said crisply, "Double."

Mrs. Domingo stared bleakly at her long pointed fingernai' "Two no-trump," she said wearily and flicked open her cigarette case.

"Pass," said Wagenseller; "Pass," said the Baron. Laura Wagenseller looked compassionate. She plucked at the buckle of her belt and said gently, "I think I'll double."

Mrs. Domingo cast a quick, appraising glance across the bridge table. Then she hugged her cards to her chest and muttered hoarsely, "Three clubs."

Both of the men passed again. Laura Wagenseller lifted her brows. There was a hint of hesitation in her voice as she muttered, "I'll double."

Mrs. Domingo looked at her fixedly. Then she snapped her cigarette lighter, leaned low over the flame, and said vibrantly, "Redouble."

The others all passed. Tony Wagenseller led the king of spades. Mrs. Domingo covered it with the singleton ace on the table, played the ace of clubs on the table, which caught the singleton king on her left, entered her hand by trumping a diamond, and spread her cards on the baize. "I'll have to give you a heart trick at the end, I'm afraid." She looked wistfully at her partner. "My hand was absolutely hideous. All I had was these miserable clubs. Eight of them, dear. Not a point in my hand."

Tony Wagenseller glared at his wife, "Will you kindly tell me what you doubled with, Laura?"

"Six diamonds and six hearts. Singleton spade and a void in clubs. What in hell," she said fiercely, "do you want me to do with a hand like that?"

"A small slam in diamonds on ice," said Tony Wagenseller. "Bid your hand, that's all I'm asking. Couldn't you see that she was trying to bluff you?"

"Three overtricks, doubled and redoubled," said the Baron amiably. He wrote it down on the score sheet. "Rather brilliant of you, Lily."

The steward set the whisky glasses on the little bamboo side table, opened the bottle of soda water, and held it poised over a glass.

"Plenty of soda in mine, please," said Laura Wagenseller with frozen lips.

"On the rocks, please, for me," whispered Mrs. Domingo.

2

Dinner was served at half past seven in the dining saloon, which was a low-ceilinged room hung with faded chintz curtains. Over the buffet at the further end hung a print of some Degas ballet dancers. There were hors d'oeuvres to start with, consisting of anchovies, sardines, and celery; these were followed by tepid mutton with lima beans and lyonnaise potatoes. For dessert there was raspberry ice with small pinkish cupcakes. The cutlery and the glasses trembled in the ceaseless vibration and a dull scent of grease permeated the hot stagnant air. There were thirty First Class passengers, and these were distributed at nine little tables, the tenth being reserved for the *Cassandra*'s captain, whose name was Abernethy. Mrs. Domingo invited Miss Eccles to sit at her table, where they were joined by her secretary, the Austrian baron. The rest of the passengers included five children, who were traveling with a governess; two elderly Scottish ladies, Miss Hough and Miss Hammersley; a trio of Australian missionaries; the American couple, the Wagensellers; and a group whom Miss Eccles immediately recognized as fellow scholars—a young Italian, a willowy Swede, and a thin little Indian.

Dinner passed listlessly. They chatted politely about the food in Colombo, the prices in Singapore. After dinner Miss Eccles wandered up to the darkened sundeck, where a mist-encircled moon shone on the row of folded deck chairs. She stood by the railing and looked down at the windless ocean, where phosphorescent bubbles played on the black heaving water. She listened to the low, incessant rustling of the water, to the creaking of the lifeboats, to the whimpering of a ukulele. She folded her fingers around the dew-dampened railing and thought: "How nice to be alone. How cool and refreshing to be alone. . . ."

At that moment a tall, pale figure emerged from the stairway. He passed the row of deck chairs, ducked clumsily under the badminton net, and came to a shy, nervous halt beside Miss Eccles. "Are you meditating, Miss Eccles?"

"Nothing so grand as meditation."

"Daydreaming, shall we call it?"

"The day has passed. Night has arrived."

"It's a different kind of dream, then. Look!" said the Baron. "How black the sea is! Here we are, gliding slowly over the surface of the ocean, but how little we know what goes on underneath!"

"You have the old Teutonic sense of mystery, I see," remarked Miss Eccles.

"A sense of terror, you might call it. Look at the blackness all around us—how infinitely peaceful, how suave and rhythmical, Miss Eccles! But beneath all that suavity there's perpetual bloodshed and endless massacre. That's what the poets keep forgetting. Hunger and terror are the keys to existence."

Miss Eccles lowered her head. "There are other things than hunger and terror."

"Lust. Avarice. Hatred."

"Beauty. Delight," said Miss Eccles. "And tenderness."

The Baron laughed thinly. "You are a scientist, Miss Eccles. It is odd to hear a scientist talking of tenderness and beauty."

"I'll admit," said Miss Eccles, "that in my zoological pursuits, if you wish to call them that, I have seen from time to time these murders and massacres, as you call them. But I have also, and far more frequently, seen the other things as well."

"I see. The delight outweighs the terror, in your experience."

"I'd rather say that the delight redeems the terror," said Miss Eccles.

"Tell me," said the Baron with curiosity, "what exactly are you looking for?"

"In Australia, you mean?"

"Well, in Australia, if you wish."

"I am looking," said Miss Eccles, "for certain curious aberrations."

The Baron glanced at her sharply. "Aberrations. I see."

"There is a form of *Troides priamus* which is quite extraordinary. Golden ocelli, ringed with blue, on wings of iridescent green. And a very rare variety of *Cressida cressida,* with submarginal spots of a brilliant silver."

The Baron's eyes grew ironical. "This is the beauty which you mentioned?"

"It is an aspect of the beauty. One of a multitude," replied Miss Eccles.

"I must say," said the Baron mockingly, "you show an amazing degree of philanthropy. Is it, Miss Eccles, because you have focused on the world of beasts rather than men?"

Miss Eccles lifted her gray, impersonal eyes and said gently, "Quite possibly. But I'd hardly call it philanthropy, Baron. One must accept the cruelties of nature. They have always existed. They will always exist. The cruelties of man are another matter. They have always horrified me."

"Then you agree with me *au fond.* You feel despair for the plight of humanity."

Miss Eccles raised her brows. "I had never been aware of it as such."

"But you feel it, Miss Eccles! I can see in your eyes that you feel it!"

"I have never felt despair, I can assure you," said Miss Eccles.

"One can feel it without being aware of it," said the Baron sententiously. His voice grew quick and passionate; he looked at Miss Eccles with a cold ferocity. "Look, Miss Eccles! Here we are, floating on a fragment of civilization—not a particularly elegant specimen, I admit, but still a specimen. We are sailing from one screaming, pullulating city to another. And below us is the sea, the silent wilderness, the primordial reality. What's your opinion? Has the progress from the old to the new been wholly desirable? This dazzling progress—well, Miss Eccles, as far as I can see, it's brought more ugliness than beauty to this idiotic world of ours. Wouldn't it be a blessing in disguise if these marvelous new bombs razed all the ugliness from the face of the earth, Miss Eccles?"

"There is always ugliness of some sort or other," said Miss Eccles dejectedly. "There was ugliness under Augustus, under the Medicis, under Elizabeth. It's a matter of personal preference. I keep trying not to think about it. Oh, there's plenty of terror in the world, but I try not to think about it."

The Baron moved his hand along the railing toward Miss Eccles. For a frightening little moment she thought that he might touch her. But he turned his head casually and looked up at the moon, which washed his pointed profile in a mercurylike brightness.

"I suppose that Lily has been talking about me?"

"Lily who? Oh, Mrs. Domingo."

The Baron's voice grew wheedling. "What did she say to you, Miss Eccles?"

"She said that you were curious to see Australia, if I remember correctly."

"That's all? You're quite sure?"

"You seem worried, my good Baron."

"I *am* worried," said the Baron carefully. "Poor old Lily is turning odd. Have you noticed the way the pupils of her eyes seem to palpitate?"

"Not especially," said Miss Eccles.

"Lily is sick. Mentally, I mean. Lily's life has been wearing. The strain," said the Baron, "is beginning to tell."

"She seems quite vigorous," said Miss Eccles. "Conversationally, at any rate."

"She has a sense of impending catastrophe. It could be the menopause, I suppose. But I wonder whether she is suffering from schizophrenia," said the Baron.

"Schizophrenia," said Miss Eccles, "is not a specialty of mine."

"Only this morning," said the Baron, "she predicted a holocaust. She kept saying, 'I feel a *cauchemar* in my bones.' Those were her words."

"Monsoon weather," said Miss Eccles. "Sticky and damp. Makes one feel edgy."

"How comforting," said the Baron, "to talk to a scientist, Miss Eccles!"

Miss Eccles drew her palm over her brow and glanced at her watch. "You'll forgive me, please, Baron? I have some letters I want to write."

The Baron looked melancholy. "Certainly, Miss Eccles. Will I see you in the morning?"

"More than likely," said Miss Eccles. She looked at the Baron with a touch of bewilderment. Then she smiled at him casually. "Good night, Baron."

"Good night, Miss Eccles."

3

The Baron lay in his hot, stuffy cabin and stared into the darkness. Suddenly he flicked on the light and started to write in his leather-bound *Tagebuch:*

Life has grown too complex. I must try to untangle my thoughts. Will this diary help? At least, I'll have *someone* I can talk to frankly, even if it's only just a coffee-colored notebook.

One thing is sure. I must be terribly cautious, relentlessly observant. I now realize that my earlier suspicions were a trifle exaggerated (this dreary vessel seems hardly the setting for an international *coup de théâtre*), but all the same, it's quite clear that we have a curious lot on board. That pitiable lepidopterous spinster, who spends her time reading detective stories. And that arrogant American couple, perpetually bickering. He's been reading Kafka. It seems ridiculous. And his carnivorous little wife. It's a deeply incongruous pair and yet there's something apt about it, as though these silly squabbles were inevitable and even harmonious.

Something rather odd happened to me on the deck this evening, after I said good night to Miss Eccles. I was leaning over the railing, staring down at the foaming water, when I noticed a young Malayan standing ten feet away. He kept glancing at me furtively. I was growing a little nervous. Suddenly to my horror I realized that he had opened his trousers and that his *membrum* was protruding, in a state of unmistakable rigidity. I thought for a moment of reporting this outrage to Captain Abernethy, but then I shrugged my shoulders and strolled back to my cabin. There were moments in my youth when I was afraid that I might be a latent urning, or at least slightly tinged with a subsidiary degree of deviation. But no. I've tried it twice, in moments of sheer desperation. That thing with the Italian boy in Cortina d'Ampezzo was an absolute fiasco. And that rendezvous with the Swedish sailor in the Tivoli Gardens was even worse. Neither *penis in os* nor *penis in anum* has the slightest appeal for me. They both strike me as visually grotesque, not to mention the hygienic aspect. Even the heterosexual act strikes me as ungraceful as well as odorous, and I certainly see no reason for exploring the variations and permutations.

What are my feelings toward Lily? I despise her and yet I'm afraid of her. I grow bored and infuriated and yet I feel an underlying tenderness. Her body revolts me sexually and yet I feel an eerie lust for her. There are moments when I positively feel a yearning to—well, never mind. There are things that even a diary might blush to be told about. What does all this boil down to? Something not very nice. And still, at the bottom of my miserable soul there is a streak of ardent purity. White and black. The blackness of my hair, as against the whiteness of my flesh. The grip of those two colors on the human fancy is more than an accident. They reflect a dilemma deep in the soul of every one of us.

4

When Tony Wagenseller awoke in the morning everything in the cabin seemed alive. Everything was rocking and slithering; squeaking, tinkling, chattering, and banging. The sea had got up in the night. The porthole was washed with spray. Laura lay motionless in her berth with her face turned to the wall. He whispered: "You all right, Laura?" But she didn't bother to answer. He grabbed at the berthpost and slid clumsily into his clothes.

When he stepped out on deck he saw that the bows were capped with spray. The sea was veiled with spindrift which was driven before the gale. He staggered along the deck, clutching at a derrick, a handrail, a stanchion. The sky was gray and mottled; the air felt heavy as lead. He heard the cry of a sea gull, and then the crazy creak of a pulley block. A great whisk of spray suddenly slapped him in the face.

Outside the lounge after breakfast he met Captain Abernethy, a corpulent man with rosy cheeks. He said brightly,

"Good morning, Mr. Wagenseller! You're having a bit of trouble? Don't let it worry you. It's just the tail end of a perfectly ordinary typhoon. Tomorrow there'll be a swell and the following day it will all be over. The whole Pacific Ocean will be as smooth as my grandmother's mill pond."

When he stepped into the cabin he saw Laura nibbling at her breakfast. A thin, mouse-gray liquid was swaying mournfully in the coffee cup.

"Nothing serious, the captain told me. Just a commonplace typhoon. All be over in a couple of days. Nothing to fret about," said Tony.

"Nothing to fret about. How restful. Were you expecting a major calamity?"

"I was trying to calm those hypersensitive nerves of yours, that's all."

"Terribly thoughtful. I feel soothed. I was tottering on the edge of a breakdown."

Tony picked up *The Castle* and made his way to the lounge. He sat down in a pink-striped davenport and stared listlessly at the opening page. Finally he tossed the book on the side table and peered gloomily at the swaying curtains. Then he folded his hairy arms, closed his eyes, and fell asleep.

It was twelve when he woke up again. The lounge was deserted. He stroked his nose thoughtfully, picked up his book, and headed for the bar. He found Laura sitting in a corner with a highball in her hand.

"Feeling better?" he said hoarsely.

"Thank you kindly. I am feeling lovely."

"Dreary boat, this *Cassandra*."

"I find it the acme of modern luxury."

"Well, it was you who picked it, Laura. We could have gone on the *Caledonia*. But no. Those Spartan tastes of yours. That penchant for the primitive."

"I can't help wondering why you bothered to come at all,

my dear Tony. All my fault, needless to say. Female selfishness, pure and simple. Bitch that I am, I tore you away from those squash-playing cronies. Sandy Hathaway, Tim Blackwelder, Bill Wintersteen—*quelle galère!* For sheer wit and cultural refinement I have never seen the likes of them."

"You've been drinking, I am pained to see."

"Most convenient. You can blame it on the alcohol."

"You cling to your grievances like a terrier, Laura."

"Listen, my love, I've hardly started. There you sit, just a wide-eyed innocent. I can hear them down in the locker room! 'That poor old bastard Wagenseller. Got roped in by a stuck-up highbrow. She's got him in her clutches. He's reading Kafka. Can you beat it?' I spent an evening once with Polly MacNamara, did I ever tell you about it? It opened my eyes to the general squalor of human existence. Oh, I knew what she was thinking! I saw the glint in those little green eyes of hers! That freckle-faced goose who spends her life swatting at golf balls. You had an affair with her, didn't you, back in those jolly old bachelor days? Pretty delirious, it must have been. All the perfumes of Arabia. What he's missed, poor old Tony, along the line of feminine allurements!"

"Boiling with hatred, aren't you, Laura? I often wonder why you ever married me. Just to prove your mental supremacy, that's the long and the short of it. Listen, Laura. You don't have to prove it. You can have it gratis on a silver platter. What wouldn't I give for a bit less cleverness and a bit more mellowness and understanding."

Laura lifted her highball glass and fixed her eyes on Tony's forehead. "It's an elevating spectacle, all this chatter about mellowness. Ripeness is all, that's your motto. Where did you imbibe that earthy wisdom? Listen to me, Tony. I never gave a hoot in hell for that background of yours. Groton, New Haven, the Social Register—you can drop it

straight into the garbage pail. There was only one reason why
I ever married you. I thought that you loved me."

"I loved you, Laura."

"You never loved me. You're incapable of loving a
woman. Oh, poor Tony, I understand you so much better than
you think! Why do you always turn out the lights when we go
to bed, will you tell me? Is it modesty? Or guilt? Come, come,
Tony. Let's get at the truth of it. Why that cold, indifferent
glaze in your eyes when it's over? Why that look of apology?
Why those dutiful wispy kisses? Be frank. You've never desired
me. You're quite incapable of desiring a woman."

"I am not a lustful man, Laura. Sad but true. It's as
simple as that."

"You're not suggesting that you're impotent? My dear
Tony, I know better."

"Impotent or not, I'll tell you one thing and it's high
time that you realized it. It's not easy to be sexually intoxicated by a woman who clings to her pedestal. Whatever you
do, even in the privacy of the loo, it's alway Laura Wagenseller, the fastidious soul, the progressive intellect. Jesus,
Laura, it's pretty difficult for a vulgar brute like me to make
love to a woman who keeps insisting on her spiritual delicacy."

"Oh. I see. Would it help if I took some lessons in
harlotry?"

"It might help if you kept your mouth shut once in a
while, I shouldn't wonder."

"Oh, the big bristling caveman with his limp little wife.
It's a touching thought, isn't it?"

"One thing's obvious, my dear Laura. You don't like men.
You utterly abhor them. You keep your eyes averted. The
masculine organ seems to repel you."

"A delightful *quid pro quo*. Well, the hell with it, I say. I

am having another drink. Waiter! *Un* whisky, *s'il vous plaît!"*
Tony winked at the Negro barman. "Make it two," he
said quietly. He stretched out his legs and stared at the ceiling
with sudden curiosity.

5

By nine o'clock that evening the gale had spent its force.
The ship continued to roll but the fury had gone from the
water. One by one the bleak-eyed passengers stepped out from
their cabins. Signor Cucci invited Herr Grönwall for a schnapps
in the bar, and the children crouched in the playroom while
Miss Hammersley read them a ghost story.

The Baron wandered slowly toward the end of the promenade deck and descended the narrow stairway that led to the
dimly lit Tourist Class. A faint whiff of onions seeped through
the doorway of the dining saloon. Two Malayans were rolling
dice in a patch of light outside the Purser's Office. The Baron
opened the door and stepped out on the lower deck. The glow
from the First Class Bar shone on the sea-lacquered railing. He
groped his way through the penumbra, following the curve of
the railing, and found himself staring at the luminous churning
of the propeller, which widened into the smooth unending
arrows of the wake. The light from one of the portholes shone
on the foamy agitation, which sparkled like snow, hurling its
flakes into the blackness. The air was strangely warm, rich and
pungent after the upheaval. Layer on layer of rotting darkness
had been scooped out of the depths. A sense of lurking
expectancy surged up in the Baron's heart, where it mingled
with another emotion: an almost suicidal anxiety. The feeling
persisted that something enormous was about to happen. Was
Herr Kleist right after all? Was there something treacherous

lurking on board the ship? Or was this feeling of alarm just one
more phase of an inner crisis? His senses held out hope, there
were inklings of self-renewal; but his nerves were sick with a
fever which found its echo in the swollen emptiness. Something vast was about to happen; something that would change
his life forever. The convulsion of a genuine passion? A
sudden blaze of illumination? Or that black *other* thing—that
wilder impulse which had always haunted him?

He leaned over the bright, boiling wake with outspread
arms. How easy it would be: one casual gesture, one tiny
leap, and his life would be assuaged forever, ennobled by all
this majesty. His hands started to shake as they clutched at the
railing. The foam down below seethed with a phosphorescent
magnetism. But the crucial moment passed. He raised his head
and sniffed at the air. The stars peeped through the clouds.
There was a whiff of far-off islands.

The *Cassandra* lurched suddenly, as though she had
struck some hidden object. The Baron noticed something
large and black and glossy floating in the water. A whale,
could it be? The ship rolled uneasily. The sound of the motors
was like a series of angry snorts. It struck the Baron that the
Cassandra, after all its watery vicissitudes, had developed a
very definite, though hardly attractive, personality of her own.
She resembled some rank and indomitable old slattern, smelly
with age, damp with neglect, and morose with promiscuity.

At that moment he heard a slow, shuffling tread on the
deck behind him. He turned swiftly and strode back to the
iron stairway, almost guiltily. For one second he saw the face
as it caught the glow from the upper bar window: the round
rosy cheeks, the startled eyes, the shell-white scalp. Then the
creature darted off, quick as a weasel, into the shade of the
corridor. The Baron gripped the door handle, which was
strangely clammy in the crisp, warm darkness. Then slowly,
panting heavily, he climbed the stairs to the upper deck.

6

The bar was quite empty except for the young Negro bartender. The spray had misted the windows, so that the room seemed dim and shadowy; the velveteen curtains swayed with the rolling of the ship. A fluorescent light shone on the bar of stained walnut, which was lined with tall stools cushioned in imitation leather. The long row of bottles rattled and danced under the mirror and the glasses kept tinkling uneasily on the shelves.

Mrs. Domingo sat down at the table in front of the bar. She dropped her bag on the table and looked intently at the bartender.

"A whisky. Johnnie Walker. On the rocks. With plenty of ice, please."

She opened her bag, from which she extracted a golden cigarette case, a golden lighter, a golden lipstick, and a golden cigarette holder. She lit a cigarette and stared at the ceiling disapprovingly.

"Funny ship," she said finally.

"Beg your pardon?" said the bartender.

"It's a *queer* sort of ship, I said. I've never seen the likes of it. There's a picture of the Mona Lisa hanging in my cabin. How did it get there?"

"It was a Dutch ship, once," said the bartender.

"I am not surprised," said Mrs. Domingo.

"It sailed to Java back in the old days."

"I can well believe it," said Mrs. Domingo. "Antediluvian, I should imagine." She cocked her head slightly. "What is your name, would you tell me, bartender?"

"My name is Ibrahim, madam."

"Quite a colorful name, isn't it?" She flicked the ash from

her cigarette. "How long have you been on the *Casssandra,* Ibrahim?"

"Eleven months, madam. I was on the *Zenobia* before that. And before that I was on the *Semiramis,* which sailed to Gibraltar."

"Gibraltar. Bless my soul. That's rather remote, isn't it, Ibrahim?" She grew thoughtful and scowled a little. "I had an ugly experience in Gibraltar."

"I am sorry to hear it, madam."

"I was robbed in Gibraltar. I was traveling to Fez with a friend of mine, a Peruvian pianist. I left five hundred pounds with the young cashier at the reception desk. On the following morning the boy had vanished, along with the money. I had the receipt, duly signed, but what on earth could I do? The manager called the police. The police checked immediately. The cashier, whose name was Fernando, had taken the ferry to Tangier. He was a soulful-looking boy but it taught me a crucial lesson. Never again, as long as I live, will I get involved with a Spaniard!"

The ship heaved abruptly; she seized her glass and held it in the air. At that moment a dusky man with gold-rimmed spectacles entered the bar. He wore a black cheviot jacket, gray gabardine trousers, and Italian-looking moccasins of coffee-hued camel's hide. He moved noiselessly across the room and said in a high singsong voice, "Would you think it terribly rude if I sat at your table, Mrs. Domingo?"

Mrs. Domingo looked at him savagely and then relented. "Do sit down, please."

"I happened to see you in the card room. Your face looked familiar. I took the liberty of asking the purser for your name. He revealed it to me."

"I see. And what, may I ask . . ."

"Oh, please excuse! Very forgetful of me. My name is Dr. Banerjee. I live in Calcutta."

"I spent only a night in Calcutta," said Mrs. Domingo. "I found it rather a bore. I doubt whether you saw me in Calcutta."

"Oh, Mrs. Domingo, not in Calcutta! Not in Calcutta, most emphatically!" Dr. Banerjee pressed his fingers to his cheeks with self-disparagement. He tittered vaguely for several moments and then inquired, "You are going to Sydney? A most implausible city for you to be visiting, Mrs. Domingo!"

"I am not expecting another Venice," said Mrs. Domingo, turning her head a little. "Australia exists. One cannot totally disregard it."

"Certainly not. It is very large. Smaller than Asia, but still large."

"And what is *your* particular purpose in visiting Sydney, Dr. Banerjee?"

Dr. Banerjee rolled his eyes. "My Australian visit is purely literary. I'll be lecturing on modern poetry at the University of Adelaide."

"T. S. Eliot and the rest?"

"Well, my period is slightly earlier. My special adoration is for Rupert Brooke. I paid a pilgrimage once to Grantchester. They still served honey with the tea, I am happy to say."

"My taste in poetry is rather elementary, I'm afraid," said Mrs. Domingo. "As a child I read 'The Raven.' And something about 'Footprints in the sands of time.' "

"I have always been puzzled," said Dr. Banerjee, "by those little footprints. Footprints in the sand do not last very long, generally speaking. But nothing vanishes completely, not even a footprint in the sand, which leads me to wonder where I've seen you before, Mrs. Domingo."

"You're quite right, Dr. Banerjee. Nothing dies away totally. Just a glimpse, a whiff, a melody—they come back at the weirdest moments."

"Angkor Wat?" suggested the Indian.

"Terribly sorry. I missed it."

"Mandalay?"

"I've never been there."

"Well, it must have been Bangkok."

Mrs. Domingo folded her arms and looked at the Indian with suspicion. "It may well have been Bangkok. But what difference does it make? You may have seen me. More likely you didn't. It's not a matter of particular consequence."

The Hindu was a lithe little man with a mouselike profile and large mournful eyes with heavy lids which half covered the irises. There was something both languorous and intensely nervous in his manner; his high, lilting voice was both arrogant and obsequious.

"No, it's not of much consequence, not in the usual sense, at least. But reality, Mrs. Domingo, is a matter of hints and innuendos. Oh, I know that you Americans are impatient of mystifications, but I might as well tell you that when I saw you in Bangkok, in the lounge of the Grand Oriental, I said to myself immediately: 'I have seen that woman in some previous embodiment.' "

"I don't believe in transmigration," said Mrs. Domingo halfheartedly.

"Your face," said Dr. Banerjee, "suggests the third of the three Alternatives. I don't suppose that you are familiar with the poetry of ancient India, but the *Satapatha* has some interesting passages about the nature of male and female. The male incorporates three basic principles, or Vital Alternatives: namely Law, synonymous with Order; Coherence, synonymous with Action; and Light, synonymous with Lucidity. The female incorporates three other Alternatives: Fluidity or Waywardness; Music, or Intuition; and Darkness, or Impenetrability. You are neither fluid nor musical, but you are quite impenetrable, Mrs. Domingo. All women have a streak of darkness in them, but with you it is rather conspicuous. I mentioned the *Satapatha*. There is also a work called the *Yajurveda*. The *Yajurveda* suggests that in each of us there are several different personalities, some of them recent, dating back to certain episodes in our childhood, and others ancient, dating back to the unfathomable depths of antiquity. Our task in life is the following, according to the *Yajurveda:* to apply six different processes in us, namely, first of all to discover these personalities, then to explore them, then to vitalize them, then to expand them, then to illuminate them, and finally to fuse them. Only when we fulfill these diverse processes do we achieve our total character. Only the lucky few, alas, ever achieve their total character."

"This is all most intriguing," said Mrs. Domingo, tapping her ash. "But what has it got to do with me, may I ask, Dr. Banerjee?"

"You are quite right in being impatient," said the Indian apologetically. "I express myself pedantically. I am used to a classroom atmosphere. And in any case, I was drifting away from the point that I started from. When I saw you that day in the Grand Oriental lounge, Mrs. Domingo, I promptly sensed that I had known you in some earlier incarnation. Oh, it was nothing so superficial as eyes, nose, or posture. It was deeper than that. It takes years of practice to get the knack of it. I won't suggest that I can put my finger on the particular species which you embodied. You may have been a snake. You may have been a tigress. Or you might even have been a peahen. There is always the possibility of a shift in sex, so that you were a peacock. I hope that you won't find these little suggestions disparaging, madam. I should add that my own embodiments were on an altogether humbler scale. The best of my previous beings was a sort of owl, with dark brown feathers. I may also have been a flea nuzzling cozily in your tail, or maybe a louse lodged in one of your wing pits. The only incarnation I have definitely identified is that of a spider. Not one of those horrible tarantulas but a neat little creature, bronze in color." Dr. Banerjee reached under his collar and drew out a golden chain. At the end of the chain dangled a gold-plated spider. "We should try and make friends with our earlier embodiments, Mrs. Domingo. I have tried to appease my spider-self by enshrining it in gold. As soon as you have established to your satisfaction your former identities, you should purchase a golden snake, or a golden tigress, or a jeweled peacock. You will be surprised by the sense of harmony and self-acceptance it will provide for you. Your nerves will be assuaged. No more insomnia. No more dyspepsia. Do forgive me for being a chatterbox but my intentions are of the friendliest." He glanced at his watch. "Half past twelve! Goodness me. I've been rambling on unmercifully. Good night, Mrs. Domingo. And sweet, harmonious dreams!"

7

A great calm fell over the sea as the *Cassandra* moved eastward. She sailed through the Bashi Channel, leaving Luzon far to the west of her, and slid into the gull-haunted realms of the real Pacific. She skirted the windworn Carolines and bore south toward the equator. Now and again a palm-fringed atoll broke the flat blue monotony. Once they saw an enormous whale spouting in the brilliance in front of them, and once a school of dolphins went scalloping over the furrows.

On the fifth day out a notice, decorated with flourishes, appeared on the bulletin board:

The S.S. CASSANDRA's Glamorous Fancy Dress Ball!
Tomorrow Evening at Ten!
Don't be shy!   *Anything will do!*

"Rather ridiculous, don't you think? With all these yokels," said Mrs. Domingo.

"Well, let's hope for something quaint. Your Dr. Banerjee, perhaps," said the Baron.

"Shall I come dressed up as a tigress? What do you think?" said Mrs. Domingo.

"Careful, dear," retorted the Baron. "The venerable doctor might come as a flea."

The bell rang promptly at ten and the doors of the lounge were flung open. Ropes of brightly colored bulbs were draped with lianas of scarlet tissue paper. The couches had been removed and the overhead lights had been extinguished. A row of wicker coffee tables stood by the wall which faced the doorway and on each of the tables a candle was burning. Some sausage-shaped balloons were bouncing idly along the ceiling and in the middle of the lounge, on a kind of dais, sat the orchestra: a Filipino with a guitar, a Japanese boy with a ukulele, an Ethiopian with a saxophone, and a young Australian at the piano. The thin, bleating tones of "Love Me or Leave Me" filled the air as Dr. Pringle, the ship's physician, clapped his hands to open the festivities. One by one the masqueraders drifted anxiously into the room, glanced about apprehensively, and took their seats at the little tables. Miss Hammersley and Miss Hough were dressed alike, swathed in sheets. Linen towels, pierced with eye holes, were carefully wrapped around their heads. "The specters of Aberystwyth," they informed Miss Eccles in playful tones, but Miss Eccles had never heard of the specters of Aberystwyth. She herself was impersonating the heroine of *Pride and Prejudice*, in a pink Empire gown and a pair of low satin slippers. She was followed by the Baron von Wolfhausen in a powdered perruque. He wore a coat of sky-blue velvet with a white satin waistcoat, a pair of nankeen breeches, and long black slippers with silver buckles. Then came a group of students from

Tourist Class, invited as a special favor: a Turk, a Siamese, three Malayans, and a girl from Lebanon. They were dressed up as gypsies, with painted eyelids and bright red scarves. The Wagensellers appeared: she in a speckled Mexican shawl with an "Aztec" belt of hammered silver, he in a Panamanian hat and a short green jacket with braided epaulets. The flute began to squeal; the pianist pounded his keys. There was a hush of expectation, a nervous glitter beyond the doorway. Ibrahim the bartender marched into the lounge in a silver loincloth and a great white turban. He was carrying an enormous fan made of mother-of-pearl and peacock feathers. Behind him came Mrs. Domingo in a gown of gold lamé, surmounted by a geyserlike hat of white ostrich feathers. There was a ripple of applause. The band embarked on "Body and Soul." Mrs. Domingo strode majestically across the floor to the far-off corner, where she joined Miss Eccles and the Baron at one of the candlelit tables.

"Champagne!" she cried to the waiter, and turned coquettishly to Miss Eccles. "Doesn't our Ibrahim look magnificent? I felt that the occasion required some chic. So I coaxed him to my cabin and wound that turban around his head. It's a strip of lush brocade that I bought in a shop in Kowloon. The fan is a bit of nonsense that I found in Benares. Lovely color he's got, isn't it? That silver loincloth was my own idea. I tried to tie it around his bottom but the little beast had a fit of modesty. Beautiful muscles, I must say. It's an earmark of his race. All these blacks are beautifully molded in the fullest sense of the term. Champagne, dear? How about it? There. You'll pour it, won't you, Hugo? My own preference is Lanson, but this Veuve Clicquot will do in a pinch. That wig looks sumptuous on Hugo, doesn't it? He's powdered his mustache. I wish he had shaved it, *entre nous*. Holy Moses. Look at those Americans. They're so miserably self-conscious. The silly oaf is disguised as a Mexican. He's better suited to a role in *The*

Meistersinger. Why do I always feel so critical of my fellow Americans, will you tell me? I am certainly not a chauvinist, but I don't consider myself an expatriate. I had some high-balls before dinner, so I must be careful with this bubbly. I've never cared for the stuff particularly. I'm just trying to jazz things up a bit. Look at that fat little man in the corner. I've never laid eyes on him before. He's dressed up like a Chinese mandarin, with that silly red kimono. Goodness, Hugo. What's biting you suddenly? Fill up his glass, Miss Eccles, won't you? He gets spasms of hypochondria on the most incongruous occasions. There's that soulful young Italian, Signor Cucci is his name. I had a chat with him in the bar. He is deeply interested in primitive sculpture. Plans to tour the breadth of Australia looking for aboriginal tidbits. I have my own little suspicions about that boy, incidentally. Not that it matters, heaven knows. In a place like Capri I'd hardly notice it, but here in this dreary community one looks around for a bit of color. Bless my soul, there's Dr. Banerjee. Dressed like Gandhi; rather cheeky of him. I'll admit that those skinny legs of his remind one of Gandhi. Isn't this hat a dream, Penelope? It's high time that I called you Penelope. Call me Lily if you like. It's hardly the name to suit my character. I've always hankered for something raffish like Consuelo or Anastasia. *Tant pis.* It can't be helped. Lily it was and Lily it is. Look at that Polynesian slut. She is laughing like a hyena. All of these people look marvelously happy. I wonder why? What's the reason?"

Miss Eccles was staring intently at the bubbles in her glass. A flake of green confetti danced through the air and lit on her forefinger. She said softly, "I'll tell you why. They've escaped from their real identities. Even Miss Hough and poor Miss Hammersley. They've turned into ghosts and they're utterly delighted. Signor Cucci has turned into Pan. Professor Shishnik has turned into a mandarin. Dr. Banerjee seems to have transmogrified himself into Gandhi. They're like butterflies fresh from the chrysalis. Preening their wings. Basking in the sunlight."

"And how long will it last, this honeymoon?" said Mrs. Domingo, shrugging her shoulders. "Will it leave a hangover, Penelope? What a beautiful name, Penelope. She kept waiting for her husband and did some knitting along the side. Well, you're doing a lot of knitting but what about the husband? You've got me worried. Make hay while the sun shines, dear. That's what they say and they're totally right. You're over thirty. And sweet in your way, with that peaches-and-cream complexion. What were you saying? That we love disguises because we're sick of our old identities? Well, it's odd, I don't mind telling you. I almost came dressed up as a nun. In the very last moment I decided to make it Lola Montez. Don't laugh, please, Penelope. My alter ego is a nun. At the bottom of my soul lurks a wide-eyed *religieuse*. I often wonder whether my life hasn't been a series of wild gymnastics just to hide the dismal truth from the rest of the world. It's not for nothing that I went to India. I did some thinking while I was in India. You may laugh at poor old Banerjee, but say what you may, he's got a point. You don't find millions of people believing in something all these centuries without there being a bit of genuine fire behind the smoke. Tigress or peacock or what have you, I'm quite prepared to consider the matter. I refuse to dismiss it as superstition. I've seen too much. I've lived too long."

A sudden pallor crept over her face. She pressed her throat and started to cough. Her eyes began to water and she whispered hoarsely to Miss Eccles, "Excuse me, dear. It's the lobster. I feel dizzy, a bit. Excuse me a minute."

She rose to her feet unsteadily and gripped the edge of the chair. Then she moved through the simmering lounge and groped her way toward the corridor.

8

Laura Wagenseller said to her husband: "There's no getting around it, dear. I've felt absolutely wretched ever since I set foot on this lousy boat."

"A touch of seasickness, I guess."

"No. Just jangled and irritable."

"That horrible greasy food."

"And the passengers," said Laura. "There's something about these people that truly infuriates me. Is it just my imagination? Or do they genuinely loathe us Americans?"

"You've always been touchy, Laura."

"Look at them, Tony. It's positively embarrassing. Just a horde of mediocrities tittering and squealing like monkeys. Gauche, I call it, when a woman of sixty starts to dress like Jean Harlow. Look at that tubby little professor. Wouldn't you think he'd mind his dignity? And that naked young Italian. He's positively dripping with narcissism."

"Don't get excited. It's just an innocent little outlet for their vanity."

"To me it has all the earmarks of a dark, macabre farce."

At that moment Tony Wagenseller had a curious sensation. The walls of the lounge seemed to be inexplicably receding. A tremor rose from below. The glasses shook; the candles quivered. The colored lights grew blurred. There was an effect of chaotic *pointillisme*. The dancers looked startled, then laughed casually and kept on dancing.

"Odd," said Laura. She put down her glass. "I almost thought, for a hideous moment . . ."

The sentence remained unfinished. Her eyes grew tense, bewildered. She turned toward Tony swiftly and bared her teeth, like a frightened animal.

9

Mrs. Domingo paused for a moment in the empty corridor in front of the gift shop. The nausea in her chest was spreading its tendrils through her system. She clutched at the handrail and stared intently at the darkened shop window. Everything started to vibrate in the tremor that shook the vessel: the cuckoo clock, the perfume bottles, the fat Tyrolean dolls. The ship gave a lurch. Mrs. Domingo lost her grip. She stumbled against the wall and fell heavily to the floor. Her wrist was caught in her necklace, which exploded in a spray of bubbles. She lay motionless for several moments and stared indifferently at the rolling pearls. Then she cautiously lifted her head and tried to straighten her feathery hat.

At that moment she caught sight of something crawling through the door of the gift shop: a ribbon of yellow smoke which went gliding across the floor and reared its head abruptly, like a cobra about to strike. She rose to her knees, snatched at the handrail and started to scream. An amber-hued glow shone through the squat, fluted bottles. The cuckoo jumped through his door; the dolls burst into flame.

Mrs. Domingo's intelligence started to work with lightning rapidity. She rose to her feet and went racing down the corridor. She opened the door of her cabin and with flawless exactitude proceeded to fling a number of scattered objects into her bag. Then she gripped the bag in her hand, stepped forth from the rattling cabin, and ran toward the stairway that led up to the Purser's Office.

10

The Baron stepped out on deck for a breath of fresh air. The sea was black and glossy, swaying idly under the starlight. The moon was just rising out of the blackness in the east. He caught sight of his silhouette reflected in one of the oval windows. The embroidery on his jacket had a corallike sheen; his wig looked incandescent; his eyes were lost in their sockets. He turned away morosely and walked slowly toward the railing, which he gripped with both hands, as though afraid of losing his balance. As he stood there something dark shot out of the sea and lit in front of him. It was a fish with wings like a bat's: it lay flapping and floundering helplessly. He picked it up gingerly and tossed it back into the sea. Then he strolled past the bar and down the stairs to the deserted tourist deck. He sauntered across the deck, turning his head left and right. He seemed vaguely to be looking for something without quite knowing what. A round, greenish bundle lay in a shadow behind the door. He walked up to it curiously, bent over, and touched it lightly. It sprang into life with a sharp falsetto squeal: it was a gray-haired little Chinese who had crawled into a corner and fallen asleep. He sat petrified with horror and stared at the Baron with gaping jaws. Then he jumped to his feet and scampered off, arms aflutter.

As he watched him disappear the Baron went through a novel experience. An optical illusion: that's what it was, quite unmistakably. The frightened little Chinese was suddenly enveloped in a rope of mist, which came welling out of the sea like a great writhing sea serpent. It swirled, opaque and luminous, around the fluttering figure; then it slid into the night again and was gone without a trace.

The Baron was quietly meditating on the nature of this vision when all of a sudden, with splitting intensity, the *Cassandra*'s sirens began to sound. He clutched the sleeves of his jacket and crossed himself hurriedly. Then he turned around sharply and started to race for the promenade deck.

11

At exactly 11:40 an elderly steward named O'Flaherty was carrying a tea tray down the corridor toward the kitchen. As he headed for the stairs he noticed the smoke exuding from the gift shop. He dropped the tray on the floor and hurriedly pressed a small red button; then he ran to the end of the corridor and ripped the extinguisher from the hook. He broke through the door and pointed the gun at the conflagration. But for some mysterious reason the extinguisher failed to work. He kept pumping away feverishly but nothing happened: the gun was dead. The flames were spreading wildly, snatching at the scarves, the gloves, the brandy bottles. A volume on Caravaggio sprang from the shelf in a fiery flutter. The smoke poured down the passageway. Somewhere or other a bell was ringing. A cook ran up from the kitchen and headed for the toilets to fetch some water. A stewardess came waddling with a blanket in her arms, followed by a pimply young officer with a bucket in each hand.

At 11:48 the fire siren started to scream. Twelve minutes later, on the stroke of midnight, the first distress message was tapped out in the radio cabin, giving the ship's exact position in terms of latitude and longitude.

The passages were already crowded with wild-eyed passengers en route to their cabins. The flames swept up the stairs and licked at the doors of the First Class Dining Saloon. A voice was speaking soothingly through the loud-speaker system: *Please report to your boat stations. Ladies and gentlemen, report to your boat stations.* . . .

12

Captain Abernethy gave the order to abandon the ship at 12:20. At 12:32 the final message was flashed from the radio cabin: *SOS from Cassandra. We are leaving the ship. Send help immediately.*

There was anarchy on deck. The loud-speakers had been disrupted and the officers were issuing contradictory orders. The crewmen were milling around in the darkness chaotically. Screams in Spanish, Dutch, Russian, Malayan, filled the air. The passengers were unable to hear the shouts of the crew and groped their way fiercely toward the smoke-enshrouded boat stations. Some of them had slipped on their life jackets; the majority had not. Most of the Tourist Class passengers were in nightgowns and pajamas. The rest were still wearing their fancy-dress costumes. The Baron caught sight of Mrs. Domingo in the distance. He raced across the deck and gripped her firmly by the arm. The brightness of the flames shone through the windows of the lounge and danced on the tangle of agitated faces. The lifeboats were being lowered; but something was horribly wrong. The chains were roughened with rust and refused to slide down the davits. None of the crew seemed to know how to lower them properly. The first one shot downward, rocked dangerously, and settled in the water. The second was halfway down when it banged against the ship. It tipped over helplessly and spilled its passengers into the ocean. The third broke loose from its chains and plunged into the water upside down. The fourth burst into flames just as it started to jolt downward. Hysteria seized the passengers. They went racing from side to side, throwing deck chairs into the sea and leaping headlong into the darkness. The gypsy-clad students were howling and waving at one another. Then they snatched at the ropes and slid frantically down the side. The water below was already mottled with floundering bodies. Miss Applebee, the Scottish governess, ran through the card room with three children, whom she dropped one by one into the flame-dappled sea. The black, sparkling bartender came rushing out of the lounge with a large canvas sack, which he threw into the floating lifeboat. Then he measured the distance, straightened his arms, and dove into the ocean. Two Malayans started to fight with lunatic fury as they clung to the railing. They barked like coyotes as they dug their nails in each other's flesh. A Japanese stood watching them; he was hugging his ukulele. He tossed it into the sea and then jumped after it despairingly. Miss Hough, ensnarled in her sheets, was screaming "Gwendolyn! Where are you?" Then she darted into the bar, which was bubbling like a caldron. A bevy of naked Hindus went racing across the tourist deck and hurled themselves en masse into the gently foaming wake. The ship was listing heavily: there was a stuttering of explosions. A sinuous paw of fire reached through the passage in front of the Purser's Office. Captain Abernethy came running down the stairway from the sundeck. He paused, spread out his arms, and was enveloped in a giant flame.

13

The lifeboat rocked listlessly on the flame-illumined water. No one spoke. All were staring with fascination at the *Cassandra*. Something curious was happening. The waves had subsided; the sea was uncannily glossy and foamless. There was a stench of burning oil, and then a sound of far-off thunder. A wild burst of flame, sulfurously blue, shot up from the hull. And a moment later, with a festive and horrifying velocity, a cascade of fire came rolling across the water, transforming the ocean into a great boiling mirror from which the ship protruded like an incandescent comb.

And then as suddenly as it had come the fiery ballet vanished again, and the sea was only a hollow, horizonless vacuum from which the ship, now nearly vertical, shot forth its cannonade of sparks. The water all around was dappled with dark, bobbing bodies, floating boxes and barrels, and the pale debris of the capsized lifeboats. Here and there a screaming face or a waving arm shone momentarily, then subsided into the deep, furrowed shade of the water. The air was still echoing with hysterical screams, which faded into a diminuendo of half-heard moans and imprecations. Hidden currents were carrying the lifeboat steadily westward from the wreck, which was smoldering in the distance like an illuminated grotto: until suddenly, with a crazy and despairing magnificence, it spat out a frenzy of burning white rockets and then sank with an eerie swiftness into the black, bubbling sea.

14

"The incompetence," said Mrs. Domingo, staring fiercely at the water. "Perfectly appalling. Seems incredible, with these modern contraptions."

"Goes to show," said Laura Wagenseller. She tightened the shawl around her shoulders. "When it comes to the ultimate crisis we relapse into barbarism."

"The behavior of the crew was quite outrageous," said Mrs. Domingo. "Did you notice? They were looting the cabins. They snatched at everything they could get hold of."

"Poor little bastards," said Tony Wagenseller. "It won't

help them much, will it? That stuff will be pretty useless down
in Davy Jones's locker."

They went drifting through the night, which now was lit
by a sultry moon. All was still. The sea was empty. Nothing
was left; not a trace, not a whimper. Three hours had elapsed
since the final catastrophe and a faint morning chill was
beginning to creep through the air. The survivors sat huddled
in the white rocking hull; Mrs. Domingo, tense and glittering,
and the lean young Baron in his powdered wig; Laura shivering in her shawl and Tony fumbling with the rudder; Miss
Eccles, primly unconquerable, and the fat Professor in his red
kimono. These were the six original occupants who had
jumped in the boat, and three others had been dragged from
the churning waters: the naked barman in his turban, a
towheaded boy in a dripping cowboy suit, and a young
Japanese who had clutched at the stern as the flames were
spreading.

There were some others who had made a last frantic effort
to reach the lifeboat, but the jets of burning oil had made
rescue next to impossible. The boat had drifted away from the
flaming wreck with strange rapidity and the swimmers had
grown invisible, and shrieks and howls were lost in the darkness. Now the sea looked dull and featureless, unnaturally
calm and dehumanized. The swell rose and sank. Not a
whitecap was visible. Once an object emerged in the distance,
pale and bulging, like a giant sack, but it vanished immediately and the ocean was sleek and black again. Once the Baron
lifted his head and looked intently at the sky: there was a
faint far-off throbbing, like the buzzing of a hornet. But the
sound faded away and the boat wandered westward while the
barman dipped his oar now and again to keep it steady.

Tony Wagenseller made a survey of the contents of the
lifeboat: a gray, dismantled sail; two water canteens and a
bucket; Laura's valise, which contained a camera and a pair of
binoculars, as well as some medicines and the last ingredients

of a bon voyage basket; the Baron's mysterious briefcase, in which an alarm clock was ticking audibly; Mrs. Domingo's leather bag, filled with a hidden and priceless miscellany; and the large canvas sack which Ibrahim the barman had hurled into the boat, and which contained on closer inspection a bottle of brandy, two woolen rugs, salt and pepper, a pot and a pan, a box of biscuits, two knives and a hatchet, a gun and a compass, a bottle of olives and a tin of matches; as well as an agate box decorated with curlicues of ivory, which Tony put back in the sack without opening it.

"How clever of you, Ibrahim," said Mrs. Domingo. "How did you manage it?"

"I kept it under the bar. I was prepared, madam," said Ibrahim.

"Rather astonishing," said Laura Wagenseller. "He sensed what was coming. And so did I."

"It's quite remarkable how our instincts come to our rescue," said Miss Eccles.

"And how swiftly," said the Baron, "the pity and terror fade from our minds."

"There was nothing we could do," said Professor Shishnik, pressing his hands together.

"Nothing at all," said Mrs. Domingo. "We did our best. We saved what we could."

"God knows what will happen next. Let's hope and pray," said Laura Wagenseller.

"Don't worry," said Tony solicitously, "there'll be some search planes out in the morning."

"Odd how quickly it all happened. It started in the gift shop," said Mrs. Domingo.

"There was definitely something queer about it," said Laura craftily. "Sabotage, perhaps?"

"Horrible, isn't it," said Miss Eccles, "how one grows callous in the face of calamity."

"There's a limit," said Mrs. Domingo, "to human compassion at certain moments."

"There! Look!" cried the little boy. He pointed eastward. "It's growing lighter."

The Professor glanced at his watch. "Dawn," he muttered. "And with dawn, forgetfulness."

15

The sea was turning from a drab slate-blue to a mottled pallor. A glint played over the waves; a shawl of mist hung on the horizon. The boat was drifting with a grim, unswerving listlessness toward the west, where a few final stars were still twinkling halfheartedly. The boy had fallen asleep with his head on Ibrahim's lap; the Professor was squatting in the prow, grinning vacuously, like a Chinese idol. The sea, now sprinkled with fog, took on the coloring of an oyster shell. Then the fog flowed away and a smoky gold oozed out of the east. The chill dropped from the air and the sea, as it swayed in the brightness, took on a delicately woven, almost lacelike exactitude. The Baron pointed into the distance; the others stared silently. An elephantine mass, violet in color, rose from the ocean. At first it looked strangely close. Then it faded into remoteness. Then it brightened all of a sudden into a rich fernlike green. They could see the rope of sand which coiled at the bottom of the mountains and the shiny white foam which played on the coral reef in front of them. Everything was swept into the huge, spectacular brilliance of the sunrise. Never had the sky looked so infinite; never had the sea looked so seething. Ibrahim the barman picked up his oar and the Japanese boy took the other, while Tony reached back and grabbed hold of the rudder. The others sat motionless, enthralled and expectant, as the boat wandered slowly toward the rock-edged peninsula.

PART III

The Beach

1

The lifeboat nudged the sand, swayed uncertainly, and came to a halt. The Japanese boy, Zenzo, jumped into the water and tugged at the rope. As Tony leaned over the gunwale he was startled by the brilliance of the water. It looked like a chaos of seething yellow diamonds. He took Mrs. Domingo by the arm and lifted her briskly over the edge. Then came the others, one by one: that queer Miss Eccles, still smiling implacably, and wide-eyed little Laura, still pallid and shivering. Then the towheaded Baxter boy and the Negro bartender Ibrahim; the swarthy Baron in his white perruque and finally the bald-headed Professor. They shuffled across the sand, sniffing uneasily, peering inquisitively, and turned one by one to look at the calm, colossal sea.

Out on the sea, a mile away perhaps, shone a ruffled white thread: it was the flash of the water as it broke over the coral reef. Beyond the end of the reef rose a rock which was shaped like a cock's comb, and two vultures wheeled slowly around the top of the rock. The sea was streaked with alternating patches of blue and green, which changed with the depth of the water, or maybe with the hidden vegetation. Tony glanced about appraisingly. The beach was a kind of promontory, a diminishing crescent which curved from a cluster of rocks to a tangle of mangroves below the mainland. The sand was a peppered yellow, finely tinted with ground-up shells, and at the mouth of a creek it darkened to slate-blue mud. Palms were sprinkled at random the length of the crescent. In the middle rose a group of coconut palms and farther down there were some fat little palms with scarlet fruits. At the end, among the rocks, there were dark, feathery bushes which were covered with tufts of lavender blossoms.

Beyond the mangroves rose the mainland, whatever that might be. There was a ribbon of swampland and behind it a cone-shaped hill which was covered with shaggy vegetation. Behind this rose a higher, more precipitous row of hills. Over a peak in the distance hung a motionless gray cloud.

The bartender and the Baron were depositing the luggage: Mrs. Domingo's cowhide bag, Laura's pigskin valise, the Baron's little briefcase, Miss Eccles's purse, and the big canvas dufflebag that Ibrahim had dropped into the lifeboat.

Mrs. Domingo walked up to Tony with outspread fingers. "Well, what do you think, Mr. Wagenseller? We must try to make the best of things. It may be a day, it may be a week. I've seen worse in my time. This place is a Garden of Eden. Look at those palms. I've never seen finer. And look at those shells. Colored like rhinestones! We're mighty lucky, Mr. Wagenseller. We ought to kneel and thank the Almighty One."

"Quite right, Mrs. Domingo. We're alive. That's what counts."

"We must plan," said Mrs. Domingo in a confidential tone. "Plans are essential. We must organize. We must keep a strict discipline."

"Not to starve, that's the main thing," Tony growled and scratched his chin.

"We won't starve," said Mrs. Domingo. She pointed triumphantly to the row of palms. "Delicious coconuts. Bananas. Fish. Lobsters. Shrimps. Octopus."

"Fresh water will be essential."

"Yes, fresh water is essential, certainly, but also our morale! Order, optimism, cooperation! Mr. Wagenseller, I don't mind telling you that I am putting my faith in you."

Three hours later, when they awoke from their naps, they all gathered under a palm tree.

Tony glanced at the sea, cleared his throat, and said solemnly, "Well, my friends, Mrs. Domingo has made some

very practical suggestions. None of us knows how long we'll be
staying on this pleasant little beach. Who knows, maybe we'll
be sitting in an airplane by sundown. Anyway, we're terribly
lucky, as I'm sure we all appreciate. We must grieve for the
ones who are lost, but our grief won't help them any, will it?
There's plenty of food; let's hope it's edible. We'll have to find
some fresh water. The sand is soft and dry. Not much danger
of rheumatism. But we'll have to get things organized, as Mrs.
Domingo pointed out. We'll all be members of a committee, if
you see what I'm driving at. Each of us here with his special
function, or hers, as the case may be. I'll tend to the water
supply. I don't know how but I'll manage. Mrs. Wagenseller
here on my left has offered to help with the food problem.
How about some nice coconut layer-cake for tonight, Laura?
Miss Eccles will handle the dispensary. If you need some pills,
apply to Miss Eccles. The Baron—excuse me, please, I don't
happen to recall your name—yes, Baron von Wolfhausen.
He'll plan your sleeping arrangements. Hammocks for such as
require them. Mats of palm leaves, anything you want. Zenzo
here"—and he indicated the Japanese boy—"will help with the
fishing. First thing in the morning we'll make a couple of rods.
How about it, old boy? Think you could catch us a marlin?
Professor Shishnik will take care of the fire. You've got plenty
of matches, Professor? Sure they're dry? Good. Excellent. Professor Shishnik, who is an expert, will also warn us about
snakes and spiders. Our friend Ibrahim will be in charge of
the *haute cuisine* and the wine cellar. Can you think up some
exotic little apéritif for tonight, Chef? Billy Baxter will look
for shells. Shells make very useful plates. Maybe he'll find
some nice little shells that we can use for cocktail glasses. And
you, Mrs. Domingo? You'll be our Mother Superior. I beg your
pardon, no rudeness intended, but you grasp what I mean.
You'll provide us with our moral and spiritual sustenance,
Mrs. Domingo. We're a pretty motley lot. But I'm sure we'll

get along. Three cheers for cooperation and a stiff upper lip! Oh, yes, one last thing. Today is Wednesday, the third of September. Let's hope it won't be long, but we might as well keep a community diary. Here's a little red notebook with a pencil attached. I'll keep it tucked in the back of this palm tree, where everybody can see it. Available at all times for entries in the space provided. The daily menu, weather and temperature, interesting phenomena, amusing incidents, flora and fauna for the Professor, exotic butterflies for Miss Eccles. Anything you wish. Maybe even a poem once in a while, how about it, Laura?"

The company dispersed. Billy went off to look for shells. Ibrahim vanished among the bushes. Mrs. Domingo opened her bag and carefully scrutinized the contents. The Baron went strolling across the sand, gathering palm leaves. The Professor sat in the shade with his leather-bound *Odyssey*. Miss Eccles moved furtively in the direction of the mangroves.

Laura sat down beside Tony with her hands in her lap. "Rather nauseating, that little speech of yours."

"It wasn't intended as a literary masterpiece."

"That sickening American smugness. Do you really think they're impressed by it? I haven't heard you talk such drivel since that night of the class reunion. Please don't underrate the intelligence of these people, my pet. They're not fools. They see through you. I watched their faces while you were talking. You sounded like some potbellied scoutmaster, I'm sorry to say. No one has appointed you as propagandist for the American way of life, Tony, and I may add that it will fall on jaded ears, if I'm not mistaken."

"There you are. The eternal pessimist."

"This has nothing to do with pessimism. Decent manners. A civilized outlook. A modicum of subtlety. That's all. Oh, darling, I do wish you would drop that silly prep school atmosphere!"

"Please, Laura. Is this the time for—"

"Oh, forget it, Tony, forget it. I'm impossible. I'm quite aware of it. It's merely that here, on a desert island . . ."

Billy came running across the beach. His arms were filled with shells. He scattered them in a heap in front of Tony and cried joyfully: "Look, Mr. Wagenseller! Aren't they beautiful? Just look at this one, it's shaped like a Jew's harp." He pressed the shell to his lips and blew vigorously into the end of it, and out came a deep, mournful sound, like the cry of a loon.

2

"This is not, strictly speaking, a desert island," declared the Baron. They were sitting around the fire and watching the sunset. "It is merely a spit of land projecting from some heavily wooded territory, maybe a part of New Guinea or even Northern Australia. My guess is that it's one of the Bismarck Archipelago. Or it might even be one of the d'Entrecasteaux Group. I happened to look at the map in the Purser's Office yesterday morning, but those distances are deceptive. Very difficult for us to judge. The point is, only if worse comes to worse, you understand, should we make some sort of effort to explore the mainland?"

"What could you possibly hope to find on the mainland?" said Mrs. Domingo.

"People, maybe," said the Baron.

"Cannibals, probably!" said Mrs. Domingo.

"Most unlikely, Lily, I promise you. There are no cannibals left in the world. Cannibalism is nothing but an obsolete white superstition. We like to shudder at the thought of being devoured by black savages. It soothes our sense of guilt. Or maybe it rationalizes our prejudice. There is no danger of your turning into a stew, I assure you, Lily."

"Well, let's talk about something a bit more appetizing, please. Look at Ibrahim fixing our dinner. Kind of picturesque, isn't it? He looks as if he'd been living in the jungle all his life. Look, he's turning a spit. I can hear it sizzling. It's that queer-looking bird that he caught up in the bushes. Looks almost like a duck. Smell that smell! What's he done to it? He's a genius, that man. I'll hire him as my chef when I get to Paris. Look quick, Mrs. Wagenseller! I'll just call you Laura, may I? Just look at that sunset! It's floating on the sea like a red balloon. Reminds me of those sunsets we had in the Bahamas. There. It's gone. Incredible, wasn't it? I can smell the night already. God, I'd love a stiff Martini right this minute, wouldn't you, Hugo? That fire gives one comfort. It's rather spooky up in the hills, I bet. Barely drinkable, this lukewarm coconut milk, *mais quoi faire?* Bottoms up, boys!"

They sipped obediently at their coconut milk and looked dreamily into the fire, which threw its twitching brightness on the circle of hungry faces.

"So you go back to Paris," said Professor Shishnik, folding his arms. "You will write down your memories, I hope, like Châteaubriand."

"I'm not wild about Paris," said Mrs. Domingo, lowering her voice a little. "All the gaiety's gone from Paris. What's left? Just a lot of tourists. And the usual smattering of lesbians and pederasts. I've tried Rome but I couldn't stand it. Capri gave me claustrophobia. Monte Carlo is a funeral parlor. Dear old Venice is a pigsty. With all its drizzle and snappishness I still prefer Paris."

"Going through an experience like this will change us all," said Laura brightly. "Don't you think so, Miss Eccles? It will give us a new perspective."

"For such as need a new perspective," said Mrs. Domingo, gleaming wickedly. "Do you feel that you need a nice new perspective, Penelope?"

"We all," said the Baron, "have been pampered atrociously. Even you, I fear, Miss Eccles. And even you, in a way, Professor. Civilized life is nothing more than a feverish kaleidoscope. Chips of multicolored glass perpetually shifting and symmetrically multiplied. One illusion after another, seductive, empty, infinitely boring. The sea, the sand, and the stars! Will they give us a new perspective? We will see. It all depends. Do we *want* reality? Do we *want* the truth? Do we really desire the healing blandishments of nature?"

"Oh, look!" cried Mrs. Domingo. "Dinner is ready. Isn't it dazzling? Positively reminds me of that *canard à la broche* at Lapérouse." She watched Ibrahim draw the bird from the spit and place it on some palm leaves. "A drumstick for Billy Baxter, if he promises to behave. Bless my soul. Smell that smell. What have you done to it, Ibrahim? What have you put into this bird?"

"I have stuffed it with some herbs and baby crabs," replied Ibrahim. He took the long knife and started to carve it apprehensively. He placed each little sliver on one of the shells which Zenzo held for him and then distributed among the diners, starting with Mrs. Domingo.

"Amusing flavor," said Laura.

"Odd, but delicious," said Miss Eccles.

One of the wings went to Tony and the other to Professor Shishnik, who regarded it with melancholy before starting to gnaw at it.

"Who would have guessed, only yesterday, what life would hold for us?" said Mrs. Domingo.

"The question still remains. The enigma dangles," said the Professor.

"The enigma will always dangle," said the Baron, wiping his lips. "Whatever happens, and there is a staggering variety of things that still *might* happen, none of us will know just *why* it happened or even exactly *what* happened, let alone what

might have happened if the tiniest detail had been different—
a cigarette dropped into a tray instead of a wastebasket, for
example."

"Poignant thought. An inch to the right, that burning
little cigarette, and we'd all be sitting safely on the *Cassandra*," said Laura.

"There is no safety, ever," said the Baron.

"Only in the spirit," said the Professor.

"Good Lord, we're turning into a bevy of philosophers,"
said Mrs. Domingo.

The flames leapt and crackled but a sudden weariness
swept over the company. They yawned, their eyes grew filmy,
and one by one they crept into the darkness where each had
prepared his own little nest. Only the Baron and Mrs. Domingo were still sitting by the fire.

"I've been wondering, my dear."

"What about?" said the Baron.

"My jewelry. Where do you think that I ought to hide it,
Hugo, pet?"

"It's hardly likely that someone will stage a robbery here,
I think," said the Baron.

"One never knows. They all look honest. One or two I'm
not quite sure about."

"You are chronically suspicious, Lily."

"One can't be too suspicious. Do you remember those
pearls that suddenly vanished in the Villa d'Este?"

"You're still wondering about those pearls? It's only
because you forgot to insure them. You could lose ten thousand pearls without noticing the difference, my good Lily."

"Well, I'll think about it tomorrow. I've been thinking
enough today. This sea air is very fatiguing to my mental
processes, I've noticed."

"Good night. *Dormez bien*, Lily."

"You too, dear. Beautiful dreams."

And all was still on the sandy peninsula.

3

When Laura woke up in the morning a bird was singing from the top of the palm tree: a bronze-breasted bird with a bright blue comb and a long black tail. The sun was a big red eye peeping out of the ocean. The leaves dripped with dew, a wasp darted by, and a dank smell of slime welled up from the mangroves.

Tony strolled across the sand with a little cluster of plumlike fruits. "Found these down by the rocks, dear. Quite tasty. Here, try one of them."

They tasted like persimmons: sweet but tart, slightly gluey.

"Well," said Tony, "they're all getting into the spirit of the thing, I'm glad to see. Ibrahim is building an oven, Professor Shishnik is looking for mussels, and Zenzo's been whittling away at some bamboo fishing rods."

"Very cozy, isn't it?" said Laura. "Almost like Moosehead Lake, I should imagine."

"There you go, with those delicate shafts of irony—is that what they call them? Christ Almighty, what's wrong with you, Laura? Everybody else is pitching in but there you sit, looking sour, picking flaws in everything I do."

"Was I picking flaws? I am terribly sorry. I am bubbling over with admiration."

"Listen, Laura. It's high time you learned a bit of humility. We're sitting on a desert island and not in a Bryn Mawr dormitory, as it happens. Those sly little digs have a very sophomoric ring."

"I just try to keep my balance, lovey dove," murmured Laura. "Do forgive me. I apologize. It's the bitch way deep down in me."

Now the sun rose over the sea and the dampness fled from

the air. A soft breath of wind passed over the palm-edged inlet and the sea glaze was broken into a thousand sparkling wavelets. Shapes, colors, even sounds took on an exaggerated vividness. Everything swung into being with a sharp, prismatic exactitude. Laura strolled toward the cove and then back to the palms again. She saw Ibrahim digging away in the little nook behind the rocks. He still wore his turban, metal-white against his wet black shoulders. The Professor was kneeling on the shore, rummaging peacefully among the shells. His shiny bald head looked like an enormous white egg and his poppy-red kimono looked alive, almost flaming. The Baron had tossed his wig and velvet coat over a bush; he was still wearing his buckled slippers and green nankeen breeches. Miss Eccles had on her bonnet and her pink Jane Austen dress. She was wandering in the treeless distance, gazing wistfully across the sea. And now Mrs. Domingo came striding in Laura's direction, her gold lamé gown flashing in the sunlight barbarically.

"Kind of stimulating, isn't it?" She crouched in the shade next to Laura. "Slept like a log, I must admit. It's this wonderful ocean air. What I mean is it's a vivid little assortment that we've got here. A cosmopolis in miniature, I'd call it. It will end by making us all a bit more tolerant, that is certain. As long as things go smoothly. Your husband is a gift from heaven."

Mrs. Domingo had removed her hat, which was poised on top of a dune. Her streaky black hair stirred in the wind in gypsy strands. She turned and peered at the shaggy green hills on her left. "It's a benevolent little paradise, no ants, no mosquitoes. Too good to be true, almost. But those hills over there. Can you imagine what they're like? Worms and maggots, poisonous centipedes. I had a glimpse of all that nastiness down in Jamaica, quite enough of it. No, thanks. I see no reason for poking around in that festering darkness." She looked intently at Laura and murmured, "You are an intelligent woman, Laura. There you sit, cool as a cucumber, thinking rational, coherent thoughts. I wish I had your brain. I am governed by my instincts. Much too much so."

"There is nothing wrong," said Laura rather indulgently, "with instincts."

"Well, I wonder. I often think that a beautiful woman lives under an awful handicap. She doesn't bother to use her brains. Her looks are amply sufficient. Don't misunderstand me, please, Laura. You have a charming, elflike face. What I mean is that it's ghastly to lose one's beauty if one's always depended on it."

"You're still beautiful, Mrs. Domingo."

"My beauty is wilting," said Mrs. Domingo. She stared at her fingernails, which gleamed like blood on her wrinkled fingers.

"Beauty like yours never wilts. You'll be beautiful at ninety," said Laura.

"I am fifty-nine," said Mrs. Domingo with a birdlike expression.

"Still young," said Laura softly. "It's the drive that counts. The *élan vital.*"

"There are times," said Mrs. Domingo, "when I feel that my marriages were tragic blunders. They seemed wise at the time. There were advantages, no doubt. I'm not complaining. But we live only once and the thought of it haunts me, Laura, it haunts me."

"What sort of man was Mr. Domingo?"

"A kind of cripple. Incapacitated. It grew worse as the years rolled by. Toward the end he could hardly move."

"Why did you marry him? Was it pity?"

"He loved me, dear. He proposed to me."

"But did you love him, Mrs. Domingo?"

"Do call me Lily. Yes, I loved him. I really did. He was a gentleman. Beautiful taste in all things. He had a magnificent

Velasquez and I'm miserable that I ever sold it." She tapped Laura on the wrist. "Look, child. Here comes Penelope."

Miss Eccles had removed her bonnet, which was dangling from her forefinger. She was wandering rather thoughtfully toward the coconut grove.

"Tell me, Laura," said Mrs. Domingo, lowering her voice, "what do you think of Penelope? I mean, does she seem quite normal to you, somehow or other?"

"She seems amiable. Sad, a little."

"Diana-like is the word. I wonder why. I have my suspicions," said Mrs. Domingo.

"She has accepted," said Laura, "spinsterhood."

"She has fled from life," said Mrs. Domingo. "Some unmentionable sort of tragedy must have struck that poor girl."

Miss Eccles sat down under the palm tree next to Laura. Her face was pink with the sun. Beads of sweat shone on her temples.

"I was just saying to Laura here," said Mrs. Domingo with suavity, "how lucky we all are. With such a mingling of human types, I mean. It will be sad when we finally drift back to civilization. Back to the Danube, the Thames, the Susquehanna, and all the rest. We must promise to keep in touch. After an intimacy like this."

"Professor Shishnik seems to be fascinated with shells," observed Miss Eccles.

"He is like a child. Scholarly, brilliant. But an infant," said Mrs. Domingo.

"It's astonishing," said Laura, "how people change on closer acquaintance. Professor Shishnik used to strike me as a middle-aged nonentity."

"It's this air," said Mrs. Domingo. "Like litmus paper, if you see my point." She suddenly cocked her head. "There! Listen! Do you hear it?"

"What?" said Laura.

"A kind of throbbing . . ."

Laura stared at the sky intently. "I don't see anything, Lily."

Mrs. Domingo looked piqued. "Not a plane, Laura. *Drums.*"

The three women sat motionless and stared at the jungly hills. Finally Miss Eccles said, "No, I hear nothing, nothing at all."

"Bullfrogs, maybe," said Laura.

"I could have sworn there was something or other. Goes to show," said Mrs. Domingo. "It's this wild, glittering air. Puts queer fancies into one's brain."

"Well, of course, it might have been drums. There is nothing wrong with drums," said Laura.

"Even if there were, there is nothing we can do to keep them from drumming," said Miss Eccles.

"The savages use drums like telegrams. To send messages," said Mrs. Domingo. "It wouldn't surprise me a bit if they were sending a sinister message."

"Sinister how?" inquired Miss Eccles.

"My dear girl," said Mrs. Domingo, "if there are niggers up in those mountains, you may rest assured they are aware of our presence."

"But does it follow," said Miss Eccles, "that they have sinister intentions?"

"The time has finally arrived," said Mrs. Domingo in husky tones, "when we whites will pay the penalty. *Vae victis,* as they say. All these hundreds of years we've been living the life of Riley. Well, the worm has turned, I tell you. All those blacks feel a terrible vengefulness."

"My dear Lily," said Miss Eccles, "you do have a way of instilling uneasiness."

"The tides of history," said Mrs. Domingo, "sweep on remorselessly. There is nothing to stop them."

"Well," said Laura, "I quite agree that there has been considerable injustice, but I trust that they won't seize on this particular island to settle their scores. We have Ibrahim with us, luckily. And that little Zenzo, who is faintly lemon-hued."

"We must hope," declared Miss Eccles, smiling bravely, "that there weren't any drums. I refuse to think there were drums. I heard nothing, Lily, nothing."

4

The Baron squatted in the secrecy of the bamboos and wrote in his diary:

Well, here we are. A sandy beach, shells and crabs, corals, coconuts. It seems unreal to the point of absurdity. There were moments when the wreck itself struck me as merely a gaudy display of fireworks. And this spectacle of a bunch of masqueraders landing on a palm-fringed peninsula—it seems like a rather banal novelistic contrivance. The curious thing is that along with my feeling of relief, almost of triumph, I also feel a queer little twinge of guilt, as though I myself were responsible for the wreck. I admit that I felt a certain *frisson* when I saw the flames shoot over the bridge. Pure destructiveness, vengefulness? No, it is more than that. Or maybe less than that. That *other* thing in me, that dark, prowling *Doppelgänger* whom I've tried so intently to ignore all these years. Well, there's no point in brooding over it. There's nothing to be done. Let's try to forget it.

Still, this business of the *Cassandra*—I keep brooding about it. I am haunted by suspicions—hundreds of crazy little suspicions. I am chronically suspicious by nature, of course—even as a child I used to wonder what my Tante Adelhaid kept in those funny old boxes of hers, and what my Onkel Willy did in the woodshed with the gardener's boy. All these thoughts keep stabbing at my brain like a cloud of mosquitoes. Kleist warned me

that there might be an agent on board the ship keeping his eye
on me. There were moments when I even suspected that Captain
Abernethy was looking at me queerly. And that shriveled old
Chinese wrapped up in a bundle—was *he* spying on me? And
Shishnik? The more I think about it the more puzzled I am by
his role. It was him that I saw that night in the Cavendish Bar,
beyond a doubt. I'm sure he'd been following me. Of course it's
quite possible that there's something *else* at the bottom of it. Not
likely, though. He doesn't strike me as a sodomitic type. I will
have to assume that this drab little man is my deadly enemy.
Whatever happens, I must prevent him from discovering my
precious envelope, which now lies safely buried under the roots
of a banana palm. And of course I mustn't risk anyone peeping
at this diary. I keep it safely tucked in its little nook beneath my
sleeping mat. What a catastrophe it would be if poor old Lily
ever got hold of it!

I've been watching the Wagenseller couple. There's something
bloodthirsty about that woman. When I look at her I know what
they mean by the female impulse toward castration. He's obviously a bit of an ass. I've noticed his behavior with that Japanese
boy. He thinks that he's fooling us all, his shrew of a wife included. It's quite clear what they're up to on those "fishing ex-
peditions." The American male would appear to be basically
ambidextrous. Burly athletes, boxers, cowboys, all exuding a
hairy virility, but all of them with a streak of the transvestite deep
down in them.

And Ibrahim! I find myself watching him with rage and fascination. He's undoubtedly the most beautiful creature that I've
ever laid eyes on. If I weren't so sure of my heterosexuality I
would almost begin to wonder. And the strange thing is that I
cannot help hating him for his beauty. It's quite obvious that
poor Lily finds him physically irresistible. I strongly disapprove of
her attitude, scarcely becoming in a woman of her age, but I
somehow rather doubt whether anything sexual will materialize.
He's incurably naïve. A genuine innocent, unless my judgment
has deserted me. And it's this innocence, along with his beauty,
which so piques and enrages me. He strikes a dangerous note on
this overcivilized promontory.

I'm beginning to find this little diary of mine rather useful,
therapeutically speaking. Not only as a confidant, to whom I can

confide my secret thoughts, but also as a father confessor, to whom I can whisper my sins. How few of us grasp the real meaning of our sins! They are like pus bursting from a wound: better squeeze it out into the open, transform it into action and do the heinous deed, than let it keep festering, haunting our dreams, poisoning our blood stream. There are plenty of things I've longed to do but never quite dared. I remember one summer in Zell-am-See when I was eleven. My cousin Rita, aged twelve, lured me into the dark, deserted bathhouse. I still remember the water glittering through the little knotholes in the wood. She ordered me to kneel in front of her. Then she lifted her skirt and spread her legs apart. "Kiss it!" she snarled. "Kiss it, you *lausbub!*" I was numb with disgust and horror. I shall never forget the menacing expression of that dark little crevice. I felt a wild impulse to grab the fishing rod that stood in the corner and ram it up her vagina: it seemed like an apt sort of vengeance. And to this day I must frankly confess that the female pudendum strikes me as aesthetically inadequate, both in shape and coloration. Is it all the fault of my cousin Rita? (She later became a distinguished contributor to the musical column of the *Wiener Tageblatt,* and the foremost authority on the works of Ditter von Dittersdorf.)

5

Soon after dawn every morning Tony would cross the creek with Zenzo, he with his gun and Zenzo with a sack, and climb into the shadowy thicket. He found a rock-strewn little stream that followed a dent between two hills and here they used to wait for the birds who came to drink. Once he shot down a duck with a crimson crown perched on its head, and once he shot a hare that was as big as a terrier.

Ibrahim's cooking grew more ingenious as the days went calmly by. Roasted fish of all hues, sprinkled with herbs or baby crayfish, and certain curious mixtures such as crabs stuffed with bananas, or a casserole of wood pigeons, bread-

fruit, and sea urchins. The Professor kept the fire going faith-
fully all day. The smell of burning twigs and sizzling seafood
gave them an appetite. The ladies went bathing in a nook behind the palms, while the men swam every morning in the
cavernous cove below the rocks, where the water was deep
and Zenzo dove from a jutting ledge.

For the first seven days life was calm and idyllic. Little by
little they all grew used to the thought of a longer stay.
Ibrahim and Zenzo, under Tony's direction, built a hut for
the ladies. Six stakes were driven into the ground and a web of
twigs was laid on top of them; then palm leaves were woven
amongst the twigs and tied with lianas. A roll of canvas was
ripped from the lifeboat, which lay stranded on the beach,
and a shady marquee was built for their noonday siesta. Billy
Baxter decorated the columns with his many-colored shells
and Miss Eccles wove an octagonal carpet of bamboo leaves.
Tony carried a bucketful of water from the stream thrice a
day. Knives and forks were carved by the Baron from the twigs
of a banyan tree. The Professor dug a pit behind a cluster of
thorny bushes, with a heap of dry sand and a palm broom
beside it. This served as a latrine. Laura's Mexican shawl was
draped over a bough to give it an air of seclusion.

Mrs. Domingo spent her hours watching the others at
their chores. She watched the Professor fanning the flames; she
watched Laura scaling the fish. She watched Tony splitting
coconut shells and Miss Eccles weaving her mats. She watched
Billy building his sand castles down by the shore, and she
watched Zenzo, stripped to the waist, squatting on a rock with
his fishing pole. And she took a special pleasure in watching
the beautiful black Ibrahim, who still insisted on wearing his
shiny white turban day and night.

Once she said to Ibrahim softly, "Tell me, Ibrahim. Are
you a Mohammedan?"

"Oh, a little," said Ibrahim airily.

"How can you be a *little* Mohammedan?"

"I was a Mohammedan baby, madam, but much has changed since I was a baby. I was born up in the mountains by Aïn-Sefra. I had six brothers and nine sisters. I was taken to the mosque. I recited the Koran. When I was twelve an English lady took me to Fez and taught me English. She was a very luxurious lady, very rich, very wise. She read books in every language—Russian, Spanish, Japanese. I brought her coffee in the morning and her tea in the afternoon. Her name was Lady Satterthwaite. Lady Satterthwaite had no God. And she seemed quite happy without a God. So after a while I stopped praying to Allah. After two years in Fez Lady Satterthwaite took me to Cairo, where we lived in a houseboat on the shore of the Nile. And two years later we went to Kandy, where we lived in the hills. Life was always full of luxury and amusement with Lady Satterthwaite. She bought a Rolls-Royce and I learned to be her chauffeur. I drove with much skill and wore a gold-braided uniform, but one morning up in the mountains the car jumped into the valley. The Rolls-Royce was smashed. Lady Satterthwaite was broken to pieces. I was sad but still alive and I started to think about Allah again. And that is why I say that I am a *little* bit Muslim."

"I see," said Mrs. Domingo. "And what did you do when the lady died?"

"I went to Colombo, where I worked in a shoe shop, and then to Bangkok, where I worked in a silk factory. Then I sailed down to Singapore, where I cooked in a restaurant. I was twenty, but very puzzled. I had no money and not even a God, and I often thought of suicide."

"A terrible thing, suicide," said Mrs. Domingo darkly. "It's an unforgivable sin, my boy. You must never commit suicide."

Ibrahim nodded his head with a crafty look. "I have stopped to think of suicide, madam."

"We must be grateful that we were born. We must smile at adversity," purred Mrs. Domingo.

Ibrahim folded his night-blue arms and looked thoughtfully into the distance, where a sea bird was diving into the mirror-smooth inlet. His white satin turban was darkened with sweat. He had discarded the rest of his costume and wore only a burlap loincloth.

Mrs. Domingo rested her eyes on his lean, shining body and said, "You are rather black for an Arab, aren't you, Ibrahim?"

"The men of Aïn-Sefra are very black," said Ibrahim suspiciously.

Mrs. Domingo was still for a moment and then murmured, almost sorrowfully, "You are unusually handsome, Ibrahim. Tell me something, please, won't you?"

Ibrahim grinned. "What, madam?"

"Do you yearn for whiteness, Ibrahim?"

"I do not grasp you quite, madam."

"I mean, do you suffer from being black? Do you grieve at not being white, Ibrahim?"

Ibrahim licked his upper lip. "Not often, I think, madam."

Mrs. Domingo said quietly, "Have you ever lusted for a white woman?"

Ibrahim peered slyly through his eyelashes. "I think *politely* about white ladies."

"And if a white lady were to offer her body to you, would you rise to the occasion, Ibrahim?"

Ibrahim scratched his navel thoughtfully. "Ah, madam, it is very complicated. There are millions of ladies in the world, some of them white, some dark, some medium. The color does not matter. I like ladies who are wise and gentle. . . ."

That evening the Baron passed around a drink which he had made from the juice of a fruit: those bright scarlet balls which grew on the palms beside the inlet. The flavor was like cassis, rather smoky and slightly cloying, but it had an exhilarating effect on the company. The Professor told of his experience with a burglar in Lisbon. The Baron chatted of chamois hunting in the hills of Carinthia. Miss Eccles described the capture of fritillary in the Pyrenees. Laura told of a week she had spent in the Andes among the Indians.

Mrs. Domingo spread her arms and rattled her bracelets with joy. "Fascinating, my child! I never dreamed that I'd be thrilled by the Andes. Alas, we'll soon be back in the whirl of civilization and this calm, lovely isle will be just a beautiful memory."

"It will seem like a dream," said Laura.

"A Fata Morgana," said the Baron.

"But it isn't a dream, it's the genuine reality," cried Mrs. Domingo. "We are bursting into bloom. We are communing with Mother Nature. We are peering into the heart of things. And look! Just look at us! We are utterly happy!"

6

Eight days after the shipwreck a streak of oil appeared on the beach, a liverish sheen that ran the length of the promontory. Lumps of tar dappled the shore and stuck to the feet of the bathers. Little chunks of charred wood came rolling in on the wavelets, as well as a rubber elephant and an empty vodka bottle. Billy Baxter discovered a ping-pong ball afloat in the foam.

Mrs. Domingo found the Professor kneeling at the edge of the water. He was peering at a stranded cushion, the kind that was used on the *Cassandra*'s deck chairs. His kimono drooped untidily; it was stained with sweat and charcoal.

"Please forgive me, Professor Shishnik, but do stop being

so reticent, won't you? In this lazy seaside atmosphere we should try to relax and confide a little."

"I have nothing to confide, madam. I wish that I did," said the Professor wistfully.

"I refuse to believe it. You are a man of vast experiences. What is your opinion about love, for example? You must have a philosophy. What is your philosophy?"

Professor Shishnik dropped the pillow and looked at Mrs. Domingo dejectedly. "So you want the truth about me? I will tell you, Mrs. Domingo. There is no truth, there is no falsehood, there is nothing, nothing whatever. I have never become a person. I float around in a psychological vacuum. I am still a raw red baby, or even a foetus if you wish, a groping mass of flesh which has never found its definite shape. I am neither this nor that, neither wicked nor virtuous. Love? I have never been in love. Philosophy? I don't know what it means. My mind is as amorphous as that jellyfish out there."

Mrs. Domingo glanced at the jellyfish and murmured, "Come, come, Professor. You're not fooling me in the least. Your eyes have lonely depths in them. You look like a figure in Dostoevski. Maybe it's just that you're Russian. You give me a feeling of endless spaces. But still, you must have a specialty. What is your specialty?"

Professor Shishnik looked at her dimly with his rabbitlike eyes. She had tied up her hair in a shiny black knot. The sunlight flashed on her earrings; her bracelet tinkled with amulets.

"I have only one specialty, Mrs. Domingo, and that is hope."

"What kind of hope?" said the woman eagerly.

"Hope for man, shall we say?"

"Are you a Communist, by chance?"

"I have no politics, none whatever. I refuse to be trapped in the purely contemporary, madam, and all politics are by their nature incurably contemporary and therefore temporary. Ah, yes, my feelings are swayed now and then by a flicker of partisanship. I feel rage, disgust, impatience, but I brush it all aside. I have never believed in missions, in crusades, or conspiracies. Our only salvation lies in the arena of the spirit."

"You have put my point of view into a perfect nutshell," said the woman, sparkling.

"I did not wish to sound crude or evangelistic," said he gently, "and the salvation to which I refer is only to be found in the deepest solitude. Solitude—that's what the modern world has so brutally annihilated. For the poetry and insight of the child, for the wisdom and lucidity of the old, it has substituted the cheap clichés and vapid mimicries of the adolescent. It is fashionable nowadays to say that no man is an island, but it is wrong: man *is* an island and will forever remain an island. He is born and will die an island and his misery lies in being perpetually invaded. You ask me what I do. I am a scholar, Mrs. Domingo, but a scholar who is floating in an absolute void. I write erudite articles. On the snakes of Sumatra, or the witches of Bali. Sometimes they are printed. More often not. I have no money, in case it interests you. I despise and fear all money. That is one thing about this place. There is no money. There is no commercialism. It is a monumental blessing."

"And what exactly is wrong with money, may I ask, Professor Shishnik?"

"I won't embark on a dissertation on the horrors of money, Mrs. Domingo. It is money, with all its corollaries, which is mankind's degradation."

"But money must exist, surely?"

"Money is totally unnecessary, madam. Look at us, for example. We are doing splendidly without money. We are in the act of creating a beautiful new society out of nothing but palm leaves, sea shells, and coconuts. Have we all gone mad, madam? No. We are slowly becoming sane again. We are building a new Utopia, a land where men are free yet equal!"

"It is stirring," said Mrs. Domingo, "to listen to such old-fashioned idealism. I wish I could believe in the marvels of poverty, Professor." The palm leaves above her swayed in the heat, crackling faintly. She folded her arms and gazed accusingly at the Professor. "Tell me, Professor. What is it that you have against me, quite frankly?"

"What makes you feel that I have something against you?" said Shishnik softly.

"You seem to recoil from me, I've noticed. I have a feeling that you despise me. You think that I'm just a pampered millionairess, don't you, Professor?"

"I do not place human beings in such casual categories, Mrs. Domingo."

"You'd be perfectly right, what's more. I *am* pampered. I *am* frivolous. But I'm other things as well. Secret, unexpected things. I may talk like a silly schoolgirl but I can assure you, Professor Shishnik, that a feeling of mystery has been gradually creeping over me!" She scratched her wrinkled neck and peered connivingly at the Professor. "There is always so much more than meets the eye, *n'est-ce pas*, Professor?"

Zenzo came running across the beach. "Professor Shishigo! Quick! Quick, please!"

Mrs. Domingo followed Zenzo and the Professor to the end of the promontory. They crossed the jutting rocks and climbed down to the shady cove, where Tony Wagenseller was kneeling beside a dark, mottled object.

Mrs. Domingo looked into the shadows, let out a howl, and covered her eyes. She turned and ran back to the beach, screaming "God, oh God, Penelope!" What she had seen was a naked torso, fearfully swollen and disfigured, with the limbs ripped from their sockets and the face hacked to shreds. She had recognized a thin golden chain imbedded in the neck, and at the end of it the bright little spider of Dr. Banerjee.

7

It was dusk. The first stars were already beginning to twinkle. It had grown too dark to read and the Professor closed his *Odyssey*. He had been reading about the Sirens. It gave him joy to read about the Sirens. He felt close, in this watery atmosphere, to those lonely little Sirens, with their wave-lacquered breasts and their dangerous, high-pitched voices.

Still, there was something very troubling and deeply melancholy about the Sirens. What did they want? What were they singing about? What was the secret of their misery? Was it the need for human love that drove them to such a frenzy? If so, it would be better to abandon all hope of human love. Better be a monk or a eunuch, or even a monstrosity, than suffer these frenzies of unrequited love.

Night fell. The moon rose, and Miss Eccles came wandering past. She was carrying an enormous white shell in her hand.

"Isn't it lovely, Professor? I just found it down by the grotto."

"It *is* lovely, Miss Eccles. You look as though you were carrying a bowl of moonlight."

"Tell me, Professor. What do you think? Is there any likelihood of our being rescued?"

"You sound like Andromeda, Miss Eccles. Are you sure that you'd like to be rescued?"

Miss Eccles smiled mistily. "Yes, perhaps I rather agree with you. Perhaps we are happier here than we'll ever be when we're back home again. Still, I'm haunted by a sense of—how shall I put it?—unreality."

"And yet," said the Professor, "it's the true reality we are being confronted with. Oh, not just the reality of nature, with all its beauty and brutality, but the reality within ourselves. We are finally turning into real people."

Miss Eccles stared at her shell, which looked as though it were melting under the moonlight. "Are we really, Professor? I wish it were so. But are we really?"

"Tell me, Miss Eccles. What is it that so fascinates you about butterflies, exactly?"

"Just their beauty, Professor. Merely their beauty and, of course, their elusiveness. Oh, yes, there are collectors who pretend that it's all in the interests of science—the nomenclature, the food plants, the wing structure, and so on. But who would dream of collecting fleas or mosquitoes or leeches? It's their loveliness, Professor. And their inexhaustible mystery."

"Every animal is mysterious, isn't it?"

"But butterflies even more than the rest of them. No creature on earth is so absurdly and irrationally beautiful. Perhaps the peacock, though I personally find the peacock a little vulgar. The butterfly's beauty is an end in itself. It has no purpose, no utility, not even for reproductive purposes, since an ugly insect mates just as easily as a pretty one. These lepidoptera live purely for happiness. They have no other purpose in life. I have watched the dark Euthalias in the Siamese forests, and the silver Argyrophorus in the depths of the Andes, and the bright little blues dancing in a meadow in Sussex. The one thing that is obvious is their utter, ecstatic happiness. When I capture one of these beasts I think I am capturing their beauty and happiness. That is love, isn't it, Professor? I am not a philosopher, unfortunately, but it strikes me as rather odd that the fulfillment of love should be murder. I pierce those darling butterflies with a needle in order to possess them."

"Oh, there's something very dreadful about all love," said the Professor.

"Yes," said Miss Eccles, "I feel like a murderess, killing the one thing that I love. And yet I keep right on doing it. These murders of passion become a habit."

"There's a certain complexity about butterflies, it appears," said the Professor.

"Indeed there is," said Miss Eccles feelingly. "There are subtleties and profundities, and insoluble mysteries. *Kallima inachus,* after millennia of effort, has finally perfected itself so that it exactly—you might say uncannily—resembles a dead leaf. It dangles from a bough with a drop of dew glistening on its wing, and even members of its own species occasionally mistake it for just a leaf. Just to think of all these subtle and sophisticated dramas that took place a million years ago! A bird swoops down at a butterfly, which instantly transforms itself into a leaf. But why that drop of dew? It's the sheer ebullience of mimicry. These mimics, I've noticed, sometimes exaggerate the thing in their enthusiasm. The wings of the huge Brazilian Caligo are decorated with feathers and vicious eyes. When they spread out their wings they look exactly like the head of an owl. There are butterflies that look like a death's head, or the eyes of a madonna, or a poisonous mushroom. The beautiful blue of the male Morpho, as opposed to the rusty female, has so intoxicated certain species that they are driven to homosexuality. And what are we to say of *Idea clara,* which floats through the air like a piece of rice paper, beautifully inscribed with rows of calligraphy, which are read in Formosa in the form of epigrams? I've often wondered, How did they do it? Was it centuries of accident, or centuries of intention? And how can an insect resemble an orchid merely by trying to resemble an orchid?"

"These are questions," said the Professor, "to which we'll never find the answer."

"Mind you, Professor," said Miss Eccles, "there are deadly dangers in lepidoptery. We are punished in the end for our greed and idolatry. Herr Lilienfeldt, a scholar from Uppsala, was stabbed to death by a Corsican bandit in his search for the rarest of European swallowtails, the dusky *hospiton*. The erudite Dr. Martineau, who was hunting in the peaks of the Pamirs, fell from a cliff as he was trying to net that dazzling miracle, an *autocrator*. The Baron de Jong, a wealthy amateur, was caught by a group of Naga tribesmen and torn limb from limb while he was looking for a Bhutan Glory. And poor old Madame Kempinski, the noted expert on the family of Morphidae, was devoured by a crocodile as she was wading in the swamps of the Xingu."

"All obsessions," said the Professor, "are eventually punished, I'm afraid."

Miss Eccles looked thoughtfully at Shishnik's sad, amorphous face, and suddenly she felt a wave of incongruous tenderness for him.

"Tell me, Professor," she said thoughtfully, "are we crazy, you and I, who are immune to the appeal of money and sexual success, and even fame?"

"Alas, Miss Eccles, we aren't crazy. We are marvelously sane, but we are anachronisms. Because we are children, you and I. And modern society has no use for children."

"Children can be cruel, too," said Miss Eccles.

"It's a different kind," said the Professor, "of cruelty."

"There are moments when I feel a terrible guilt."

"The guilt," said the Professor, "of being a poet. After all, in your own special way you are a poet, Miss Eccles. Not Homeric or Dantesque, nor Shakespearean: Blakean, shall we say?"

"You flatter me, Professor. I am perfectly humdrum and ordinary."

"And I," said the Professor mournfully, "am not even humdrum, not even ordinary."

"Well, good night, Professor Shishnik. It has been a most agreeable chat."

"Good night, Miss Eccles. And please don't worry about your greed and idolatry!"

8

Mrs. Domingo lay in the darkness of the hut, unable to sleep. Through the interwoven palm leaves she could see the intensity of the night outside—a sky that was even blacker than the interior of the hut and fiercely dotted with brilliant little stars. These bouts of insomnia came over her every three or four weeks, and their unpleasantness was intensified by the grimness of her thoughts as she lay awake. Instead of fixing her mind on the various charming things that had happened to her, she was haunted by memories of cruelty, of embarrassment, of general nastiness. The bottle of sleeping pills was empty, she had used up her tonic, and all she had left was a little box of crumbling aspirin tablets. She had never gone in for drugs; life, she said, was "amusing enough" without them. But there were moments in the deep of night when she would have been grateful for a wave of forgetfulness, or at least for a cozy, understanding friend whom she could chat with.

She leaned into the gloom and whispered, "Penelope! Are you asleep?" No answer.

Then she turned to the opposite wall. "Laura! Are you sleeping?" Still no answer.

She rose with a sigh and groped her way through the palms toward the inlet. The cool spicy air restored her peace of mind for a while, and she dipped her calloused toes into the star-sprinkled water.

At that moment she saw, or thought that she saw, a silhouette in the distance, where the bamboos reached down to the mud-crusted shore. A naked black man. Ibrahim? No, he was smaller than Ibrahim. And Ibrahim, of course, would be easy to recognize with his snow-white turban. The figure turned sharply, crouched low for a moment, and then went scurrying off behind the screen of bamboos.

"Holy smokes," said Mrs. Domingo in an awe-struck whisper. "It's a goddamn cannibal." And a *frisson* of horror, tinged with pleasure, ran down her spine.

But the night was so beautiful that her peace of mind returned instantly and she muttered to herself reassuringly: "Just an optical illusion." It wasn't the first time on this beach that she had suffered from hallucinations, especially after sipping an overdose of Hugo's pungent palm cassis. Even as a child she used to shudder at the notion of a man hiding in her bedroom—usually he was black and covered with hair, and not infrequently he was naked. Such an idiotic obsession: she was certainly not the spinster type, and in view of her broad experiences it was absurd to be frightened of men, naked or otherwise. She sat down on the sand and stared up at the Milky Way. The moment had come, she felt, for some restful meditations.

"Lily," said a voice directly behind her.

She turned abruptly. "Hugo. Heavens."

"What are you doing here, Lily?"

"Just thinking some thoughts, that's all."

"Sleepless again? My poor little Lily."

"Oh, I'm used to it," she said bravely. "There are worse things in the world, I suppose, than insomnia."

"As long," said the Baron, sitting down beside her, "as one feels peaceful. If one doesn't feel peaceful, then, of course, insomnia can be tiresome."

"I don't feel peaceful exactly," said Mrs. Domingo somewhat irritably, "but I've learned to put up with my own frailties and inadequacies. I used to be haunted by a feeling of wickedness, but now I know better. I'm not wicked, am I, Hugo? Tell me, Hugo, do you think I'm wicked? Oh, please, Hugo, honey, tell me that my life hasn't been evil! How can people be evil if they don't even realize that they're being naughty? Believe me, Hugo, I never in my life did a thing that I knew was evil. My heart is basically kind. I've lied and I've cheated and my sex life has been on the giddy side, but I've never wounded a soul, not deliberately anyway. God knows what evil is. Are *you* evil? I wish I knew. There was something kind of evil about the *Cassandra*, I can't help feeling, but I never discovered exactly what it was. There were times when I felt suspicious about Signor Cucci and even Mr. Banerjee, and once or twice it crossed my mind that maybe even you had something to do with it. Let me tell you a secret. It's something that I've never mentioned to anybody. That night of the shipwreck I was feeling sick and sort of dizzy, with all that champagne on top of the whisky, and I've never even cared for champagne especially. Well, I was tottering down to my cabin when I saw that smoke oozing out of the gift shop and I realized instantaneously that the goddamn ship was on fire. I recovered my wits immediately. My brain worked like a machine. I saw, quick as a flash, someone scurrying down the corridor. I never saw his face, he was gone before I knew what had happened, all I can say is that it was definitely and unmistakably an Oriental, with shortish black hair and sort of baby-blue overalls. Sounds bizarre, but I can remember it just as vividly as when it happened. What does it prove? What's at the bottom of it? Do you have a theory about it, Hugo?"

"Well," said Hugo, "we'll never know the truth about the *Cassandra*, that is certain. All the evidence, if there *was* any evidence, is safely tucked in the bottom of the ocean. I cannot personally believe that there was anything sinister about it, like sabotage. What on earth would there be to sabotage on a dreary tub like the *Cassandra?* One grows suspicious, it's only human, one tries to detect some sort of motive; but the fact is that the poor old vessel was coming apart at the seams. Somebody dropped a cigarette, my dear, it's as simple as that, and the miracle is that we're still alive and sitting peacefully on this lovely island."

"Lovely island?" said Mrs. Domingo. "Well, I'm glad that's the way you feel about it."

"We should be grateful," said the Baron sententiously, "for every blessing, however tiny."

9

Tony was careful never to prowl too deeply into the thicket beyond the beach. He followed the brook through a veil of ferns and up toward a statelier array of foliage—a grove of eucalyptus trees, which shed a strong scent of curry, and some writhing old banyans which were studded with mushrooms. He found some sturdy banana palms as well as a type of *Artocarpus,* a tree of small, beady fruits which tasted like pumpkins. Beyond the eucalyptus grove rose a chaos of blue-gray boulders which gradually dipped into a flinty ravine. In this treeless ravine the air shook with heat. A dark narrow chasm guarded the end of the ravine and beyond it shone the gonglike blue of the ocean. It was here, in an inlet lined with brightly colored pebbles, that he and Zenzo spent their mornings sitting in the shade, fishing peacefully.

"How long you think we stay here, Mr. Wagasala?" said Zenzo, grinning.

"Your guess is as good as mine. Getting worried, are you, Zenzo?"

"No, not worry. Quite O.K. Where you live, Mr. Wagasala?"

"I was raised in an evil old city called Philadelphia."

"Evil how, Mr. Wagasala?"

"People drank. People gossiped. They played golf. They played bridge. They threw their lives into the gutter."

Zenzo jerked at his line. Then he swung it into the air. A large brownish fish, leopard-spotted, danced on the end of it.

"That's a new one," said Tony.

"Mighty fine, eh?" said Zenzo.

"Tell me, Zenzo. Are you bored? Are you homesick for Japan?"

Zenzo giggled and shook his head. "I never bored. I always happy!"

"You could live here forever? Just swimming and fishing?"

Zenzo grew solemn. "I like fishing. But I no like killing."

"We must kill if we're going to eat. If we didn't eat we'd all be dead."

"Please no joke, Mr. Wagasala. To kill is bad, very bad thing."

"Well, it's better to kill a fish than a man, isn't it, Zenzo?"

Zenzo shook his head solemnly. "No, no, Mr. Wagasala. All killing be bad. Fish, bird, man, everything. Fish and bird very happy. Even butterfly very happy. A very bad thing to kill happy fishes."

"Well," said Tony, "we could live on bananas, I guess. But who knows, maybe a banana is also very happy."

"Please no joke, Mr. Wagasala! Me and friends up in Tokyo, we all happy when we live alone in woods eating berries."

"Oh, I see. So you think it's time we returned to nature, do you, Zenzo?"

"Look," said Zenzo. "Everybody happy who live quiet in nature. Professor happy. Baron happy. Lady who chase butterfly, Miss Ecky, she happy. No hard to be happy. Why no everybody happy?"

"I didn't know that the Japanese were so crazy about happiness."

"Oh, yes, Japanese folks all crazy about happiness."

"Well, then, why do they go and commit hara-kiri, Zenzo?"

"Just so, Mr. Wagasala! Because sadness be like a sickness. My friend pretty Sado fall in love with American gentleman. His name Mr. Spencer. Mr. Spencer jolly old man. Mr. Spencer very fat. Mr. Spencer have very fine beard. But Mr. Spencer no love Sado. So Sado turn sick with sadness and poor Sado go falling into sea by Yokohama."

"Yes. I see," said Tony thoughtfully. "Little Sado couldn't cope with it. I don't wonder. Having a crush on a phony bastard with a beard."

Zenzo glanced at him teasingly with his glittering black eyes. "You afraid, Mr. Wagasala? Why afraid, Mr. Wagasala?"

"Afraid? I'm not afraid. There's nothing to be afraid of, is there, Zenzo?"

"Ah, yes. You afraid! You full of afraidness, Mr. Wagasala!" And he burst into an uncontrollable fit of laughter.

They climbed down to the beach and Tony brought the fish to Ibrahim, who was stirring a bright yellow sauce in a hollow coconut shell. Zenzo wandered along the shore and found Laura under her palmtree.

"Me catch beautiful fish," he said. "Mighty tasty, I think, Mrs. Wagasala!"

"Tell me, Zenzo. Where did you pick up that funny American accent?"

"I make friend with many American in Tokyo," said Zenzo proudly. "I go to their home. I read their magazine. I listen to their music. *St. Louis Blues, Mood Indigo.* I have a big wish for U.S.A., Mrs. Wagasala."

"I think you might be disappointed in the U.S.A., a shade," said Laura.

Zenzo looked at her slyly. "I think no, Mrs. Wagasala. In Tokyo I learn much and think much about U.S.A."

"Such as what, for example?"

"Such as love, Mrs. Wagasala. Much strangeness and afraidness of love in U.S.A."

"They are frustrated, a bit," said Laura.

"Look," said Zenzo, "at Mr. Wagasala."

"Yes? Go on, please," said Laura.

"Mr. Wagasala very strange. Mr. Wagasala full of afraidness. Poor Mr. Wagasala want love but afraid even to touch me!"

Laura lifted her head and looked quietly at Zenzo. He smiled back at her and cocked his shiny head with curiosity. And for the first time she noticed something charming about Zenzo: the broad merry face, the powerful swimmer's body, the stubborn black hair, the guileless black eyes.

She turned around slowly and looked down at the blazing sea. Some gulls shot down from the rocks and hung bickering over the cove. Billy Baxter was sitting in the stranded lifeboat with the Professor, who was reading aloud, with roaming gestures, from *The Odyssey.*

10

Billy and Ibrahim were building castles out of sand beside the water. Billy's castle was medieval, with a moat all around it. He built a drawbridge over the moat with little stalks of dry seaweed and on top of the castle he placed a crenellated tower. Ibrahim's castle had a whimsically Moorish look about it: a mosquelike dome and a minaret which was studded with sea shells.

"How old are you, Ibrahim?"

"I am twenty," said Ibrahim.

"That's exactly twice what I am. I'm just ten," declared Billy.

"Your real name is William?"

"William Oglethorpe Baxter."

"An elegant name," said Ibrahim. "You played ping-pong on the *Cassandra*, didn't you?"

"I played with Tommy Ross and Eileen Merriweather," said Billy.

"I saw you play with your sister too."

"My sister is dead," said Billy softly.

"Don't be sad," said Ibrahim, agitated. "You must smile. You must look at the prettiness. Look at the water! Isn't it pretty? Look at the shells. Aren't they pretty? You must try to be full of joy on this pretty beach, Billy Baxter."

Billy nodded his head reflectively. "We were going to Sydney, Australia. I wonder what it's like in Australia. Are kangaroos dangerous, Ibrahim?"

"No animal is dangerous," said Ibrahim.

"Not even a tiger?" said Billy.

"Not even a tiger. The only dangerous beast is a crocodile," said Ibrahim.

"And cobras? Aren't they dangerous?"

"Only when you scare them they're dangerous."

"Spiders! Those awful hairy ones!"

"Yes, spiders," said Ibrahim thoughtfully.

"And rats. I'm scared of rats."

"Rats are ugly," nodded Ibrahim.

"And sharks! What about sharks?"

"It is a fable about sharks. Sharks eat fish but not people. They are puzzled but scared by people. I saw a shark once by

Singapore. I was standing on a rock in the water. The shark came very close. It was curious, that is all. It looked puzzled but not dangerous. It flicked its tail and swam away again."

Billy pointed to a rock which jutted from the sea in the distance. "What do you think is on that rock, Ibrahim?"

"Nothing," said Ibrahim. "Just a lot of sea urchins."

"Could we swim to that rock?"

"It's too far for a swim," said Ibrahim, bored a little.

"Come! Swim with me!" cried Billy. "Teach me the back-stroke, please, Ibrahim!"

"Tomorrow," said Ibrahim, yawning. "Today I am full of laziness."

He lay down on his back beside the castle and fell asleep. His mouth fell half open, his belly rose rhythmically. Billy studied the dark, slumbering Ibrahim with curiosity: the crisp, puckered nipples, the curls in his armpits, the pointed finger-nails. There was a sheen in the corners of his eyes, as though he were peering through his eyelashes. A fresh, pleasing odor, like pineapple, rose from his body.

Billy leaned very close and looked at Ibrahim's skin. Very dark but not quite black, with a violet sheen, like certain butterflies. He touched him lightly on the arm and then on the belly. He could feel the blackness of Ibrahim, warm and cozy, but also frightening.

Billy thought, "What a wonderful island," and waded lazily into the water. A jellyfish, translucent, the color of amethyst, was floating near him. It looked infinitely frail and insubstantial, like a little ghost. And for some mysterious reason he was reminded of his sister Sally. Had he loved her as much as he should have, poor little Sally? Had he grieved for Sally sufficiently when she sank beneath the waves? Why had he nearly forgotten Sally if his feelings were the right ones? Was there something in his soul which was wicked and deplorable?

Far away, on the smooth horizon, something curious wa

happening. A shiny black ribbon was fluttering on the surface
of the sea. It seemed to be moving in a series of lazy undulations. The undulations came nearer and went skimming past
the promontory: seven, nine, eleven, thirteen of them, very
sleek, the color of eggplants. Billy Baxter stood motionless and
held his breath as he watched them. He felt a passionate
longing to turn into one of those glossy creatures, whose lives
were a ceaseless dance of delight.

He cried, "Ibrahim! Porpoises!" But Ibrahim kept on
sleeping and the porpoises vanished behind the rocks, gone
forever.

Billy wandered along the beach toward the thorny bushes
down at the end. Laura's Mexican shawl was draped discreetly
over a twig. Billy tiptoed behind a bush and peeped through
the foliage. Miss Eccles was crouching on the sand with a
distant expression. Her eyes were strangely intent as they
stared into space; her lips were pursed grimly, her fingers
curved daintily. She scooped out a hollow in the ground with
a stick and into it she dropped what looked like a blood-
stained bandage. Then swiftly and fastidiously she filled up
the hole with sand again.

Billy felt troubled and full of pity for poor Miss Eccles,
with her hidden wound.

Mrs. Domingo was sitting alone beside the hut as he
wandered by. She smiled and waved briskly. "Billy Baxter!
Come and sit in the shade here! Goodness me, you'll be
getting a sunstroke, my boy. Do be careful."

She tossed off her slippers. Her toenails gleamed luridly.
Billy noticed the efflorescence of lilac veins on her calves. In
her lap lay a dark leather case, half open.

"Would you like to see my jewels, Billy? They are exceptional. Come. Take a peep at them."

Billy stood at her side and gazed silently over her shoulder. She drew out a bracelet. "Eleven rubies and twenty-two
sapphires, child. It used to belong to the Empress Eugénie."

And then a necklace: "Just look at those diamonds! Worth eighty thousand dollars." And then a brooch. "The biggest opal I've ever seen, I don't mind telling you." And then a ring. "This emerald, Billy, belonged to the Gaekwar of Baroda. And look. Do you see this egg? Lapis lazuli, by Fabergé. Flick it open and out pops a teeny golden rooster."

Her fingers moved caressively through a tangle of stones and metal: great amethysts and topazes and strangely tinted aquamarines, green tourmalines and pink ones, golden chains, anklets, amulets. They kept squirming and flickering like a horde of beetles under her touch. "They're not just pieces of brightness," she muttered, almost savagely. "They have power! They're bits of magic! You can take my word for it, Billy. A diamond cures rheumatism. Rubies protect you against gossip. Sapphires help you make decisions. An emerald brings love." She whispered darkly, "You must promise not to tell a soul about them, Billy. They're worth—well, I shudder to tell you what they're worth, my dear child."

11

The Baron wrote in his diary:

The worthy Mrs. Wagenseller brought us some flowers this morning. A mass of beach magnolias, which wilted immediately, as well as a magnificent spray of *messerschmidia*. She keeps looking at me rather curiously. What is happening in her mind, I wonder? As for Shishnik, all is going more or less as I expected. He has succeeded in taming the little parrot which Zenzo brought him. He has called him Elijah and is teaching him to swear in Russian. Miss Eccles has made a butterfly net, very cleverly I must say, out of one of Lily's semitransparent negligées. She caught an amazing specimen yesterday—tomato-red striped with gold. I didn't realize that such insects existed. Why do they exist? I am mystified. To give pleasure to each other? To give pleasure to the

birds? Or does nature revel occasionally in producing a preposterous, pointless beauty?

Our diet is improving. Last night we had a parrot fish. It
tasted like a *poulet de Bresse* with a subtle hint of turtle. We
have also had a surgeonfish, a goatfish, and a convict fish, as well
as a *gratin* of coconut crabs, a great delicacy. My own invention,
my palm cassis as I call it, is a definite success. Lily has become
quite addicted to it. It induces a state of euphoria, which unfortunately seems to be followed by an acute irritability. . . .

He glanced about cautiously, scratched his nose with the
pencil, and went on writing.

I can't quite rid myself of the notion that we are still on the
Cassandra, sleeping peacefully in our cabins. Will I wake up
tomorrow and peer through my porthole at the sizzling sea? Will
my food start tasting dreary again, will every color be tinged with
gray, will these people slip back into a bickering anonymity? No.
Of course not. I am merely looking for an excuse. *That thing*
is creeping over me again. I feel the telltale symptoms: dizziness,
headaches and tremors, a sudden loss of breath. Never mind.
Here at any rate there's nothing to worry about. I feel like laughing aloud when I watch dear Lily and our learned Professor.
So sly they are, so calculating, but *au fond* as naïve as children.
A hideous thought occurs to me. Is it *I* who am naïve? No. I
refuse to accept this climate of smirking camaraderie and empty
hedonism. The Enemy still exists. He will always exist. I still
hate, I still fear. I refuse to become a vegetable. . . .

He slipped the diary back into the pocket of his nankeen
breeches and sauntered toward the fire, where Ibrahim was
cooking dinner. He was spooning a brownish juice over a
salmonlike fish. A pan of stewed breadfruit was bubbling over
the flames.

And suddenly an uncontrollable emotion swept over the
Baron. Ibrahim was leaning over the flames, frowning a bit as
he basted the fish. He looked up, grinned, and nodded. "Very
good tonight, Baron." Sweat burst from the Baron's brow. His
hands started to tremble. He longed to reach down and seize

Ibrahim by the throat and feel that living flesh squirming desperately in his grip. And then? Ah, yes, then? He would kneel by the corpse and meditate on its beauty. He would stroke the cooling brow, he would close the stiffening lids. Then he would lift it in his arms, bear it tenderly to the shore, and drop it crisply into the big blue ocean.

"*Jesus Christus,*" he thought feverishly. "*Wieder einmal. Und immer wieder. . . .*" He turned and walked quickly, almost running, to the edge of the water, where he flung himself breathlessly on the soft yellow sand.

All was still under the fruit palms. The beach was deserted. The rest were still lingering in the shadows, waiting for sunset. A fruit dropped with a thud; a bumblebee buzzed by. The Baron heard footsteps. He peered from the corner of his eye without moving. Miss Eccles crossed the dune, unaware of the Baron's presence, paused by the edge of the inlet, and spread her arms joyfully. Then she slid her carnation-tinted dress over her head, tossed it casually on the sand, and tiptoed into the shallows. There was something rather poignant about her lanky white body, with its flat, sexless buttocks and long skinny legs. She flung herself forward and splashed about ecstatically. The air flashed with drops as she kicked up the foam.

The Baron felt touched, vaguely ashamed, and subtly humanized. He lay back and closed his eyes again. "God help me," he muttered.

12

He woke up in the middle of the night. A half-moon was shining. The sand had a pale broken glitter, like salt. No wind; not a ripple; the palms were black and motionless. His temples throbbed queerly, his whole body was soaked in sweat. The scar in his cheek began to burn, as it often did before a thunderstorm. He got up from his mat and walked slowly across the beach. Footprints lay sprinkled all around him, unnaturally clear in the snowy sand. They were easy to recognize, and the Baron amused himself by identifying them: the Professor's Siamese sandals, Lily's high heeled French slippers, Mrs. Wagenseller's tennis shoes, and an assortment of bare feet: Billy's the smallest and Wagenseller's the biggest, with Zenzo's and Ibrahim's in between. He glanced about for footprints of his own. Curiously enough, he found none. He went sauntering down toward the ladies' hut, somewhat dreamily.

He peered through the lianas. Mrs. Domingo was lying directly in front of him, her mouth wide open and her hair all disheveled. Beyond her lay Miss Eccles, straight and pale as a tombstone, with Mrs. Wagenseller in the corner, curled up in a ball. Very slowly, almost hypnotically, he reached through the lianas. He touched Lily on the elbow, and then on her neck very lightly. She didn't stir. He reached under her mat, groping intuitively, and drew out a key. Then he lifted her leather jewel case, which lay tucked under a shawl to the left of her, and placed it very gently on the sand outside the hut. He paused and glanced at the sky. His heart was beating painfully and there was an ugly taste on his tongue, like raw liver. He slid the key into the lock and flicked open the lid. After a moment's hesitation he plucked out an opal brooch. He locked the case again and slipped it back through the screen of lianas, covered it deftly with Lily's shawl, and slid the key back under the mat.

A cloud had covered the moon when he reached the edge of the inlet. He was standing by the clump of bamboos where Ibrahim had slung his hammock. He paused by the hammock and stared at the Negro intently, then calmly slipped the brooch under a fold in Ibrahim's turban. He meditated for several moments over the motionless black body, sniffing the smell of Ibrahim's sleep, sensing the depths of Ibrahim's dreams. He uttered a sigh, half regretful and half exultant, and then wandered back toward the coconut palms.

13

"I've been having some rather extraordinary dreams," said Miss Eccles.

"Perfectly natural, isn't it?" said the Baron. "Considering the circumstances."

"Do you believe that dreams can have some kind of premonitory function, Baron? I mean, that they might be not just an echo of our hidden anxieties but something a bit more definite, a piecing together of scraps of evidence, a reinterpretation of humdrum incidents into a deeper significance? So that they have a certain validity with regard to the future as well as the past? I don't believe in fortunetellers, mind you, but dreams are a different matter."

The Baron looked thoughtfully as Miss Eccles's pallid face. He was suddenly struck by something strange in her eyes. Poor Miss Eccles was distinctly plain, but her eyes were very lovely, of a pure delphinium blue that seemed both innocent and coldly impersonal, in which he detected a visionary gleam which was almost savage in its intensity.

He nodded his head and said calmly, "I thoroughly agree with you, Miss Eccles, that the world of dreams has scarcely been explored. Certain facets have been cleverly investigated but it's only the top of the iceberg. Do we dream about things that we could never have heard about or read about, but that nevertheless occurred to someone or other in the past? Do our dreams reach into space and capture fragments of far-off happenings, maybe something that took place a hundred years ago in Madagascar? I hardly know how else to explain certain strange and recurrent dreams of mine."

"Last night, for example," said Miss Eccles, lowering her voice, "I dreamed that I was standing on top of a mountain, encircled by a bevy of naked savages. Suddenly I noticed that my nose was turning into a beak, and fuzzy little feathers were sprouting out of my arms. Obviously this was something that has never happened to me, nor to anyone else I know of, nor is it something that I'd be able to invent all by myself. I have a rather limited imaginative capacity, unfortunately. Well, there I was standing—"

"Hugo! Please!" It was Mrs. Domingo; her voice was shrill with excitement. She came running across the sand toward the tree where Miss Eccles was sitting. "Hugo! Do you mind if I speak to your privately for a minute or two? Excuse me, Penelope. It's a confidential matter. . . ."

She took the Baron by the elbow and led him swiftly across the dune. "Something ugly has happened, Hugo. There's a thief on this beach."

"Why? Are you missing something, Lily?" The Baron's voice was slyly disparaging.

"I most certainly am. My lovely opal brooch. The one that Pancho bought at Boucheron's for our wedding anniversary."

"Where did you keep it?"

"In the jewel case, naturally. With the rest of my stuff, as always."

"Was it locked?"

"Of course it was locked."

"And opened by force?"

"Well, not exactly." Her voice grew hesitant. "Rather odd, when you stop to think of it. The case was still locked when I picked it up this morning. But that brooch has very definitely and undeniably vanished."

The Baron smiled indulgently. "Come, Lily. Try to remember, please. It doesn't make sense, quite. That brooch had no wings, and I doubt if it could fly, nor did it have mandibles with which it could bore. And the case was still locked. Rack your brains, please, Lily."

"I wish you would kindly remove that condescending smirk from your lips, Hugo. Are you hinting that I've gone blind and that the brooch is still in the jewel case?"

"I am quite prepared to take your word, Lily. If you say it has vanished I am sure it has vanished. Still, let us be sensible for a moment. When did you last see that brooch?"

"I was looking at it last night, just before I went to bed. So obviously . . ."

"Quite," said the Baron. "And you are sure that you put it back in the case again?"

"I am not in the habit of leaving my jewelry scattered in the sand, Hugo."

"Excuse me, Lily, but remember that you drank quite a bit of that excellent palm cassis, which is mildly intoxicating."

"I most distinctly was not drunk, if that's what you're insinuating," said Mrs. Domingo.

"Very well," said the Baron gently. "Let's try to analyze this curious business. Someone or other got hold of the jewel case. How did they open the jewel case, Lily?"

"Well, they must have found the key."

"Where was it?"

"Under my mat."

"Can you explain, my dear little Lily, how they possibly could have obtained the key and extracted the brooch from the jewel case and then returned the key to its hiding place, and all without your being aware of it, in the middle of the night? The thing seems rather improbable, doesn't it, Lily?"

"Well, it does, I guess, dear," said Mrs. Domingo with a touch of bleakness. "But those are the naked facts. I have no theory. Have you a theory?"

They were standing on the brink of the inlet, which lay

clear and unruffled. Tiny crabs were edging their way through the coral-shaped greenery.

"Whom," said the Baron, "do you suspect?"

"Oh, Lord, it's all so ridiculous. Who on earth could use that opal? It seems so absurd. Why not the diamonds, while they're at it? Less easily identified and much more negotiable. And besides, to do a thing like *that* in a place like *this*. I am baffled, Hugo."

"Either you were robbed or you weren't, my girl. And if you were robbed, well, somebody robbed you. And that somebody was obviously very sly and ingenious."

"The Professor, you mean? I utterly refuse to consider—"

"I did not say it was the Professor," murmured Hugo with indifference. He stooped to pick up a shell which was shaped like a lion's paw.

"We can exclude Penelope, naturally."

"And the Wagensellers, I think."

"Which leaves . . ."

"That Japanese boy and our Negro chef. And Billy Baxter."

Mrs. Domingo grew thoughtful. "Should I make a public announcement, dear?"

"Wait," said the Baron. "Don't be hasty. Let us meditate on the matter. The situation will require considerable tact, my dear Lily."

"Why do you look at me so strangely?"

"Am I looking at you strangely?"

"I do believe," said Mrs. Domingo, "that you suspect me of hiding that brooch, or of losing it on purpose just to build up a crisis."

The Baron took her hand and lifted it to his lips, rather ironically. "Nonsense, child. I know how you shrink from any sort of vulgar melodrama."

"You don't trust me. You don't believe in me."

"I love you, Lily. I love you passionately."

She looked at her pointed fingernails, which were gradually turning into claws. "You've said it so often that I almost believe you, dear boy. One day I think you're a saint, and the next I'm sure you're evil incarnate. A sadist or a masochist—which is it? Or are you both?" She threw her arms around him and buried her face in his neck. "Oh, Christ, Hugo darling, we've got to stick together, whatever happens! Let's rot away together and to hell with the rest of the world!"

14

"Have you noticed," said Laura, "something funny about the light? Maybe I need a pair of glasses, but I tell you things look different. Prismatic, if you see what I mean. The colors keep shifting. The green turns into blue and the blue into violet, and the red kind of wiggles, like something that's going to pounce on you. And not only the colors. I look at a tree and all of a sudden it starts to squirm, as if it were turning into a boa constrictor. And look at that rock out there. I've been watching it carefully, Tony. It's only a rock, of course, but I'd swear I've seen it moving."

"Optical illusions," said Tony. He flicked a ladybird from his wrist.

"Very well, be prosaic. I'm sure you're perfectly right, of course. Just the sunlight playing on microscopical particles in the air. All the same, it gives me an eerie sort of feeling now and then. Look at the shore down there, for instance. Do you see Professor Shishnik? He's still wearing that filthy kimono of his. Well, honey, you'll think I'm mad, but I give you my word that five minutes ago, as I was quietly sitting here, he just vanished into thin air. There he was, stooping down to pick up a shell, and *poof!* Gone. Just like that. I was petrified.

But a moment later there he was again, poking around with those dreary shells. Oh, I know it sounds ridiculous but I guess it's like the Sahara. All those fountains and oases suddenly coagulating out of nothingness."

"Just a mirage," murmured Tony, stroking the tip of his nose.

"And mind you, that's not all. This place is driving me loony. It's not only the mirages, it's the *people,* darling, the *people.*"

"The people?" said Tony.

"Listen. I'll tell you what I mean. Back on the *Cassandra* all these people seemed reasonably normal, more or less, didn't they? Not commonplace, exactly, but quite human and comprehensible. And now I'm beginning to wonder if it's me or they that's crazy. Me, no doubt. I can't help it. There's something eerie about them all."

"Go on, dear. I'm listening carefully."

"Take that Baron, for example. On the boat he merely struck me as a kind of anachronism, a passé aristocrat. A bit of a sissy, maybe, with all those gestures and innuendos. A castle in Carinthia, hunting chamois, and all the rest. But now I'm not so sure. There is something satanic about the Baron."

"Well, of course, if he's a pansy . . ."

"Don't be gross. He's not a pansy. He's been sleeping with Lily Domingo and there's probably an *arrière-pensée,* but still, those curious mannerisms are not effeminate, they're merely Austrian."

"Has experience taught you, Laura, that every faggot uses lipstick?"

"There you go. Hipped on the subject. You ought to go on a crusade. You seem to think that there's something poisonous about sexual deviation."

"Not in the least. It's you who keeps harping on the subject. It seems to fascinate you."

"Well, I think it's high time that you broadened your horizon a little, Tony. For a person of your intelligence you show surprisingly little subtlety. Take Mrs. Domingo. You think she's just a *déclassé* society woman. It's much more complicated, I assure you. There's more than meets the eye. Her mind lacks discipline and orderliness but she's shrewd, Tony, she's penetrating. I'm not suggesting for a moment that she has mastered her Schopenhauer, but as a judge of human nature I'll put my money on Mrs. Domingo."

"Very interesting. Go on, dear. What do you think of the Professor?"

"Frankly, Tony, I have no opinion whatsoever about Professor Shishnik. Head high up in the clouds, the dreaming naturalist, and so on. Brilliantly intelligent, I suppose, if you can get at the intelligence. He was talking about Kierkegaard yesterday. Very impressive in a way, I'm sure, but I had a feeling that he was really thinking about the price of eggs in Alaska. His eyes—have you ever looked into his eyes from close up, Tony? They're shifty. Or maybe not shifty but kind of slippery, like drops of mercury."

"Thank you, Laura. Most illuminating. I can't tell you how intrigued I am. Everything's wiggling and squirming, the poor old Professor does a disappearing act, Mrs. Domingo is suddenly a genius, and the Baron's turned into Lucifer. Listen, bunny. I think that the two of us had better get the hell out of here. You're right. This place is definitely driving you witless."

"That wonderful sanity of yours is most refreshing, I must say. Everybody's out of step but you. Including poor little me, naturally. You do manage to wear your blinkers in an astonishing fashion. I don't suppose that it ever occurs to you that you too have your little oddities? Could it be that there's a skeleton tucked away in a teeny closet? I don't wish to sound crude but there are times, Tony Wagenseller, when your facial expression is exactly that of a babe in diapers."

Yellow flames were leaping up into the twilight beneath the palms. Ibrahim was jabbing at the logs, getting ready to cook dinner.

"Darling, forgive me, please," said Laura. "My tongue keeps running away with me."

"Forget it, Laura. Forget it. Just relax. Don't get hysterical."

15

They came gathering around the fire for the banquet, one by one. Tony had climbed into the woods that morning and had caught a wild pig, a small speckled beast that couldn't have been more than two months old. A spit had been whittled out of eucalyptus by Ibrahim, and jets of golden fat burst from the pig and hissed in the flames. There was an air of festivity. Mrs. Domingo wore her rubies, which reflected the flames like the eyes of a cheetah, and the Baron von Wolfhausen was wearing his velvet jacket. He looked crisp and almost dandyfied as he passed around the palm wine.

"If you could fly on a magic carpet," said Mrs. Domingo, lifting her bosom a little, "and could dine wherever you wished tonight, which spot would you choose, Penelope?"

Miss Eccles scowled a little. "I remember a place in Srinagar. I'd been looking for some female *Teinopalpus imperialis*. We were sitting in a houseboat, eating trout fresh from the Dal and watching the moon rise up from the Himalayas. . . ."

"Terribly romantic, I'm sure," said Laura. "Do you remember that place in Capri, Tony? Way up on top of a cliff, with Naples shining beyond the bay? We had some marvelous scampi and a *pollo alla diavolo*."

"And you, Professor Shishnik?"

"My tastes are humble," said the Professor. "There is a

village called Rozemberok in the mountains of Ruthenia. I used to sit under a fir tree while the cows mooed in the distance and the ducks waddled past on their way from the pond. They had sausages and noodles, and a very good Pilsener."

Mrs. Domingo sipped at her palm wine and said gaily, "And how about you, Ibrahim?"

Ibrahim looked up from the flames. The firelight shone in his eyes. "I remember a night we all rode into the desert, madam. This was by Aïn-Safra, where the mountains touch the desert. We rode for four hours and came to a place by an oasis. It is night and the men of the desert are sitting around a fire. They are roasting a baby camel and the man with the beard is singing a song. Each man reaches out with his knife and carves a slice from the camel and nothing has ever tasted so good as that camel."

He leaned down to rake some embers under the sizzling pig, and at that moment a glowing object fell from a fold in his turban. He picked it out of the ashes and gazed at the opal with perplexity.

Mrs. Domingo turned slowly and looked at the Baron without moving. No one spoke for several moments. Ibrahim glanced at the tree above him, and then again quizzically at the jewel in his palm.

Mrs. Domingo whispered, "Ibrahim."

Ibrahim smiled bashfully. "Yes, madam?"

"Will you please," said Mrs. Domingo, broadening a little as she spoke, "tell us immediately where you obtained that piece of jewelry, Ibrahim?"

Ibrahim rolled his eyes speculatively. "You saw it, yes, madam? It dropped from the palm tree and fell on my head!"

Mrs. Domingo's voice grew tremulous. "Stand up, Ibrahim, and look at me. You seem to take us all for a bunch of dithering idiots. That brooch in your hand was removed from my jewel case last night and everybody present saw it dropping out of your turban."

"Very funny, yes, madam. I think it fell from the coco-nuts."

"That will do, thank you, Ibrahim. I don't think we need to go further. I'm sure that the Professor and the Wagensellers will agree with me, as well as Miss Eccles. We saw what we saw, and a thief is a thief. Tell me, what do they do to thieves in Mohammedan countries, please, Ibrahim?"

Ibrahim dropped the opal brooch as though it were a tarantula. It tumbled among the ashes, pulsating faintly in the dance of the flames.

He stared at the ground and said, "Excuse me, madam. I am not a thief."

Mrs. Domingo got up and stood by the fire, facing Ibrahim. Her damp, oily hair flowed over her brow and down her shoulders. She had grown a little plumper; her breasts shook with excitement. She lifted her arm in a regal gesture and pointed at Ibrahim.

"I'll tell you what they do to a thief in Mohammedan countries, Ibrahim. They cut off his hand! That's what they do and quite rightly. You are a savage, that's all you are, just an illiterate little Negro, and when a Negro starts to steal he is slithering beyond salvation. Here we are, a bunch of cast-aways, trapped on the brink of the wilderness. We need some discipline and order or we'll all be swallowed up in the jungle. And discipline means punishment. We will have to punish you, Ibrahim. Please leave us. Go back to your ham-mock. We'll be seeing you in the morning."

16

Ibrahim was lying in his hammock among the bamboos, meditating. The flames had died into ashes and a hot, dank stillness was settling on the promontory.

He meditated on the strange, sad confusion of human

existence: on its unpredictable calamities, its pointless tyrannies and gratuitous cruelties. He felt no hatred toward Mrs. Domingo, only a mournful bewilderment, and concerning the opal he felt no suspicion, only a childlike incredulity. He was incapable of hatred, of suspicion or bitterness. Instead of these he felt, when confronted with evil, merely a yearning to withdraw into secrecy. It had never occurred to him to be ashamed or resentful of his blackness: he serenely knew that he was beautiful, that he was strong and a part of nature. And nature, of course, could hold no sort of evil. In his sweetness and simplicity, he could not conceive of the roots of evil. What might seem evil to others was to him merely absurd. He lay in his hammock and stared at the stars. They too were a part of nature. What was it like to live on a star? Were there cruelties and calamities on a star, and puzzles?

There was a rustling among the stalks and a voice said, "Ibrahim! Are you sleeping?"

Ibrahim said nothing. Billy Baxter crept up to the hammock and said, "Ibrahim . . ."

"I feel scared, Billy," said Ibrahim.

"I hate that Mrs. Domingo!"

Ibrahim whispered, "I am not a thief, Billy."

"Oh, I know you aren't, Ibrahim."

Ibrahim took hold of Billy's hand and held it tenderly in his own. There was a shrewd, evil glitter in his enormous black eyes. They were silent for several minutes and then the Negro said, "I am going away, Billy."

"Going away!" said Billy, agitated.

"They will cut off my hand," said Ibrahim.

"I won't let them! I'll kill them!"

Ibrahim whispered, "Hush. Come along with me."

He led Billy by the hand along the inlet toward the mangroves. They waded through the mud and twisted their way through a clump of roots. Finally they stood on the edge of the sea and Ibrahim pointed: "Look, Billy."

A thick hollowed log, some ten feet long, lay afloat in the water. It was pointed at both ends, and hewed into flatness across the center. Two thin stakes carved into paddles lay in the middle of the log and underneath, half covered with leaves, lay something pale that looked like a sack.

"It's a canoe," said Billy, "isn't it?"

Ibrahim grinned. "I found the log. I chopped at the log until it turned into a boat."

"You never told me! When did you make it?" said Billy excitedly.

"A little bit each day, Billy. I saw a usefulness for a boat. A boat will help for fishing. A boat will also help for other things. And now I feel scared and I will use the boat for other things."

Billy tugged at Ibrahim's arm. "Oh, Ibrahim, please! Can I come along with you?"

"No. Not now. I will go to the rock and I will see what is on the rock. If all is well on the rock I will come in the night and get you, Billy."

He groped among the roots and then jumped nimbly into the boat. He picked up the sack, opened it cautiously, and put it down again. Then he took one of the paddles and dipped it silently in the murky water. The boat creaked and trembled, then slid gently into the sea.

"Ibraham! Ibrahim! Oh, wait for me, Ibrahim. . . ."

"Not now," said Ibrahim calmly, and he crouched in the boat and lifted his paddle.

"Ibrahim! Please!" cried Billy. "Ibrahim!"

"Good-by, Billy," called Ibrahim softly, and the boat moved silently under the starlight.

For a long time Billy Baxter stood on the edge of the swamp and watched the tiny vessel gliding slowly across the sea. The rock rose in the distance like a petrified wave and the blackness of the boat was lost in the blackness of the ocean. All that Billy could see was the shining whiteness of Ibrahim's turban and then that too was gone and the sea lay empty and impenetrable.

17

The following morning Tony and Laura went for a stroll along the cove.

"Well, I've made up my mind," said Tony.

"Thank the Lord," said Laura dustily.

"I talked it over with Zenzo. He's the only one who's got any sense. He agrees. And he's right. We'd better go while the going's good. It's not just a matter of conscience, Laura—"

"Spare me your conscience, please, dovey."

"It's common sense," said Tony. "It's a question of survival. Oh, it's perfectly conceivable that we could hold out for another year. The climate is good, the food's digestible, no snakes, no mosquitoes. It's the mental part that worries me. There is bound to be an explosion. Don't ask me what it is, but there's something rotten in Denmark. That woman is going to end by driving all of us nuts. So there we are. It's us and Zenzo and to hell with the rest of them."

"You're fond of Zenzo, aren't you?"

"He's a clean, well-balanced fellow."

"Cultured, too. Loves music, he told me."

"Nothing wrong with that, is there?"

"Kind of cute, wouldn't you say?"

Tony looked at her for a moment. Then he said, baring his teeth a little. "Look here, Laura. What's wrong with you? You've been sinking your claws into every goddamn person on this island."

"Seems to me that you've done a bit of clawing yourself, sweetie pie. Did I hear you use the words 'lousy old bitch' about Mrs. Domingo?"

"Are you trying to defend that disgusting exhibition of hers?"

"She was overexcited, Tony. She'd been drinking that sickening palm juice."

"Overexcited. I see. I'd call it downright bloodthirsty."

"Good heavens, Tony. Be sensible. Stop taking things so literally. She was just being theatrical about chopping off his hand. I'm not defending her, God forbid, but to treat her as a menace is ridiculous."

"Well, you see what that harmless bit of theatricality has done. The poor bastard's run off into the jungle. Good-by to our *maître d'hôtel*."

"God Almighty, a human being's gone to perish in the wilderness and you stand there complaining that we've lost our chef! Compassionate, aren't you?"

"Listen, Laura. I'm good and sick of hearing you spout about compassion. In Spain it was the peasants, in Sicily the poor little donkeys, in Calcutta the starving babies. And all the while you were congratulating yourself on that wonderful compassion of yours. One would think that an experience like this one would knock some realism into you. But no, it takes more than a shipwreck to shake you out of that Bryn Mawr smugness."

"Thank you, dear. Most instructive. You've always displayed great perspicacity. When you're through with your fulminations, do you mind calming down and being more explicit about this little plan of yours?"

They were standing on a flat gray rock above the water. A glittering school of fish, ruddy gold speckled with indigo, went swarming into the shadows, paused for an instant, and then shot out again.

Tony picked up a pebble and tossed it idly into the sea. "I've made a list of the essentials. We'll be taking along two sacks. Food and medicines in one of them. Aspirin, iodine, quinine, vitamins of course, salt and pepper, the rest of the brandy, and that tin of marrons glacés. Some chocolate and tea of course. Anything else you can think of?"

"And the other sack?"

"In the other I'll pack the knife and the little hatchet. Rope, matches, compass, gun, that copper pot and a couple of blankets. You can carry the water jug and the binoculars. They're bound to come in handy. Twice I've noticed a thread of smoke rising out of the valley and I'll bet my bottom dollar there's a village there somewhere. It's worth the risk, anyway. We can't go far wrong. If worse comes to worse we can always turn back. Four days ought to do it. Maybe less. Fifty miles, let's say. Those hills look pretty tough but I'm sure that they're navigable."

"And that charming little village? Suppose they decide to cut our throats?"

"You've been listening to Mrs. Domingo. These native islanders are basically affable."

"What about snakes?"

"There are no snakes. I haven't laid eyes on a single snake."

"Food?" said Laura.

"That's my problem. I'm not worried about the food."

"And Zenzo's coming along. It all sounds frightfully cozy. Are we taking along some marshmallows to roast over the fire?"

"Well, I'm glad you're getting back some of that old campfire spirit. When we're through you can give some edifying lectures, Mrs. Wagenseller. 'Fertility Rites among the Aborigines of the New Hebrides,' that sort of thing. I'm sure they'll lap it up in Bryn Mawr if you handle it boldly. Look. There's Zenzo. He's caught some fish. We'll have to think about lunch. Do you think you can steel yourself to grilling a fish or two, Laura?"

PART IV

The Jungle

1

When he awoke in the morning Ibrahim looked around with amazement. Two great stones met overhead, forming a triangular archway, and in the shade of the arch some moss-like flowers were blossoming. He rubbed his eyes. This was his kingdom. No one would ever invade his territory. Here he was Prince, Sheik, Sultan, Pope, President, and Maharajah. Everything glistened in the sunlight. Flakes of mica shone in the pebbles. The ripples at his feet were alive with dancing gold pieces. He listened to the roar of the breakers on the reef ten yards beyond, and watched the rainbows hovering in the spray hurled from the corals. He had never expected to find all this splendor, this variety. Instead of a black and dismal rock he had found a shining cathedral. He picked a tuft of moss from the shade and pressed it to his nose. He caught the smell of the sea, of sun-baked rocks, and of something else—life lurking in the silent distance, things stirring in the invisible wilderness.

He peered through a crack in the rocks: he could see the line of the wide peninsula, strangely small, with its wispy palms stuck like feathers in the dunes. Nothing was stirring on the beach. They were all still asleep. His whole body was tingling with joy. He started to sing out of sheer pleasure.

But then he thought: *"Get busy, Ibrahim! Survey your kingdom! Build your fortresses!"*

He climbed to the top of the rock. The isle was bigger than he had expected. Not big in circumference, perhaps, but full of crannies and indentations. The south looked on the reef, which sloped toward the water, smooth as marble. The drops thrown by the breakers flashed like diamonds and vanished instantly. The west faced the peninsula: a single cliff that jutted from the sea. To the north lay a maze of shallow little pools and trickling tributaries, which snickered and gurgled with each gently passing wave. It was in the east, he knew immediately, that he would build his tiny palace. It was here that he had landed on a thin strip of sand which was shielded from the sea by a kind of jetty and shaded from the sun by a cavernous rock.

He pulled his boat higher and rammed it firmly into the cavern. He tossed out the paddles, then the rope and the fishing pole. Then he took out the sack and laid his treasures in a row: the kitchen knife from the *Cassandra,* with the fork and the pepper shaker; his silver cigarette lighter, a tin of caviar, and a jar of olives; nine coins, which included six rupees, two gulden, and a Hong Kong dollar, and finally his agate box, engraved with a cupid and a dove.

He climbed over the jetty toward the maze of little pools. They looked like tiny craters, some of them deep, most of them shallow. In some he could see the ultramarine spines of the sea urchins. In others lurked tiny crustaceans which darted like hornets. He crawled out to the edge and stared down into the sea. A wilderness of corals completely surrounded the rock. They were shaped like great convolvulus, or luminous cacti, or wands of celery. Their colors kept shifting under the play of the water from lilac and mauve to nasturtium red or canary yellow. Through this jungle flowed a ceaseless parade of little animals—greenish prawns with wandering antennae, squids with long amber tentacles, slate-blue eels as sharp as razors, curious artichokes, laborious crabs, crouching sponges, pimpled sea-cucumbers, translucent jellyfish, and layer upon multitudinous layer of plankton, tiny creatures no bigger than fleas or mosquitoes.

Now and then a larger fish would come prowling through the recesses, some slow-moving predator grimly surveying the lesser hordes, and once a school of minnows swooped down through the labyrinth: pausing for an instant, suddenly immobilized into rows of silver knives, then lanquidly gliding into an array of blue-finned ballet dancers, and finally darting into the depths with electrical speed as a black-snouted beast with pronglike eyes swung into sight.

Ibrahim dove into the sea and swam about delightedly. He was the lord of the ocean; these were his multicolored minions. They fled in frightened droves at his dusky approach. He circled the rock in slow, easy strokes, weaving his way above the corals, scattering the shiny wake behind him, until he saw something curious which was caught in the shade of the cliff. He moved closer: white as snow and heraldically symmetrical, a human skeleton lay trapped in the shallow water. The skull nodded gently and rhythmically on the sea sway; the outspread fingers kept stroking the corals. Ibrahim reached out his hand and touched the dead man on the brow. He felt a pang of wonder, a small flicker of curiosity. Then he spread out his arms in the exultation of being alive and swam back to the barnacle-crusted jetty.

2

A haze hung over the promontory when they stepped across the dunes and followed the damp strip of sand that bordered the inlet. The sun still lay hidden beyond the rock in the eastern distance but a honey-colored brightness was beginning to flow from the western hills. A small grayish bird shot out of a palm and vanished instantly. A fish jumped up from the water. A parrot started to scream.

"Just a minute," muttered Tony. "Maybe I ought to leave a note."

"Only fair, I guess," said Laura. "Try to make it tactful, sweetie."

Tony ripped a page from his Kafka and scrawled across it hurriedly: *Heading for the hills. Will send help on arrival. Best of luck. T.W.*

He placed it under a pebble in front of the marquee and then quickly followed the others toward the shadowy mangroves. They crept around the swamp and climbed through a dewy thicket and came to a halt in the grove of eucalyptus trees. They dropped their sacks on the ground and Tony glanced at his compass. Through the tapering gray trunks they could see the sickle of yellowish sand and the blue sea beyond with its solitary rock.

"I feel qualms," said Laura suddenly.

"They'll be tickled we're gone," said Tony. "They all hated my guts. And they weren't exactly in love with you either."

"Still, we might have talked it over with them," said Laura, scratching her collarbone.

"Waste of time," said Tony breezily. "I'd made up my mind. There was no point in shilly-shallying."

At that moment they saw a figure emerging from the shade of a palm tree, very tiny at this distance but as brilliant as a hornet. A squeaky, desolate voice rose very faintly from the promontory: "Oh, Laura! Laura Wagenseller! Come back, dear! We need you!"

Laura glanced at Tony thoughtfully, then she sighed and shrugged her shoulders. Zenzo tittered in his strange little way, and picked up his sack.

They climbed over a barrier of smooth, tawny rocks and then down again into a treeless ravine. The air was still cool in the nooks of the estuary but the boulders gave out a warmth like a beast's. They walked across the pebbles and again started to climb, this time into a forest which was studded with underbush. Sprays of orchids, salmon-colored, dangled from the low-hanging branches and the boughs higher up were filled with the twittering of birds. Threads of gold-dusted light started to seep through the foliage. The air grew warm instantly. It was seething with mosquitoes.

3

"Absolutely caddish, I must say. I wouldn't have thought it of Mr. Wagenseller. In a crisis like this the least one can expect is a grain of loyalty."

"It was their privilege," said the Baron. "And also their risk. I do not envy them."

"It was treachery," said Mrs. Domingo. "They might have told us about it, at least. And I think it was downright loathsome for them to steal the blankets and the brandy."

"*Sauve qui peut,*" said the Baron. "I prefer this sandy beach of ours. They will have their little problems in those leech-ridden jungles."

They were sitting under the palms. The sun was low, the sea was glassy. Billy Baxter had gone to bed, Professor Shishnik lolled by the fire, and Miss Eccles was wandering among the rocks, looking for moths.

"They have gone and I doubt whether we will see them again," said the Baron. "It was bound to happen, Lily. They were not of our world."

"True, my boy, like everything you say. We are the butterflies and they are the bees. Theirs is the world of good hard labor and ours, alas, is a world of frivolity."

The Baron stretched his long, tapering legs across the sand. "We are the exotica, the eternal exiles. We are no longer a part of the world. And this island merely emphasizes what was already sufficiently obvious. When we get back to civilization, what will we do, my good Lily? Hurl ourselves into the maelstrom? Join the great modern struggle? Or at least, in common decency, shed salty tears for the oppressed ones? No, alas. We'll be sitting in the Casino, mildly tipsy, placing our chips."

Mrs. Domingo raised her arm. "Look at those hills out there, Hugo. Just look at them. Can't you see the deadly menace oozing out of those humps? Don't tell me that I've wasted my life, Hugo, please. I know better. I've had my moments. Rare but precious ones, believe me. I've been brushed by magic wings! And it wasn't all just laughter and kisses. I've wept tears, bitter tears! Once in Capri I held the razor against my wrist. It was nip and tuck, Hugo. And in Claridge's there was that overdose of sleeping tablets, and with plenty of reason. Damn it, Hugo, it wasn't all just a glittering pantomime. Now of course all is different, there's nothing left to remind me of anything, but oh, the hauntings! The harrowings! The self-disgust, the humiliations! I was the richest woman in Tennessee, but what did it matter? Everything that I did was beginning to stink with decay. Any why? Why, I ask you? Merely because I once was beautiful. Oh, yes, I was lovely, I was perfectly exquisite, Hugo. But if I ever were born again, let me tell you, I would pray to be ugly!"

The Baron leaned over and kissed her on both cheeks. "I am going to bed now, Lily. We have had a trying day. Those *coquilles Saint-Jacques* of the Professor were rather depressing. Good night, *mein Schätzchen.*"

4

"This, you see," said Miss Eccles, plucking a specimen out of her jar, "is a member of the Ornithoptera, or the family of Birdwings. They are the biggest butterflies in the world, and the rarest and loveliest. In Amboina the ladies keep them as pets, tied to their wrist. In the Solomons they are regarded as the souls of the dead."

"Amazing," said Mrs. Domingo, leaning out of her hammock. "Have they a value? Can you sell those little beasts for real money?"

"Oh, a good *paradisea* would probably bring in eighty pounds. Most of the things I've been catching are much less impressive." She moved closer to Mrs. Domingo and lowered her voice a little. "This morning I saw something quite extraordinary, Lily. There are some big eucalyptus trees on the other side of the inlet. I looked up and there in the sunlight, trembling on the edge of a bough, was the most magnificent creature I've ever seen. Gold and blue."

"Goodness me. Did you catch it?"

"It was heart-breaking, Lily. I stalked it for several minutes. It was out of my reach. It kept fluttering above that bough; it couldn't decide where to settle. I kept waiting and praying. I can't tell you how I prayed. I saw it quite clearly. A velvety blue lined with black, and dotted with a row of brilliant golden eyes. Ten inches across, I'd say. An unknown species, definitely."

"Yes. And then?" purred Mrs. Domingo.

"What could I do?" said Miss Eccles. "I prayed. Then I jumped. Alas, dear Lily, I am not an athlete. I missed. The thing went soaring away into the sky."

"Console yourself, Penelope. There must be others. You'll be catching one."

"I shall write a little note for *The Entomologist*," said Miss Eccles wistfully.

"Listen, dear, there is something that I'd like to discuss with you, if I may. Sit down under the palm. It's a delicate matter."

Miss Eccles lifted her brows, patted her skirt, and sat down quietly.

"You're so ethereal, my dear girl, it's not easy to be blunt with you. I'm afraid you'll just flutter away, like one of those pretty butterflies. You look like a Vestal Virgin, with that ash-blond hair of yours. I keep wondering, Penelope. Have you ever been in love?"

Miss Eccles smiled calmly and pressed her fingers into a triangle. "How can one answer such a question? What is love? Can you define it, Lily?"

"There you go, being equivocal. Lord Almighty, Penelope, when one really falls in love there are no two ways about it. It's one thing of course if the love is reciprocal and quite another, alas, if it isn't. Walking on clouds, tingling with eagerness, everything aglitter like waves in the sunlight. That's the reciprocal variety, needless to say. Sleepless nights and horrible pangs, sickening visions, loss of appetite. That's the other. Which is worse? A ridiculous question, I'll admit, but it's the first kind dwindling into the second which is really the horror. Well, one has to go through it. It's a *sine qua non*. The trouble with you is that you've never let go of yourself. I can see it in your eyes. I'm not suggesting that you're a virgin, maybe you are and maybe you aren't and it's none of my goddamn business. But what's that little poem? 'Gather ye rosebuds while ye may.' It won't be long before the rosebuds are all shriveled, Penelope Eccles."

There was a brief silence. Then Miss Eccles said brittley: "I'm a little bit puzzled, Lily. Do forgive me if I'm stupid. It's all fine about gathering rosebuds, but we are what we are. I'm not the type, I'm afraid, and that's all there is to it."

"True enough. *With* reservations. You were born, well, slightly frigid, but are you sure that you've explored the deeper realms of your emotional capacities? Are you sure that there isn't another Penelope Eccles slumbering inside you?"

"There may quite possibly be, Lily, and in fact I'm sure there is, but frankly, I have no intention of waking up that other Penelope."

"Good God, my girl, why not? There's nothing wrong with a bit of hanky-panky, even if it's on the outré side. In your schooldays, back in Salisbury . . ."

"Shrewsbury, I'm afraid."

"You played *games*, I suppose?"

"Badminton, a trifle."

"Ah. Badminton!"

"And hockey."

"*Hockey* . . . I thought so."

"Please, Lily . . ."

"There. You're blushing. Don't deny it! Something is stirring way inside you. Listen, my angel. If you could only learn to accept that thing that's lurking in you, if you could only stop recoiling from the fleshly realities. I know I'm putting it crudely and I have no desire to meddle, but be human, Penelope, for Christ's sake, be human. Join the whirligig. Kick up your heels. Do you want the plain truth? You're thirty years younger than I—don't deny it, it's a fact. Thirty years hence you'll be like me. And I? I'll be a skeleton. Cold white bones. Oh, how I long to be just bones, immaculate white bones, no wrinkles or secretions, no ugly humiliations or dismal hankerings. It isn't especially appetizing to be a woman, *entre nous*. Once I was beautiful. Now I am garbage. Look at my breasts. I could scream. If you only knew one tenth of the things that I've gone through, dear girl. It was different with poor old Pancho, he was a cripple and an invalid. But before that it was Rinaldo and before Rinaldo it was Archie. That sneaky black Rinaldo! That illustrious ancestry of his! Oldest family in Palermo! What a sickly little farce! Do you know what he used to do? Well, I'll refrain from spoiling your appetite, but it was nauseating, I tell you, nauseating. Oh, the squalor you've been spared. You've lived in your ivied cloisters with just an occasional nip into the jungle. You've never had to cope with these aboriginal lusts. That pitiful, grotesque Archie. Archie was a monster, I don't mind telling you. Not a pig like Rinaldo but a swindler and a vulgarian. He bought me the way he bought his diamond cufflinks at Cartier's. Sexually, of course, he soon grew weary of me, the way he wearied of all the rest of them. All he wanted was those bosomy blond harlots in the Casino. But only once, of course. Never a second time. *L'homme d'une nuit*, they all called him. He was insatiable, mentally at any rate. Squat and broad, nine-tenths Indian, with broken teeth and eyes like bullets. Oh, a gilt-edged heterosexual, a vulture, a killer! He stayed at the best hotels, wore striped blazers and blue suede shoes, had an aluminum-colored Mercedes and a pretty Brazilian secretary. All he lacked was a heart. Oh, Archie, what an utter louse you were! His equipment was like a donkey's, more preposterous than truly impressive, however. He showed it to all and sundry at the drop of a hat. He tried to drown that jungle stench of his in Cuir de Russie. You can see that poor old Pancho was rather a rest after Archie McGillicuddy. When Pancho died, believe me, Penelope, I decided I'd had enough of it. Time for a change of personnel. Out with the old, in with the new. I moved into the circles of manqué artists and half-starved gigolos. I was a queen in my own realm. Wasp-waisted fairies, Turkish surrealists."

She belched and scratched her elbow. "And now it's dear old Hugo. I met him in the Dolomites. Very dashing he did look, I'll say, as he swooped across the snow. Hugo is altogether a different kettle of fish, as you can see. He is not just a cad or a sponge, it's much more complicated. There's a mystery about Hugo. Don't ask me what. He's inscrutable. Do be careful with Hugo, Penelope. I have noticed the way you look at him. Oh, have your little fling, I don't begrudge it. I'm not the jealous type. Far from it. But let me tell you one thing. He secretly despises all of us and that means you too, my dear Penelope. He despises every woman who reveals the slightest interest in him. He was talking about you yesterday. He wasn't exactly flattering. Men are treacherous. Be on the alert, child. Gather your rosebuds but be circumspect."

She laughed a grim little laugh and patted her belly dreamily. "Nothing is simple, nothing is clear in life. Everything is blurred, or speckled, or mottled. Here I'm raving about love to you, and it's nothing but filth and misery. Look at me. Just a dried-up harpy with a hundred million dollars. I'm tired. I long for peace but, Christ, will you tell me where to find it?"

5

Miss Eccles dropped her net and knelt on the sand beside the water. The wavelets licked at the sand very lightly, almost inaudibly. The palm wine had left her pleasantly alert yet subdued; solemnly attentive, bemused by the evening air. She felt that she was gliding from the grayish torpor of an anaesthetic into a deeper and statelier daze, savage but calm, like the sea itself. The light died in the east. She caught a whiff of the crumbling fire. The rock out in the sea looked like a black, gigantic rat.

"Do you mind," whispered the Baron, "if I sit with you for a moment?"

Miss Eccles gasped, recoiled. "Oh, goodness, you *did* frighten me. You looked like a specter. Oh, certainly, do sit down, please."

"Beautiful, isn't it?" said the Baron. "You were born, Miss Eccles, on an island, a big and powerful island but still an island, with water around it. I was seventeen years old when I first laid eyes on the sea. That was on a visit to my Aunt Hedwig, who had a villa on the Adriatic. And after all, the Adriatic isn't quite like the Pacific. It is a very gentle and humanized piece of water, as I remember it."

The Baron glanced at Miss Eccles with his sloping eyes, then quickly away again.

"Tell me, Miss Eccles. You are a cool and sensible person. What do you think of me?"

Miss Eccles felt a flickering of warmth deep inside her. She said sedately, "I don't form my opinions until I am sure about them, Baron."

"You aren't sure yet what you think of me? Very tactfully phrased. You are wavering between approval and disapproval. Is that it?"

"Not wavering. Merely suspended. You are very conceited, I think, Baron."

"Conceited? Yes. Disgustingly so. And I am deeply ashamed of it. But don't you see through the mask? Don't you see the face beneath it? Conceit is a camouflage. Haven't you seen through the camouflage?"

"You are such a virtuoso at analyzing yourself, my dear Baron. Why on earth should you listen to what I might contribute?"

"You are a naturalist, Miss Eccles. You pierce your insects with a pin and study their wings, their antennae, their proboscis. You have formed an approach which is both spacious and miscroscopic, framed as it is in the timeless grandeurs of entomology. You are not easily deceived, I am sure. You can identify the various species."

"It's rather difficult," said Miss Eccles, "ever to be sure of what you mean, Baron. Your camouflage isn't conceit so much as an all-enshrouding irony. When everything is veiled in irony a truth becomes a half-truth. All things become ambiguous. I have never cared for ambiguity."

The Baron's voice grew solicitous, almost imploring. "Very well. I shall try to be candid. May I tell you about myself? Not with irony or conceit but perhaps with the tiniest tremor of panic? I was born in a beautiful and lonely forest near Klagenfurt. Twittering birds in the summer, sparkling streams full of trout. Silent snow in the wintertime, decorated with hoof prints and claw prints. I wore a black velvet jacket. I was taught to play the oboe. I floundered through adolescence, baffled by the riddles of the stars and frightened to death of my own emotions. I was shy, insanely so. When I was sixteen years old a dark little mustache crept out on my lip. I decided never to shave. I was determined to reform the world. But my father did not agree. He had no wish to alter the universe. We had terrible scenes. I even toyed with the thought of killing him. And then one day my father died and I fled to Vienna. I took a room in a pension not far from the Prater. I still remember the view of Tivoli which hung in the hallway and the wax gladioli on the piano in the drawing room.

"I was struggling! I groaned and sweated. I was locked in a grip with my demon. I was fighting my way toward the *real* reality. I read Plato and Aristotle. I read *Hamlet*. I read Kant. I learned Italian because I wanted to read Dante in the original. I used to go to the Café Mozart with a notebook in my pocket and jot down all the thoughts that kept swarming through my brain. I finally decided that our world is a bestial world—or rather, worse than bestial: sterile, dehumanized. Not very original, you say? Maybe not, my good Miss Eccles, but it shook me like an illumination of the Ultimate Evil. I decided to take a stand. One day I was quietly sitting there. The violinist was playing a waltz by Waldteufel. An elderly general with a beard walked by with a dachshund. I closed my notebook firmly. It was a heart-rending moment. I succumbed to Nazism, Miss Eccles. Out of sheer, plain despondency."

Miss Eccles placed a finger against her cheek and said: "Despondency? I can visualize a life much more despondent than yours, Baron. I think you could call it just a fit of childish rebelliousness. Are we to regard those hysterical conversions, to no matter how vile a cause, as the genuine upheavals of a tortured idealism? No, thank you very much. I reject your explanation. You were very far from ignorant. It was sordid, Baron. It was ludicrous."

"I fear that I haven't made myself clear," said the Baron rapidly. "It was more than sordid, Miss Eccles. It was downright catastrophic. It was spiritual suicide. I was hurling my Dante into the flames. *Mon Dieu,* Miss Eccles, I have no intention of trying to justify the thing. Quite the contrary. I was trying to say how ludicrous it was. It was like deliberately fouling one's body with a sickness—syphilis, for example. I have tried ever since to cure myself of that spiritual syphilis."

"You are cured, are you, finally?"

"Are we ever *really* cured?"

"You have paid a penalty. Is that what you mean?"

"Oh, if only it were that simple! Some pay their penalty with imprisonment, or the gallows, or God knows what. Others pay it with loneliness or hara-kiri, or quiet lunacy. I am living a life of continual self-torment. That is my penalty."

"Most convenient," said Miss Eccles. "If I grasp your real meaning. You call your mode of relationship—I won't be specific, Baron—you call your life of luxury hotels and fashionable casinos just a Spartan exercise in self-laceration. Quite. I see."

"But *do* you see, do you really?" The Baron's voice grew deep and quivering. The scar in his cheek had turned to a deep, accusing purple. "Day in, day out. The torture. The boredom. You cannot imagine. To keep smirking in front of a woman whom I utterly abhor! You may sneer at the décor but believe me, Miss Eccles, it is anything but paradise."

"Thank you, Baron. At least you are making your position quite obvious. I am charmed that your political dabbling has brought you nothing but disillusionment, and I am touched that your amorous liaisons are—what were your words? Boredom. Torture."

The Baron very discreetly took Miss Eccles's hand in his own. "Just as I said. Precise. Impersonal. The faultless lepidopterist! I have never talked like this to anyone in my life, my charming Penelope. Human contacts—what are they? As frail as spiderwebs! One breath and they're gone. I have felt a miraculous proximity, but so misty, so ephemeral. Will it all be gone in the morning, like the dew on the bushes? Penelope, my beautiful friend, I must sound like a silly poetaster. I am stepping out of my camouflage. Maybe I *am* a silly poetaster!" He lifted her hand to his lips and rose to his feet, a little clumsily. "Good night. And please forgive me. You won't betray me, that I'm sure of. Because you know, you know quite definitely, however ridiculous it may seem to you, you know it, don't you, Penelope? That I deeply . . . that I utterly love you!"

He stalked off into the darkness, groping his way past the bamboos.

Miss Eccles sat in the sand without moving and stared at the sea.

6

Now at last they saw the river shining through the tree trunks in front of them, swiftly flowing but strangely silent as it passed through the trees. Tufts of blood-colored foam bobbed along on its braids; lumps of driftwood floated by, still and eerie as ghosts. Further down the water narrowed into a churning red torrent but then the banks flattened again and the stream grew wide and smooth as glass. The bank was a tangle of ugly black roots but on the opposite shore a strip of sand shone through the reeds.

"Bigger than I thought," muttered Tony. He put down the sack and grabbed hold of a bough. "Won't be easy. Looks treacherous. What do you think about it, Zenzo?"

"I try wading, O.K.?"

"You'll sink in the mud to your hips, boy."

"I try swimming," said Zenzo.

"You won't make it," said Tony.

"And the bags," said Laura nervously. "We can't risk it. No use trying, dear."

"Let's stop chattering," said Tony. "We need a raft. There's no way out of it." He took the hatchet out of the sack and started to chop at a withered tree while Zenzo tugged at the sagging limbs. Laura crouched on the ground and wound the rope around the logs. They worked for three hours. It was late in the day when they finished. All three of them pulled together as they dragged the raft into the water. The wood was brittle with rot but the raft stayed afloat. Tony had whittled a pair of stakes and a spatula-shaped paddle and the men started to punt while Laura fastened the sacks. They guided it slowly through the barricade of mangroves. Then they slid into the mainstream. The raft shook in the onrush and the rope squeaked and chattered as it tightened around the logs. Now Zenzo maneuvered the vessel into a calmer stretch of water and Tony took the paddle and finally gained control of the raft. They turned a bend in the river and moved on the smooth, even current. The sun was low and ruddy when they reached the shade of the opposite bank. Clouds of big red mosquitoes welled out of the cattails. They kept floating downstream; the river grew gentler and broader. Once Laura cried "Look!" and it seemed that the sea shone in the distance. But then the river curved suddenly and the banks grew steep and wooded. Dusk fell and they headed for a ribbon of dry, brownish sand.

A bird dove out of the thicket, screaming hysterically. Tony reached for his gun: the bird spun like a top and then dove into the water, where it bobbed in the darkening foam. Tony steered the raft closer and Zenzo seized the floating bird, which was a bronze-winged pheasant with long purple tail feathers. They landed and slung the rope from the raft over a stump. The air was cool and fresh, free of insects, smelling of bay leaves. They climbed up the bank in the last light of the evening and spread out their blanket in the middle of the clearing. The twigs were thin and dry; the fire burned easily and briskly. Laura plucked the fat pheasant and cleaned it out and pierced it with a stick. It crackled and spat as she turned it over the flame. The smell of roast fowl went floating through the air and they felt almost gay as they settled down for dinner, slicing disks of fresh breadfruit and letting them fry in the grease of the pheasant.

"All we need," said Tony festively, "is some Châteauneuf-du-Pape."

"I don't think that you know your wines as well as you should, love," said Laura.

"I had a pheasant in Avignon with a lovely Châteauneuf-du-Pape."

"Do you remember that beautiful pheasant we had in Pamplona?"

Zenzo tossed his wing in the flames. "We have bird in Hokkaido."

"A special kind of bird?"

"We call it moon bird," said Zenzo.

"Is it tasty?" said Laura.

"Oh, we never eat moon bird. It come swooping at night with balls like a man and bosom like a lady."

"A queer sort of bird."

"Very sad bird," said Zenzo. "Always alone. Not man, not lady. Not bird, not person. Very lonely."

They sat silently by the fire and listened to the sound of the river flowing. A black incessant whisper as it tugged at the reeds, and then a sly little gurgle and a burst of low, malicious laughter. The fire shone on the reeds; sharp red arrows flashed on the water. The men lay down on the blanket and Laura sat alone by the fire as the last of the embers spluttered and died. Zenzo was twitching in his sleep and Tony lay motionless as a corpse. She felt lost in the wilderness, sad, unloved, like Zenzo's moon bird.

The shriek of a parrot woke her up the next morning. She opened her eyes and saw him sitting on the end of a bough. He ruffled his shiny wings and then flew low over the river where the mist was already melting in the yellow-speared inlets.

Tony and Zenzo were down by the shore, dismembering the raft and winding the rope. Zenzo was naked and dripping but when he saw Laura coming he giggled apologetically and slipped on his shorts.

The fire was already burning. Laura filled the pot with water. They silently sipped their tea and carefully wrapped up the sacks. Then they started uphill through the dewy forest.

7

They climbed all day long, heading for the wavelike ridge of hills from which they saw a column of smoke slowly rising. Behind the hills, some twenty or thirty miles beyond, rose the snow-capped summits.

Tony shifted his sack and glanced back at Laura. "Tired, darling?"

"I'll manage."

"It won't be long now."

"Let's hope so," said Laura.

"There are people up in those hills, I'm sure."

"Let's hope they have nice manners."

"Beautiful manners, I'm sure," said Tony.

"And beautiful souls, I trust," said Laura.

Zenzo was walking behind her and every time she looked back he smiled his shiny, conspiratorial smile at her. The walking was easier now, the underbrush had gone and the ground was smooth and dry under the casuarina trees. Laura felt a rush of dizziness when they moved through the open sunlight, but when they stepped into the shadows she felt firm and refreshed again. In the late afternoon they came to a tree-crested hillock and Tony dropped his sack and lay down in the shade. He divided a bar of chocolate, soft with the heat but still edible, and Zenzo took the binoculars and climbed to the top of the hillock.

"Anything special?" said Tony.

"Something wiggle," said Zenzo.

"A man?"

"More like beast."

"One of those pigs?"

"No," said Zenzo. "It stand on two legs and wave long ugly stick. Maybe man with head like a monkey. He dance like a shimmy."

"Sounds unpleasant," said Laura.

"Some sort of ritual, I guess," said Tony.

"Not exactly reassuring. Do you think," said Laura, "they can see us?"

"What if they do? There's nothing to worry about. All men are friendly if you treat them decently. That female down on the beach kept on raving about cannibals. It's that Mrs. Domingo who's the cannibal, if you want my opinion."

"You seem obsessed with Mrs. Domingo."

"I detest vicious lunatics."

"You hate women, that's your trouble."

"Stupid generalities, that's *your* trouble."

"You don't deny it, do you, sweet?"

"What are you trying to insinuate?"

"Oh, nothing," said Laura wearily. "All this claptrap

about humanity, about its decency and unquenchable sweetness even when it's just a bunch of savages. But when it comes to actual people, the people you see around you, all that tolerance evaporates. You grow red in the face with fury. You loathe humanity in the bottom of your heart, and you hide your loathing with this smirking tolerance."

"Clever, aren't you? Oh, how wonderful to be an intellectual! Such insight!"

"The plain fact, Tony Wagenseller, is you're a bigoted Philadelphia puritan. You keep traveling around the world but you're still stuck in your provincialism."

"The plain fact, Laura Wagenseller, is you're a sour Milwaukee bluestocking. With all your clever chatter you're just a bundle of small-town prejudices."

"Oh, God, how you fatigue me," said Laura softly. "That male conceit."

"Thanks," said Tony. "Male. Conceit. It's a beautiful way to win an argument."

He grunted and closed his eyes. Zenzo lay on the grass beside him. Laura looked at them with something like hatred as they lay there: the carefree Japanese and the anxious, arrogant American. "I mustn't think. I refuse to think. Oh God, just let me stop thinking!" She fixed her gaze on the tapering tree: a column of ants was climbing the trunk. A bird started chirping; a spider hung by its thread. "Not to think. Just to accept. That's the way to survive." A tiny worm lit on her wrist. She looked at it dreamily, then scooped if off with a twig and crushed it viciously under a stone.

It was growing cooler when they started out again, still heading for the north. They crossed a broad savannah and once again they started to climb, this time through a forest of dark, stunted evergreens. Zenzo kept looking for birds, but the only birds were no bigger than sparrows: quick and twittering little creatures with azure wings and yellow tails. But then suddenly Laura whispered, "Look, Tony!" An enormous hare sat under a bush, raised its ears and looked at them gravely, then bounced away through the underbush. Tony aimed, pulled the trigger. "Yes, you got him!" cried Zenzo and he scrambled into the thicket and seized the hare by its long brown ears.

Low clouds shaped like catfish were gathering above the valley. The sun sank: the clouds brightened; the air grew brisk, smelling of pine needles. They came to a circle of trees laden with prickly green fruits, and here they decided to camp for the night.

Laura sat and peeled the fruits while Tony skinned the hare. It was dark when they crouched beside the flames for their dinner. The meat was tough and tasteless but they were ravenously hungry: Laura roasted the curious fruits, which were dry and inedible, but they split them and extracted the kernels, which were crisp and delicious.

"Two more days," said Tony, nibbling at a bone, "should see us through. Keeping one's nerve, that's what counts. Not to fret. Not to get emotional."

"I've seen nothing," said Laura, "to grow emotional about, particularly."

"No, there's nothing that needs to worry us. Everything's working out beautifully. There are people up in the hills. That I'm sure of. I'm not worried."

"You sound worried just a bit, all the same," hinted Laura.

"I'm just worried about you, dear. But you're holding out marvelously."

"I'm wiry," said Laura, mousey-eyed.

"You're amazing," said Tony.

The night was very clear, wonderfully spacious and calming. The sky was speckled with stars that shone in the dew that hung from the pine needles. Nothing stirred. The embers died. A small black skeleton lay in the ashes. Zenzo sat beside Laura and looked at Tony, who was fast asleep.

"He try to be brave. But something frighten him," said Zenzo.

"All his life there's been something that scares him," said Laura.

"What, maybe?" said Zenzo.

"The truth, maybe," said Laura.

Zenzo whispered, "What truth?"

"God knows," said Laura desolately.

"You love him, Mrs. Wagasala?"

"Yes," said Laura after a moment. "Sometimes he maddens me. And sometimes he baffles me. But maybe I love him because he baffles me."

"He mix-up," said Zenzo gently.

"And terribly vain," said Laura acidly. "Oh, if he weren't so ridiculously conceited. Men are so boring when they are conceited."

"Poor Mr. Wagasala," said Zenzo.

"He is like a ghost, or an optical illusion. There he is, clear and vivid, and a second later he darts into the shadows. Is that love? Do I really love him? Or do I love an optical illusion?"

"In his heart a little snake. And that snake," said Zenzo, "scare him."

"It's a snake called guilt," said Laura. "It lies coiled deep down in his heart, and, oh Lord, it's so exhausting to live with somebody else's guilt. Especially when the guilt is just a silly little guilt, just a schoolboy taboo, an American stupidity. He needs something or other to shake him out of his guilt. To wake him out of his stupor and make a grown-up man out of him."

"And still," said Zenzo softly, "you no tell me why he guilty."

"Oh, damn it," said Laura angrily, "it's not anything that

he's done. It's the things he hasn't done. It's that childish moral cowardice."

Zenzo chewed at a blade of grass. "You think I wicked, Mrs. Wagasala?"

"I'm sure that you're wicked, Zenzo," said Laura, smiling inwardly.

Zenzo's teeth shone white in the darkness. "You forgive me, Mrs. Wagasala?"

"I'll thank you and I'll bless you, Zenzo, if you wake him out of his stupor."

They sat silently for a while, snatching at their own elusive thoughts—sly, spasmodic little thoughts that shot through the darkness like fireflies. "Yes," thought Laura, "I must accept things. I'll be saved only if I accept things."

Zenzo whispered: "Sh! Listen!"

Laura lifted her head and listened.

"There. Again!"

"A falling twig . . ."

"Or a creepy beast . . ."

"It's the wind in the bushes."

They waited but all was still again. The boughs were motionless and the stars were brilliant. Laura lay down on the blanket and breathed the cool clean smell of the pine needles.

And as she lay there she felt something that she had never felt before. Utter physical exhaustion: but under the exhaustion something else. Peace. Harmony. Indifference. Nothing mattered any longer. The past slid away till it faded into the jungle distances, no bigger and no louder than a leaf falling in the darkness. Tiny fragments emerged from its shadows: a cry at dusk in the lonely dormitory, a yellow scorpion in the hotel bathtub, the bells at midnight in the snow-lit village. All unreal, utterly unreal, like tiny handkerchiefs waving good-by from a black and heartless, irrevocable past. What was her crime? Self-hatred? Self-distortion? Self-laceration? Had all her intellectual gestures, her love of Bach, her hatred of Beethoven, been merely a camouflage to hide the anguish of her bodily inadequacy? Never mind. All was past. Nothing mattered any longer. Let them do as they please, as long as they're happy, as long as they're silent, as long as they leave her alone in her own little cistern of nightmares.

8

"Butterflies, again?" said Mrs. Domingo.

Miss Eccles nodded and waved her net.

"Your outfit," said Mrs. Domingo, "looks rather incongruous, I must say. The monkeys will be amazed. But the mosquitoes will approve, perhaps." She wiped her neck with a handkerchief and fixed her gaze on the sea. "I was looking into my mirror this morning, Penelope."

"You are still a very fine-looking woman, dear Lily."

"Alas, I wish it were so. My past is written on my face. Our faces are our diaries, but truer and sadder. Everything we've done is written down there. Especially all the nasty things—the cruelties and the betrayals, the drunken self-indulgences. Bless my soul. Here we are, just flotsam and jetsam, castaways from civilization, gradually turning into beasts. Away with the masks and pantomimes! Just flesh, fur, and frenzy!"

"We must try to be patient, a bit," said Miss Eccles.

Mrs. Domingo laughed hoarsely. "Please don't talk to me about patience! I've been patient for twenty years with all these sycophants and sponges! Cannes, Salzburg, San Remo—it was always the same old story. I've been looking for someone with a heart, someone with a flicker of innate decency. Sounds pathetic, doesn't it, dear? Well, I tell you, Penelope, it's like looking for a needle in a goddamn haystack. What's wrong? Is

there something horrible about me? Something that my best
friends won't tell me? Do I stink? Do I exude? All I ask for is
honesty and loyalty. Do they exist? I seriously doubt it. I have
decided once and for all that the *membrum virile* is an over-
rated commodity. They're a dime a dozen, all sizes, black and
white, bloated and weazened. Do I shock you, Penelope? Quite
the contrary is intended. Those fleshy excrescences which set
the whole world aquiver—oh, if people only realized how
totally dismal they can be! There was a rat in San Sebastián
who called me a nymphomaniac. His name was Alfonso. Well,
my dear little Alfonso, if only you knew how unutterably
tedious your performance was! It's a thing that a woman
normally refrains from telling a man: it might damage that
idiotic roosterlike conceit of his. There they are, strutting like
cocks along the esplanades and ramblas, so proud to be male,
so proud of those dangling participles! Oh, God, that the fate
of humanity should repose on such a squalor! That love
should reach its pinnacle in those greasy acrobatics! It baffled
me as a child. And, by Jesus, it still baffles me. You won't
believe me, Penelope, but the whole of my sexual career was
just a dedicated effort to discover what the hell it's all about.
Oh, I won't deny that there's a certain little thrill now and
again, but I can state with finality that the whole thing's far
from what it's cracked up to be. One of these days, when I've
finally retired to my little cottage on the moors, I'm going to
sit down and write my autobiography. The whole harrowing
truth from beginning to end. No holds barred, I can tell you.
No detail too excruciating. It should turn into a work of
considerable piquancy, don't you think? Oh, Penelope, dear,
you're such a saintly little person, with those lovely clear eyes
and that silly old net of yours! I warn you. I'm not joking.
There are poisonous vipers lurking in the shadows. Must you
prowl in slimy nooks looking for those frivolous little insects?
Well, all right. It's a kind of destiny, I guess. Better than most,

when you get right down to it. But hurry back, my child. I
have something interesting to tell you."

She flicked her red forefinger, closed her eyes, and lay
back in the hammock. Miss Eccles followed the beach in the
direction of the bamboo thicket. The Baron was crouching in
the shade of a palm, splitting a coconut. The instant she saw
him she felt something extraordinary: a sharp, ugly pang, as
though a rib had cracked in two.

He looked up as she passed and smiled at her teasingly.
"The illustrious zoologist, eh? Looking for some marvelous
new rarity?'

She smiled back at him amiably and walked quickly
across the dune.

9

She climbed through the web of bamboos and down to
the water. The smell of mussels filled the air: a lazy breeze
ruffled the inlet. She knelt at the water's edge and took off her
slippers and cautiously dipped her foot in the tepid water.
Then she started to wade, holding her slippers in one hand
and gripping the insect net in the other. The mud oozed up
through her toes, smooth and oily as butter. The water rose to
her knees. She tucked up her skirt. A tiny beast, a shrimp
perhaps, nipped daintily at her ankle. A fat purple eel darted
past her and vanished. The water grew suddenly cool. A
barricade of roots lined the shore of the mainland, leaving a
crisscross of black slimy streaks on her calves. She stepped
ashore gingerly: a powerful smell hung in the atmosphere—a
stench of old burial grounds, of prehistoric cellars. She put on
her slippers and climbed up the bank. Fingery blossoms, blood-
colored, drooped from the overhanging vines.

She entered the forest. A vegetable hush welled out of the darkness. The trees grew stupendous, taller than any she'd ever seen. From the peninsula they hadn't looked nearly so tall, so dark and bearded. A swarm of catopsilias sat in a patch of muddy sunlight. They rose as she approached, a cloud of shattered, chaotic brilliance. The trees looked startled for a moment, their leaves attentive, like millions of ears.

The place was full of a sessile animation, like the bottom of the sea. She saw hoof prints in the mud, crisp as a doe's but more pointed. There was a ceaseless rustling of birds and once there was the screech of a cockatoo. Under a bush she caught sight of some bulletlike dung. She had the feeling of being watched by myriads of little eyes. Once she had the impression, too blurred and fleeting to be definite, of a long, blackish beast darting off through the underbrush. And everywhere there were butterflies—great sulphur butterflies and dark little satyrs, the iridescent danaids and red-spotted swallowtails.

Then suddenly she saw it. Blue and gold, as big as a swallow. She caught her breath. A blissful panic, a rush of delirium shot through her. *Papilio penelope!* Or *Troides penelope,* to be more accurate, a cousin to *Troides alexandria,* but still vaster, still more exquisite. It swam idly among the saplings, now in sunlight, now in shadow, the gold on the dark-blue velvet catching the quick molten light. *"Oh God,"* she thought quickly, *"Dear God! Just this once, please!"* She felt dizzy, close to swooning with desire and desperation. The insect came to rest on a twig eight feet from the ground. It spread its mighty wings and peered at her with a queenly curiosity. Tears welled into her eyes; her hands shook uncontrollably. She tiptoed closer; jaws frozen, net uplifted, holding her breath. Something stabbed at her knee like a needle: she scarcely noticed the sudden pain.

She stood directly below the bough. The enormous creature was half hidden, but she could see the pointed shadow of its wing on the sunlit leaf. Her longing was so intense that it was tinged with a creeping nausea. *"For God's sake, calm down! Take it easy, Penelope!"* She raised the net slightly. *"Now! Now! Please, oh please, God!"* The forest began to sway, to whisper, to palpitate. She struck: but simultaneously the birdwing dove into space, floated motionless for one second, and went soaring into the treetops.

She stood shaking for several minutes, moaning softly, panting violently. Her cheeks were wet with tears. Her body was soaked with sweat. *"Gone,"* she thought. *"Gone forever."* Slowly she wandered into the wilderness, pale and rapt and blinded with grief, inconsolable as a sleepwalker.

Suddenly she felt, as she paused for a moment, a red-hot stab in her leg. She looked down and saw a scrawl of half-dried blood on her knee. "Well, at least it's not a snake bite," she thought with relief. A thorn or a broken twig. But the pain was sharp, like that of a cigarette burn.

And now she saw, with a queer little pang, an orange blaze beyond the battalion of tree trunks. Sunset. Mercy, was it possible? How long had she been wandering about like this? There was a smell of approaching dusk, tart, resinous, like dying embers. For a moment or two the light blazed out like a conflagration. The rays shot through the boughs in jets of reddish gold. The butterflies had vanished except for some low-flying crepusculars, the iron-blue *Thaumantis*, the furtive Amathusidae.

Miss Eccles grew frightened. The tropical dusk swung down like a curtain. The trees seemed to multiply. The boughs reached out silently. *"Careful,"* she thought. *"Careful, Penelope. You mustn't lose your way, dear."*

She drew a deep breath and glanced about appraisingly. Which was the way she had come? There, to the left, by the clump of bushes? Very likely. That would be eastward; and the beach lay eastward, more or less. *"No rush,"* thought Miss Eccles. *"Take it easy. There's nothing to worry about."*

But then, with a hideous rapidity, the woods grew impenetrable. Night had fallen. The bushes were drowned in a sea of slate-blue shadow. Miss Eccles closed her eyes and stood motionless for a moment, trying to calm her troubled nerves and to think with lucidity. *"The thing is to be rational,"* she thought intensely. *"Don't get panicky."*

She sat down on a fallen trunk, laying her net in her lap. The feel of the bamboo handle reassured her a little. Her eyes grew used to the darkness. The woods receded again. Bright stars were beginning to peep through the overarching boughs. Insects started to chirp. Somewhere in the depths a monkey screamed. And the forest, which three minutes ago had seemed so threatening and sinister, took on a strangely intimate, almost conversational flavor.

"Well," she thought, *"I'll have to be patient. There's nothing to be afraid of. Nothing at all. It's happened before. You're not a baby, Penelope."*

For several minutes Miss Eccles felt positively contented. She felt fortified, resourceful; she felt wise and at one with nature. She folded her arms and looked about for a place to sleep. *"No mosquitoes, thank God,"* she thought. *"Dampish, a bit, but not too bad."*

A feverish weariness swept over her. She slumped down on the springy moss, still gripping her net as though it were a weapon. The squabbling of the monkeys and the whine of insects lulled her to sleep. Once she opened her eyes and saw that the moon was shining through the branches. The monkeys had stopped their chatter; the only life was the life of the moths, who had gathered in velvety hordes, fat-bodied sphinxes that darted like hummingbirds and the long-tailed

Actias that floated like phantoms; hundreds of moths, vast and tiny, dancing in the moonlight with a lunatic aimlessness. She watched, enthralled and comforted; and finally she fell asleep again.

10

"I am afraid," said the Baron, "that she got ensnarled in that mass of jungle. The footprints stopped at the inlet. She must have waded across the inlet. I scrambled through those mangroves but of course there wasn't a trace. Then I looked higher up among the eucalyptus trees. Not a clue. Nothing at all. I kept calling. No answer, of course."

"We will try again tomorrow," said the Professor, looking owlish. "Miss Eccles is a sensible woman. She has walked in jungles before."

"I was climbing over the rocks," said Billy Baxter very softly. "I saw Miss Eccles down on the shore with her butterfly net. She put down her net and took off her slippers. I saw her wading into the water. She was carrying her net and her slippers."

"I am terrified," said Mrs. Domingo. "Penelope was shrewd but she was fanatical. Those insects were her love life. I know how she felt about those butterflies. Now it's night and she's trapped in the woods. Snakes. Centipedes. Orangutans."

"We can only hope and pray," said the Baron, rather balefully.

"We must wait for the morning," said the Professor, stroking his beard.

"And not only the animals, mind you! The *men!*" cried Mrs. Domingo. "Don't tell me there's nobody living there. I've heard those drumbeats throbbing. I've heard voices—yes, distinctly. Far-off echoes across the valley. Penelope is brave, but after all she's a woman. I quake when I think of those prowling savages."

"Maybe you exaggerate the sexual appetites of those natives," said the Baron. "I doubt whether our Penelope needs to worry about her chastity."

"I'm not thinking about chastity. I am thinking of more sinister appetites. You'll think I'm hysterical but I feel ill when I think of Penelope."

"Look at the moon," said Shishnik, pointing. "Nearly full. All round and silvery. We must try to think of something more refreshing to talk about."

"Exactly," said the Baron. "First it was Ibrahim and then the Wagensellers. And now poor Miss Eccles. We must smile. We must look at the moon."

"Please, Hugo, don't be ironical. Professor Shishnik is talking sense. We have got to be optimistic. Think of something pleasant, please, Professor."

"Well, there are many pleasant things still left in the world," said the Professor. "Even now, with all the terrors of our time and all the vulgarity. There are still places I would like to visit. The hills of Delphi, for example."

"I have a yearning for Ispahan," said Mrs. Domingo, looking skyward. "The vastnesses of Asia. The deserts. The steppes. The pinnacles. Untouched, I'm sure, by modern machinery. And the names! Bokhara, Samarkand. They remind me of poems I read as a child. Say what you may, there still is beauty if one knows where to look for it."

"I should like," said the Baron, "to visit the Straits of Magellan. No one will ever try to vulgarize the Straits of Magellan."

"I'd love," said Billy Baxter, "to climb to the top of the Himalayas."

"You will find it very mournful on Mount Everest," said the Baron.

"Here we are," said Mrs. Domingo, "chattering away about these far-off places. Do you know what I'd really like? I'm fed up with the exotic. I'd just love to settle down in some cozy spa in the middle of the woods. Baden-Baden, that sort of thing. No more curries, no more rickshaws. Just a croissant with my tea out on the lawn, under an umbrella. A bit of bridge in the afternoon. Two Martinis before dinner. I'm sick of gadding about. I want peace. Peace and order. I am well past maturity. I want to find out what I'm really like. I mean, way deep down in the unexplored depths of me. Oh, Professor, you're so right to scoff at the world of materialism. It is so difficult these days to elude the phantoms of materialism. But here in this lonely spot some funny thoughts have been crowding in on me. I'm sure that it sounds naïve to you, but I feel there's a destiny awaiting me. There must be something or somebody, I don't quite have a name for it, it's all much too complicated to give it a name, but I'm sure there's something or somebody who feels an abiding interest in me. Nobody else has ever felt it, as far as I've been able to see, so what's the point in living if that certain somebody doesn't care?" She raised her hands to her temples and stared intently at Professor Shishnik. "It's so wearying to be a woman, especially a woman like me, Professor. No children, no absorptions, no achievements, just a lot of money. I've always felt a wee bit desolate about being a woman. An aching, quivering emptiness that's waiting to be filled. So frightened of being filled and still so scared of not being filled! Look at Billy. I don't care if he listens. It's high time he learned a thing or two. There should come a time in our lives when we can throw off our sex and become something else, betwixt and between, half man, half woman. We could relax and just be human. Aft all, it was only a stray little spermatozoon that decided it

Haven't you felt a bit disgruntled with being a male sometimes, Professor? And you, Hugo, hasn't it struck you as rather
limiting occasionally? Oh, how I long to be just human and
shed this dribbling femininity, these breasts, these disguises,
this hypocrisy, this horrible worrying."

Billy Baxter pointed suddenly toward the sea and cried,
"Look!"

Way out on top of the sea there was something shining
feebly. At first it was just a small yellow gleam, like a
fisherman's lantern. Then it moved, ever so slowly; the gleam
grew brighter, multiplied.

"Good God," said Mrs. Domingo.

"A ship! A ship!" cried Billy.

The Baron and the Professor jumped to their feet without
a word. All four of them went racing down to the edge of the
water. There they stood, waving and shouting, watching the
ship move slowly southward. In that glittering chain of lights
the whole wide world lay savagely concentrated: the leap of
hope and the poignance, the terrible withdrawal, the final
blackness.

Mrs. Domingo knelt on the sand and cried, "They can't!
Oh Christ, they can't!"

Then she shook her fist at the sea and howled, "The
bastards! Oh, those bastards. . . ."

PART V

The Village

The moment she opened her eyes she sensed an alertness in the air. The moonlight was so strong that the leaves looked phosphorescent. The brightness on the ground gleamed like freshly fallen snow. A twig snapped suddenly. Miss Eccles stared into the darkness. Slowly, like a fish rising to the surface, a slender figure materialized. It looked like an emaciated idol, half human, half cockatoo.

She called crisply, "Hello there!" The shape recoiled a little. Then it seemed to pick up courage and crept out from the underbrush. It was a man, black as pitch and quite naked except for the headdress: a spray of green feathers bursting over a large sculptured beak. He tiptoed toward Miss Eccles in gingerly, mincing spasms and sank to the ground in front of her, peering up with awe-struck eyes.

"You friend?" said Miss Eccles in a cool, casual tone.

The Negro grinned mournfully and clawed at the earth.

"Me friend," stated Miss Eccles, and she pointed to her bosom.

The Negro spread his arms and fluttered the tips of his fingers.

She caught the smell of the savage and knew that he was frightened. She smiled, baring her teeth. He cringed and shuddered slightly. "Well," she thought, "I dare say I look rather odd to the little fellow."

"*Mingali!*" murmured the Negro, plucking at the hem of her skirt. The whites of his eyes were unnaturally large and luminous. The look on his face was childishly abject, yet cold and cunning.

He muttered in prayerful tones, "*Djungalali! Djungalali!*"

"Well, there's nothing to be worried about," thought Miss Eccles. She picked up her net. "He is trying to help me, obviously. Or maybe it's *he* who is looking for help. . . ."

The Negro got up and pointed to an opening in the trees. A misty gray light was beginning to seep through the leaves. "Dawn. Thank God," thought Miss Eccles. "Well, we'll see what he's up to."

She rose, feeling stiff and slightly dizzy, and followed the Negro. They entered what looked like a well-frequented path, which circled uphill along the edge of a narrow stream. The trees grew sparse and stunted. A mountain rose in the distance. The light grew lemon-hued. The sun was about to rise.

The Negro came to a halt. *"Djungalali!"* he purred ceremoniously. Some fifty yards ahead of them a man stepped out of the shadows. Miss Eccles was puzzled. He was tall and skeletally thin, not black but a grisly white, with a wispy beard which hung to his navel. He wore faded khaki shorts from which his legs protruded like stilts. His head was totally bald. White hairs hung from his nipples. A large pair of spectacles was perched on a long, pedantic nose.

He strolled stiffly toward Miss Eccles and bowed his head politely. Then he said in a clear, clipped English, "Can I be of use to you, madam?"

"Oh, thanks. Very kind of you," said Miss Eccles, taken aback. "I've lost my way, I'm afraid." She added quickly, "I've come from the peninsula."

The bearded man, who looked like some crazy old hermit, said placidly, "It's not serious in the least, I assure you. A two hour's walk, three at the most. Excuse me for meddling. May I ask you your name?"

"Penelope Eccles."

"Ah. English?"

"I live in Shrewsbury."

"A lepidopterist, I gather," said the stranger, peering at

the net. "We have some extraordinary species hereabouts, as you may have noticed."

"Indeed you do," said Miss Eccles, brightening a little. "Some dazzling papilios."

"We are rather proud of our insects," said the man. He smirked coquettishly. "Unique in size and brilliance. Much sought after by the collectors."

"Are you English, too, by chance?"

"No, alas," said the stranger. "My name is Djungalali. A Melanesian name of debatable origins. My real name is Krauss. Doktor Willibald Krauss, from Tübingen. A doctor of philosophy and not of medicine, I must hasten to add. I am happy to make your acquaintance. Will you pardon my casual attire?"

The little Negro stood behind the white man, slightly to his left, rolling his eyes. The sun was rising. The far-off hills shone salmon-pink in the spreading brilliance. Miss Eccles was able to see things with a greater exactitude: the emerald feathers in the Negro's headdress, the bluish sheen of his penis. She saw the analytical gleam in the eyes of the white man, which bulged like a trout's behind the thick-lensed glasses.

"You are here," ventured Miss Eccles, "on a scientific mission, Herr Krauss?"

"Scientific? Yes and no," said Herr Krauss, chuckling amiably. "Merely existing in this place is anthropologically edifying, if I may say so. There is an endless accumulation of data. But the deductions are equivocal."

"You speak impeccable English, I must say," said Miss Eccles.

"I was in Oxford for two years. Balliol. Oriental Studies. I always revered the English. Truly civilized: not rational but *easonable*. Not profound perhaps, but *flexible*. Ah me. Perfidious Albion! It's my spiritual dwelling place." He took her by the elbow. *"Ach,* forgive me, Miss Eccles. I am wasting your valuable time. Let me accompany you to the village."

The path led through a clearing on the edge of a hill and down a pebbly slope into a spoon-shaped valley. Way below, among some palms, rose a cluster of little huts. Nothing stirred, no life was visible except for a plume of brownish smoke.

They paused on the edge of a precipice which guarded the neck of the valley. The Negro lurked behind them, picking mushrooms and chewing them dreamily.

"Have you been here long, Herr Krauss?"

"Forty years, my good Miss Eccles."

"You prefer this place to Tübingen?"

"It's a complicated tale, Miss Eccles. I left Tübingen when I was thirty. I am an old man, as you see. When I was thirty, I thought I was wise. I knew the history of all mankind—not only Assyria, Persia, Babylon, but the very beginnings, the killers of mastodons, the vast migrations, and so on. I came here to add some corroboratory footnotes, so to speak. I discovered my abysmal ignorance. I decided to linger on. Little by little, year by year, I grew aware of the infinite subtleties. *Ach,* they're ignorant and childlike, they're gentle and naïve, but I assure you, Miss Eccles, they have a system of divinations, a whole hierarchy of intuitions more intricate than anything you'll find in Europe!"

"And you're happy here, Herr Krauss?"

"I am necessary," he said with finality. "To them I'm the great magician. They would be utterly lost without me. I help the women give birth. I circumcise the boys. I pierce the festering boils and saw off the gangrenous legs. Not particularly easy, as you can imagine. I used up my ointments thirty years ago. Now I use primeval instinct, the wisdom of the ages, you might say."

He turned to her and smiled: an appalling little smile

The cold, fishy eyes, the piercing nose, the swooping beard, and under it all this dried-out loneliness, this clutching fanaticism. Was it that? Or had he merely deteriorated into an empty shell, a spiritual fiasco?

He took her by the arm and helped her carefully down the precipice. They walked through a field of ferns still soaked with the morning dew, and then, abrupt as a gong, the light of the sun flooded the valley. A bevy of pigs scurried past them, nuzzling and squealing.

"You are very blond," remarked Herr Krauss. He grinned toothily at Miss Eccles. "Almost albino. Very fortunate. They will think you are a white, all-healing god-lady!"

2

As they entered the village Miss Eccles realized that they were expecting her. Children were squatting among the shrubs, half hidden, peeping impishly. A group of wrinkled elders stood under a palm with folded arms. As they strolled past the huts the assembled villagers drew back solemnly, fondling their bracelets, whispering furtively, gazing raptly at Miss Eccles. Their black protruding eyes were shining with terror and adoration.

Miss Eccles felt touched, slightly puzzled, vaguely obligated. She felt that something benevolent or even miraculous was expected of her.

She glanced at Herr Krauss. "They knew I was coming, it appears."

"Oh, yes, they were informed. They were fully aware," said Krauss whimsically.

They walked side by side through the village. There was a hush of ceremonial excitement. Mothers peered through their little doorways, holding their babies in front of them. A trio of feathered warriors stood in the clearing, spears upraised. Their bodies were gleaming with oil and their hair was caked with mud. They were quite naked; even the hairs had been plucked from their bodies. They stood frozen like statues. Only their eyeballs moved suggestively as Herr Krauss and Miss Eccles wandered slowly across the clearing.

"Where are we going?" said Miss Eccles.

"Ah," said Krauss, stroking his Adam's apple, "there is a charming little bungalow awaiting you, Miss Eccles. They are profoundly flattered, you understand. They are expecting you to stay a while."

"Well, I doubt whether I can afford . . ."

"*Pazienza*, Miss Eccles. You will find your sojourn in this village highly rewarding," said Herr Krauss.

He paused in front of a hut at the edge of the village. It was shaped like a mushroom, squat and windowless and circular, with the dangling roof grasses almost touching the dust. The skull of some beast, painted blue, hung over the doorway.

Miss Eccles lowered her head and stepped through the doorway. She glanced about in the darkness. Some logs were smoldering in a stone-ringed oven. The rafters and the roof were black with the smoke of the casuarina firewood. Smoke-blackened gourds hung on the walls. The floor was strewn with kunai grass. There was a pleasant smell of smoke and dried grass and fresh pig grease.

A middle-aged woman was sitting by the oven, arms akimbo. She too was naked except for a tiny round apron made of bark. Her whole body was tattooed with whorls of small yellow dots.

"This is Kayakalali," said Herr Krauss. He took off his spectacles and wiped them with a rag. "Kayakalali is wise and experienced. She will tend to your various requirements

Relax, Miss Eccles. You need a rest. I will see you shortly. *À bientôt!*" And he twisted his bony body and half crawled, half darted, through the doorway.

The woman Kayakalali stared lugubriously at Miss Eccles and pointed to a large mat of leaves beside the wall. Miss Eccles felt strangely dejected all of a sudden. She sat down on the mat and placed her chin on the palm of her hand. Kayakalali stood by the oven and lifted a pot from the embers. A smell like roasted almonds went drifting through the hut. Kayakalali lifted a large, pear-shaped melon out of the pot, carefully peeled off the rind and split it into segments, like an orange. These she placed on a leaf in front of Miss Eccles. "*Karuka,*" she said.

Miss Eccles nibbled cautiously. The flavor resembled eggplant and the little black kernels tasted of cinnamon, sweet and spicy. Kayakalali looked pleased. She knelt beside Miss Eccles, drew off her shoes, and started to knead her aching toes with a yellowish oil.

A strange, tingling lassitude crept over Miss Eccles. The smell of the smoke and the crackling of the embers, the taste of the melon, Kayakalali's massage, all had a profoundly soothing, even somniferous effect on her. She lay back on the mat with a little sigh and closed her eyes.

From far away came a sound like great waves breaking on a beach. A breeze stirred the air. A cock crowed; a pig grunted.

When she awoke she saw Kayakalali sitting beside her, shelling beans. She turned over and lifted her head, and was startled to see that she was naked. Her faded pink dress was pinned to the wall with a long black knife. Her underclothes had vanished. Her slippers hung by the oven.

For a moment she felt puzzled, then piqued, then indignant. "Kayakalali!" she cried, and pointed angrily to her dress. Kayakalali grinned blandly and went on shelling her beans.

Miss Eccles glanced at her body, which looked unhealthily white in the darkness. She started to get up but Kayakalali grasped her shoulder and gently but firmly pushed her back on the mat.

At this moment a small, hairy figure darkened the doorway. A very old man with a frizzy beard limped into the hut. He was followed by a second man, tall and young and extremely muscular. Miss Eccles shrank back and covered her breasts with her hands. The older man, who gave out a powerful smell of bananas, nodded affably to Miss Eccles and crouched beside her on the mat. His face looked like a lizard's: bat-blue eyelids, quivering nostrils, features melting into a maze of scaly dry wrinkles.

Very deftly, as though probing a vegetable, he touched her belly and then her calves. He leaned down and sniffed at her thighs. He scraped at her nipple with his fingernail. Miss Eccles felt too totally disconcerted to resist. She stared blankly at the strange old man, and then at Kayakalali, and then at the young man.

The old man nodded to the young one, who drew closer, muttering *"Akabbe."* He placed an earthenware ewer filled with oil in front of Miss Eccles. He dipped his palms in the ewer and then placed them on her bosom. With great solemnity he anointed her body with the fragrant green oil: her breasts, and her shoulder blades, her kneecaps, her buttocks. The older man kept nodding and muttering and gesticulating, pointing now here, now there, picking his teeth with satisfaction. Finally the ceremony was finished. The young man picked up the ewer and followed the old man out through the doorway. Kayakalali scratched her head, shrugged her shoulders, and sat down by the fire.

Miss Eccles, to her own amazement, felt neither shame nor indignation. She felt marvelously relaxed, at peace with things, drowsily serene. She glanced at her flesh, which looked suddenly warm and alive. She sat on the mat of pandanus

leaves and watched Kayakalali, who was squatting beside the
oven and kneading a thick grayish paste.

Time passed. She dozed off, dreaming incoherent dreams:
she was clutching at a huge umbrella, wafted gently over a
tropical desert. Far below she could see the tribesmen and
their camels beside the firelight. She sank to the ground and
found herself in a kind of mazelike kasbah. Some bearded men
were sitting on a café terrace, rolling dice. She hurried down
the street and stepped into a candlelit cathedral. Naked
cherubs were fluttering down the nave, singing joyously.
There was a sudden clap of thunder. The cathedral doors
swung open. Outside, instead of the street, yawned a vast
boiling chasm; a woman in a kind of wedding gown was
waving frantically from the edge of the crater.

She woke up. There was a delicious smell of freshly baked
bread. Kayakalali was sprinkling a fine yellow powder over the
loaves. She turned toward Miss Eccles and grinned at her
toothlessly.

"*Mukule?*" she whispered.

Miss Eccles smiled and nodded. She suddenly understood.
She got up and stepped to the doorway, no longer ashamed of
her pallid nakedness. She was surprised to see that it was
already late in the afternoon. A rich burnished light hung
over the village, accentuating the shadows.

The village had grown animated. The feathery warriors
were strutting in the distance. A crowd had gathered near the
hut and in the palm grove behind the hut. When Miss Eccles
appeared in the doorway a kind of spasm passed over the
crowd. There was an awed undulation, a ripple of murmur-
ings. An armless old woman started to chant. Miss Eccles
grasped the fact that she was instilling the crowd with secret
joyousness, and she continued to stand in the doorway. She
felt no trace of shame. She felt potent, almost regal.

The people in the grove, she now realized, were the sick

and the afflicted ones. They crouched or lay supine among the trees, moaning softly. Some had crawled to the edge of the stream and were dipping their faces in the water. Others sat in the shade, heads sunk forward, plucking at their sores. The stench of suppuration mingled with the scent of the banana palms. Some of the stricken ones crawled nearer, eyes fixed on Miss Eccles. They looked like animated plants, with their shapeless faces and withered arms. In their eyes there was a look of unfathomable stillness and concentration. Miss Eccles could feel a great wave of longing that rose from the lepers; the desperate lull of watchfulness, the hush of an expected miracle.

The young athlete who had visited her earlier now strolled through the trees, carrying a water jar. He beckoned to Miss Eccles and followed her back into the hut. Seeing him more clearly in the oblique sunlight she noticed something strange about him. He was much taller than the rest of the villagers and altogether more handsome: he had tender, intelligent eyes and a sad, snowy smile.

He placed the jar in her hands and gestured to her to drink. Miss Eccles peered at the liquid, which was gritty, brown, opaque. She lifted the jar and sipped. It was sweet and pungent, like licorice. She took a second and a third sip and gave back the jar. The young man looked at her thoughtfully. "*Kani. Kalluli,*" he said and departed.

Dusk fell. Miss Eccles lay down again on her bed of pandanus leaves. She felt dizzy and vaguely exultant. A pleasantly burning sensation flowed through her. She felt her body being lifted to a new and more rarefied level. Her arms floated like wings. She felt weightless, ethereal. She felt herself rising above the zones of space and time. Forgiveness, perception, harmony, divination, purification: they danced in the air like entities, interwoven in golden strands. She felt transfigured, superhuman. She was like a soaring, birdlike deity.

3

Everything started to rot. The shoes were gray with mold. Mrs. Domingo's leather bag had grown furry with fungi. The knives and shears grew rusty, the aspirin disintegrated, and the Baron's alarm clock was filled with little bugs. The Professor strolled about in his fiery kimono. In spite of the whimsical diet he was growing a little fatter. The Baron had grown thinner. His beautiful breeches were ripped and faded, and his lavender shirt was coming apart at the seams. His mustache drooped from the sides of his mouth like a Chinaman's. As for Mrs. Domingo, she had abandoned all pretense. Her hair was white at the roots and hung down to her waist. To make up for her lost cosmetics she dappled her body with jewels. The glint of emeralds and sapphires flashed on her long, darkening arms, and one morning she strode forth in her diamond tiara. Billy's hair was matted with salt and his cowboy pants were covered with stains, but he was the only one who retained some slight semblance of normality.

One morning the Professor climbed into the forest to fetch some water from the stream. As he knelt on the moss he caught sight of a little monkey which sat huddled in the shade of a eucalyptus tree. It had honey-colored fur, with violet rings around its eyes. The Professor stepped closer. The monkey cringed and blinked its eyes, and then looked at the Professor with a curiously intimate expression. It was a baby, he realized. Was it ill? Had it lost its way? He lifted it gently. It fondled his eyebrows inquisitively. He stroked its silky ears and carried it lovingly down to the beach, where he laid it on his mat and fed it a banana.

After this the Professor and his monkey, whom he named

Yuri, were inseparable. All day long it crouched on his shoulder, plucking daintily at his hairy earlobes, or hung dangling from his neck with a look of anguished solemnity. At night it slept on his belly with its tail curled round his wrist. A sweet and subtle change crept over Professor Shisknik's character.

When he woke up in the morning and saw the light flow over the sea and the palm leaves overhead shining faintly in the rosy light, what he felt was sharper than pleasure: it was an aching expectancy. Little by little he was discovering a new dimension in life. The abstractions, the generalities, the intricacies of theory shriveled away. As he wandered along the beach he no longer kept mumbling, "Precisely . . . incontrovertibly . . ." The peninsula was no longer a place with a definite geography and geology. It had turned into a cornucopia of colors and sounds and fragrances. The birds wove threads of music through the thunder of far-off breakers. The musk from the jungle was filled with a dark rejuvenation. He would sit for hours on the rocks that jutted over the cove, just looking at the ripples as they trailed their shadows over the sand. Or he lay on his back on the sand with Yuri nuzzling at his armpit, and stared at the palm leaves swaying idly in the breeze. He felt the balmy air slowly sapping his will power, perpetually sucking away at the very roots of his personality. He stopped thinking of himself as an ugly, lumpish personage with certain higher obligations, a Duty to Science, a Mission in Life. He stroked Yuri's coiling tail and scratched him gently under the chin. He felt exquisitely immobilized, like a giant chained in cobwebs.

He whispered to Yuri in Russian: "Good God, Yuri, do you know what's happened? It is incredible! It is crazy! I feel happy, completely happy! For the first time in my life! Do you know the reason, my beautiful Yuri? Tell me the reason. Or no. Don't bother. Life was always full of question marks and

colons and exclamation points. Now it is nothing but lazy
dots. Just endless, meaningless dots. And I feel happy. Stupid
and happy! Am I losing my mind? Am I crazy, Yuri?"

The little parrot Elijah cried from the bough overhead,
in his shrill, angry Russian, *"Soukimesin! Soukine sin!"*

4

Finally the figures were finished. The Baron had spent
two whole days on them, carving away at the smooth, tawny
chips of casuarina. The pawns were simple enough, done in
ten or fifteen minutes. The rooks were a bit more difficult,
with their fragile castellations. The bishops and the knights
took an hour at least, each of them, with their tapering miters
and undulating manes. But it was the queens who were the
triumph, even grander than the kings, and when he showed
them to Lily she said, "You've missed your vocation, sweet.
They are spectacular."

The two men sat under the palm tree with the chessboard
between them. Mrs. Domingo dozed in her hammock. No
breeze stirred. Nobody spoke. The players bowed their heads
as they meditated on their armies, now lifting a little pawn
and now shifting a bishop. The Baron wore only a loincloth
made from the remnants of his shirt. His chest was burned and
bony. He looked like a sadhu. As for the Professor, he still
clung to his miserable kimono, but he had cut off the sleeves
and made himself a bandana. His eyes, oyster gray, still had
their look of foggy sadness, but a queer little smile sometimes
hovered on the edge of his lips.

They finally finished their game. Mrs. Domingo had left
them. She was down in the "kitchen" preparing a fruit salad.
Billy Baxter was prowling about in the dunes. The sun was

touching the mountains and the heat had gone from the air. The white-lathered reef sparkled snowily in the distance.

"Tell me, Professor," said the Baron, lifting his queen and peering at her thoughtfully. "You feel hope for this rotting world of ours. I feel nothing but despair. Let us assume that we're both intelligent men, perfectly honest in our convictions. Why this chasm between us? What is behind it? How do you explain it?"

The Professor sighed wistfully. "Ah, my friend. What a question. If we knew the real answer we could put a stop to these horrible massacres. If we look at history impartially, have we any clean-cut reason for regarding it either with optimism or pessimism? We take our choice as our instincts tell us. Some see a march toward a distant glory, interrupted by some vicious little setbacks, to be sure, which of course will be eliminated when we eliminate their cause, which at the moment wears the camouflage of social injustice. Others visualize a march toward an all-engulfing catastrophe, which will leave our corpses rotting in a moonlike desolation. I cannot believe in either of these extremist positions, my good Baron. Call it hope if you wish. You might merely call it indifference."

"Very tactfully put," said the Baron. "But the puzzle still remains. Why do some of us choose the first position and others the second, since it is certain that neither can be proved right or wrong? Is it obligatory for us to think of our opponents as vicious idiots? Can't we conceive of the possibility that the other one is right?"

"I am surprised to hear you talking like an Englishman, Baron. The possibility that the other is right! That is much too tolerant and reasonable! As though our lives would continue as usual if our lovely theories suddenly exploded. Human history all these centuries has been smeared with blood and terror and we live in the hope that someday there will be an end to all the terror. The irony is that the adversaries, with their little recipes to end all bloodshed, keep on spilling still

more blood in order to protect their sterile recipes. You have
your recipe, no doubt. Perhaps I have mine. Are we likely to
shrug our shoulders and murmur, '*Chacun à son goût?*' "

"It is strange, isn't it?" said the Baron. "Here we sit in the
middle of nowhere, talking of the fate of humanity as though
it were under our immediate jurisdiction. We should really be
thinking of nothing but fishes and coconuts."

"We are men," said the Professor.

"Fools. Fanatics," said the Baron.

5

The Baron sat on a rock and wrote in his diary:

This morning I was walking all alone by the inlet. Lily and
Shishnik were still asleep. I reached down to pick up a mussel and
there they were! Naked footprints! I thought of Shishnik. Much
too small. Lily, maybe? Obviously not. Or poor Billy? Quite
impossible. These feet, as I studied them carefully, were not the
feet of a civilized being. They came up from the water, half
obliterated at first, then growing crisp and clear as they followed
the edge of the inlet. Seven footprints in all. They turned back
to the water and vanished. What does it mean? Is Lily right?
On an impulse I covered them up. I doubt whether it is wise to
mention the matter.

The point is this. I must be watchful. I must keep on the alert.
I have certain definite advantages. I am younger and physically
stronger. But I lack patience. I am overemotional. This has
revealed itself in our chess games. That is the reason for this
diary. Self-knowledge. Self-discipline. I've been doing my daily
exercises—fifty knee bends, fifty push-ups. *Mens sana in corpore
sano.* But is it true? I can't help wondering: the stronger and
healthier I feel the more troubled I am by that *other* thing. Never
mind. I must go on. I am not an idiot, after all.

Last night I remembered a lonely walk that I took one night
in Innsbruck. I was twelve years old. I was spending a week with
my Uncle Franz. I followed the little street with its blackened
gables and vomiting gargoyles. It must have been midnight. God

knows what I was looking for. Maybe I had some vague inkling even then of sexual adventure. I crossed the narrow park and wandered slowly along the Inn. A young couple was lying on the grass behind the bushes at the edge of the river. I stole up behind them. I saw it all, from beginning to end. The man—dark, handsome, maybe an Italian, I kept thinking—finally slipped off the rubber and tied a crisp little knot around it. Then he tossed it into the bushes where it lit at my feet. They walked away, laughing. (Did they know I was watching? I've always wondered about this.) I picked up the trophy, still warm and alive, and slipped it in my pocket. In the secrecy of my bedroom I cautiously untied it. The odor was tart but not unpleasant. It reminded me of chestnut blossoms. I dipped my finger into the liquid. It felt sticky, like mucilage. I carefully tied it up again and put it back in my trousers. All this was followed, naturally enough, by the usual puerile ritual. I forgot it for several days. Suddenly it burst in my pocket. The clammy fluid spread through my underclothes, spreading the stench of rotting protein. I was filled with disgust. The disgust has never left me. I am still obsessed with the putrescence and the sheer absurdity of it all. Is this stupid little episode at the root of my hatred of humanity?

Point three. (I must be systematic. Whatever happens, I *must* be orderly.) After this discovery of the footprints I walked to the stream with the bucket. A tiny blue flower was growing in the moss beside the stream. Something about this little flower suddenly struck me as amazing. I stopped wondering about those footprints. I stopped worrying about Shishnik. I felt touched, overwhelmed. I leaned down and kissed the flower. It reminded me of April in Carinthia, picnics in the meadow, cowbells tinkling. How I'd love to feast my eyes on a peaceful, speckled cow! I am homesick, is that it? A queer sensation. I have never experienced it. I feel a whole new outlook, a new personality seeping into my veins. That *Doppelgänger* of mine is turning into an Austrian sentimentalist. Is it only another mask? We will see. Time will tell.

Point four. This heat is growing more horrible every day. I see heavy green clouds bubbling over the horizon from time to time. I keep hoping for rain. But the rain refuses to come. The stream is almost dry. The water tastes rancid. The bananas and breadfruits are shriveling on the trees. Soon there will be nothing left but coconuts. Rain! Rain! I quiver at the thought of it. I can

see why these primitive tribes are so obsessed by it. I can smell
it in the distance. I feel a flickering in the atmosphere. Once or
twice I've heard thunder. But the rain refuses to fall. In this
scorching, merciless light everything seems to be magnified—
bloated and blistered, exposed, as though seen under a microscope.
My fingers look swollen. Even my pores have grown larger. Tomorrow I will start going about completely naked. Shishnik won't even
notice. Nor will Lily. They are lost in their dreams.

Final point. Things are moving toward a climax, that is obvious. I've been watching Lily carefully. She's behaving very
oddly. Is she heading for a nervous breakdown? Is she going mad,
at last? Or is she really infatuated with that fat old scoundrel?
And what about Shishnik, with that cringing little monkey? He
is masquerading as a blue-eyed innocent. Rather convincingly,
what's more. If I weren't so sure of his villainy I would almost
begin to wonder. His behavior is a marvelous piece of histrionics,
I must say. This brutal calculation disguised as a Dostoevskian
naïveté. Well, whatever is about to happen—and something is
inexorably going to happen—I will accept it as I have to accept
everything: bearable because meaningless. Only a continuation of
this awful monotony seems unbearable. Let it come! Let it happen! Whatever it is, I open my arms to it!

He put down his pencil and covered the diary with sand.
Then he strolled toward the hut. Mrs. Domingo was lying in
the shade. She wiped the sweat from her eyelids and stared at
the Baron with bloodshot eyes.

"I feel miserable today, Hugo. It's the diet. It's killing
me. Couldn't you look around a bit? A roasted bird would do
wonders."

"I found an interesting little flower up by the stream this
morning. It looked like a forget-me-not."

"I am constipated. I need oils. I need purges," moaned
Mrs. Domingo. She sat up all of a sudden and glared savagely
at the Baron. "There you stand like an ape, chattering away
about forget-me-nots! Don't you realize that we're rotting
away? We're doomed, I tell you! We're doomed to death!
Don't look at me like that! You think I'm going crazy, don't

you? Well, I'm not! It's you who are mad! Do you hear me? You're a lunatic! You hate me. I can see it in your eyes. You've always despised me. I used to think you were after my money but of course it was more than the money. You needed someone you could sneer at. Was that it? Well, it's over. If we ever get out of here, and by Jesus, I'm beginning to doubt it, you'll be back on your own, Hugo. No more qualms about being a gigolo. Just a gigolo! *Quelle blague!* It's pretty pathetic when you stop to think about it. An impecunious baron, past the bloom of his youth, hitches on to a rich American woman who refuses to face the facts. Poor old Lily, all she wanted was to keep on being loved. So she finds this miserable cad with soulful eyes and a third-rate title. Mind you, I've never revealed to anyone those quaint little activities of yours. Thought you were fooling me, did you? Dear God, the idiocy of men! I peeked at that envelope one night. Recipes indeed! What a horrible fraud! Peddling that vile murderous stuff just for the thrill of it, that's all. It's not as though you needed the cash. God knows, you had all you wanted. No, it was the secrecy, the criminality, and above all the destructiveness that appealed to you. Cocaine or heroin or whatever the hell it was, it made you feel masterful. It made you feel potent. A glamorous lover! Is that what I was looking for? What absolute balls. And serves me right. That beseeching little cock of yours, those squirming, piddling orgasms. Well, it's over, the Lord be praised. You're free. You're free! Do you hear me?"

The Baron said nothing. His jawbone started to quiver. He reached down quite casually, as though picking up a pebble and struck Mrs. Domingo across the cheek, twice, crisply. Then he turned and walked slowly back to the sea.

6

Miss Eccles woke up in the morning with a throbbing headache. Kayakalali had thrown a sow's hide over her body to keep her warm. But she had caught a touch of rheumatism. She wasn't accustomed to nudity. The curious anise drink had left a nasty taste in her mouth. Her stomach was upset. She had no appetite. She was shivering a little.

Kayakalali brought her some milk in a coconut shell, but the milk had a rancid odor; Miss Eccles recoiled. She gazed at Kayakalali anxiously and said, "Djungalali?"

The woman grinned and nodded, covering her eyes in imitation of spectacles. She waddled out of the hut and five minutes later Doktor Krauss appeared.

"Good morning, Miss Eccles."

"Good morning, Herr Krauss."

"You look solemn."

"I feel solemn. I feel definitely indisposed."

"You drank too much of that horrible kava which Bundule brought you yesterday. Nasty stuff. Bad for the morale. Only a sip next time, I beg you."

"I was wondering, Herr Krauss . . ."

"I know precisely what you were wondering. And I'm not in the least surprised. Being elevated like this, without warning, to a state of semidivinity, well, it's not the sort of thing one gets used to overnight. May I sit down?"

"Do, please," said Miss Eccles, draping the pig's hide over her torso.

"It is *Schicksal*, not *Zufall*, which has brought you here, Miss Eccles. It is *Schicksal* that you came exactly to this place at this moment. Chasing butterflies, were you? Have you ever observed how the tiniest accident, a call at the grocer's or the sting of a gnat, always leads to the momentous experience, the crucial turning point of our existence? Oh, so perfect it all is! Such a miracle of exactitude! Doesn't it make you feel blessed, doesn't it make you glow with pride? The victim of a marvelous jungle god! Such a lucky, lovely victim!"

"If you'll pardon me, Herr Krauss . . ."

"Just a moment, please, Miss Eccles. You are too practical, too impatient. Learn to accept. Learn to contemplate. All of life is a symbolism. All these rituals, what are they? I'll tell you their *raison d'être*. To make things bearable."

"Are things unbearable otherwise?"

"Yes, things are unbearable otherwise. The thought of our death is unbearable. The death of our belovèd is unbearable. Withering into senility is unbearable. The vastness of nature is unbearable. And above all, *mein gutes Fraülein,* the inscrutable pointlessness of the world is unbearable, the ridiculousness, the ennui, the unconquerable loneliness. And these savages have devised their rituals over thousands of years to make them bearable."

"Aren't you reading a bit too much, Herr Krauss, into these Negro superstitions?"

"Oh, call them that if you wish," said Herr Krauss somewhat airily. "But do you seriously suggest that men have grown more intelligent over the centuries? Ingenious and organized, no doubt. But intelligent? The evidence is flimsy. I was born in Stuttgart, Miss Eccles. Think of it! That humble Swabian pedantry! Very far from these hysterical orchids and giant insects, *nicht war?* I bought chestnuts on snowy evenings from a poor old hag down by the Schlossgarten. I collected tin soldiers and postage stamps from Baden and Mecklenburg. My sister Elly baked Krapfen, my Aunt Liese played the harp, we went bicycling into the forest, we read Rilke and Hölderlin. And, yes, I became a poet. I lived in a garret and wrote poetry. Real poetry! Inspired, I tell you! Moon-lit ruins, swans, roses!

I lived in a positive miasma of melancholy rhythms." Herr
Krauss folded his arms and lifted his spectacles for a moment.
"Well, here I don't need visions. The rhythms are lightning
and thunder. The metaphors are written in blood, and the
flowers stink of death. We take our choice. I've taken mine.
Life is horrible, but it is unique."

"Am I to conclude, Doktor Krauss, that you have no
intention of helping me?"

"Helping you? My dear Miss Eccles, I am merely the
agent of your destiny!"

"And you conspired to bring me here, did you? You have
toadied to these ignorant savages?"

"*Ach*, Miss Eccles, if we could only be birds and twitter
and dance on twigs! Just enjoying our little life and minding
our own feathery business! But no. We are men. We *think*. We
philosophize. *Jesses Maria*, what a pest! Nothing is pure any
more, nothing is vivid, fresh, our own. We excrete our filthy
theories, we grovel in a mire of dogmas, we sweat slogans out
of our pores. We're haunted, you and me, we're civilized
creatures—we're obsessed. Here we are, trapped in the naked
sun-warmed origins of the world, still clutching at our dreams,
our miserable shreds of memory. Why can't we be free? And
feel purely and clearly? No. We're people. Even these savages
lie encrusted in human dirt."

His Adam's apple throbbed, his voice shook with passion.
His face, hollow and whittled, looked almost like a skull.
Except, of course, for the eyes, which shone with a reptilian
intensity.

Miss Eccles waited a moment. Then she said in a casual
tone, "Tell me one little thing, Herr Krauss. What are these
people planning to do with me?"

Herr Krauss shrugged his shoulders. "That depends on
you, Miss Eccles. We become the roles we have chosen. Surely
you have realized that by now? You have chosen your *Schick-*

sal, without consciously knowing it, perhaps, but deep in your blood you probably did know it. Have you noticed, by chance, how in their beautiful simplicity these dear black creatures make up for their ignorance by an uncanny clairvoyance? They have a sharpness of smell like a beast's, They've smelled what you feel, they've smelled what you are. They feel a need, *verstehen Sie,* to bring order into this chaos of instinct. And thus their lives have been twisted into a series of rituals. You are witnessing one of these rituals. In fact, you've turned into one of their rituals! You should feel flattered, Miss Eccles. It is most unusual for an English lady, a spinster and an eccentric, if you'll pardon me, to turn into a Melanesian goddess!"

Oddly enough, Herr Krauss's visit had a reassuring effect on Miss Eccles. The spectacle of his absurdity distracted her attention from her own malaise. Toward noon Kayakalali brought her a bowl of yams and some cassava bread. The day was warm and dry, the twinge of rheumatism left her. In the middle of the afternoon young Bundule arrived with his kava jug. Miss Eccles smiled tactfully and pushed away the jug. Bundule sat patiently on the floor and waited. Rebuffed, he waited again. He offered it a third time. Miss Eccles took a sip. This time the flavor struck her as unusally pleasant and invigorating. She took a second sip. Bundule departed, gratified.

Toward sunset Bundule returned and sat down beside Miss Eccles. She could feel the velvety warmth of his body touching her own.

"*Ulali,*" he whispered, pointing casually to his phallus, which had suddenly grown erect and was throbbing impatiently.

Miss Eccles nodded. She understood.

"*Oli ulali,*" murmured Bundule.

Miss Eccles smiled sadly, vaguely touched, yet aloof.

"*Buru ulalali,*" repeated the visitor in a more insistent tone.

Miss Eccles shook her head, forlorn, discreet, regretful.

What she felt toward the beautiful savage was certainly not desire, nor fear, nor quite curiosity. It had grown to be something lambent and infinitely gentle, almost maternal.

After Bundule had gone away the smell of his sperm still hung in the air. Miss Eccles felt deeply compassionate. She also felt confused. To distract her troubled mind she began to make imaginary lists. The ten great poets, from Homer to Yeats. The ten great painters, from Giotto to Goya. The ten most beautiful butterflies, from *Troides supremus* to *Papilio ulysses*. What constituted splendor? Could it be dissected, categorized? Or was she merely being nostalgic? Was she clutching at flotsam and jetsam?

Toward sunset Miss Eccles detected signs of excitement in the village. There was a beating of tiny drums, a rattling of wooden rattles. Kayakalali cast furtive glances at her guest from time to time. Miss Eccles looked through the doorway: a heap of logs had been placed in the clearing, and something resembling a scaffold was being erected behind it. Three girls sat under a palm tree, painting their faces with yellow clay. From somewhere came the sharp, sickening squeal of a pig.

Miss Eccles was far from happy, but she felt no fear whatever. She thought about Herr Krauss with a new kind of compassion, a heightened degree of insight, even a wry sort of irony. Then she thought of Bundule and a wave of tenderness swept over her. He too needed pity; he too was hungry for love. And she suddenly discerned, like a school of minnows deep down in a pool, long-hidden strands in her character stirring faintly, beginning to shimmer.

Night fell. The logs were lit. The dance of the flames played on the walls and the shapes of the dancers threw long shadows all around her. A silhouette loomed in the doorway:

Bundule beckoned to Miss Eccles. She rose, dropped her sow hide on the floor, and followed him out. The villagers were sitting in an awestruck circle around the fire.

Bundule led Miss Eccles by the hand into the clearing. Three men in painted bird masks were squatting by the fire. One of the three was tossing the fragments of a pig into a caldron. Another was stirring the caldron, which was filled with mud and banana leaves. The third was busily chewing at some bits of dried ginger and then spat on the chunks of boiling meat to season them. Now Bundule prodded the caldron with a spear and fished out the pig's head. The man who was chewing the ginger decorously sliced off an ear and Bundule, with stately solemnity, presented it to Miss Eccles. She looked nervously at the ginger man. He pointed to his mouth and grinned. Miss Eccles took the ear, wincing slightly, and started to nibble it. A long sigh of wonder and approbation rose from the audience.

Little slices of pig meat were distributed among the villagers. There were low grunts of relish, greasy grins, knowledgeable gestures. A figure emerged from the circle and strode toward the fire. The moth-eaten head of a leopard was perched on top of his head, with the paws dangling loosely and the tail wound around his neck.

There was a beating of drums. Miss Eccles stood motionless. Some sort of ritual, she gathered, was about to begin. In spite of her tall white nakedness and the strangeness of her situation she made an effort to remain stoical, dignified, impassive. Two old women stepped up to the fire with pots of paint and sprays of feathers, and proceeded very nimbly to paint Miss Eccles's body. First the face, with large red circles; then the arms, all in black; then the breast and buttocks with a series of concentric rings, until finally the work was finished and the feathers were bound to her arms.

Now the chieftain pointed skyward and said crisply, "*Bangauali!*" Miss Eccles grasped what he meant. She had turned into a bird. The man was ordering her to fly in order to prove that she was a bird goddess. She had realized long since the pure futility of being reasonable, the utter impossibility of trying to prove that she was human. She raised her arms upward and prayed blindly for some sort of miracle. The drumbeats quickened rapidly. The villagers bleated. There was a clapping of hands and a slapping of sweaty thighs. For one wild moment she actually felt that she was on the brink of levitation: one more instant of fierce credulity, one more flash of magical faith. But no. Nothing happened. Her arms refused to be wings. The chieftain waited grimly with an air of deepening skepticism. Miss Eccles sank to the ground and buried her face in her hands.

7

When she awoke the next day Miss Eccles knew that her life had changed. Even in Kayakalali's eyes she detected an ominous, crucial difference. She had no notion of what had happened after her collapse in front of the fire. They had brought her back to the hut and tied her with ropes; they had smeared her body with pig dung, which had hardened to a stinking plaster.

Kayakalali, with an air of hostility, placed a bowl of water in front of her. Miss Eccles was violently thirsty. She wriggled forward in wormlike motions and lowered her head to lap at the water. Then she leaned back against the wall and meditated grimly on her situation. Kayakalali's manner made it clear that her role had deteriorated from that of a goddess to that of a prisoner. And why? Because she had failed in her flying test?

Or was it deeper than that? Well, at any rate, it was obvious that her position looked ugly. She would have to be very clever, very ingenious to get out of it.

The day passed uneventfully until late afternoon. Miss Eccles slept in fits. She felt chilly and neuralgic, but something or other, maybe the kava, made sleep a little easier. She instinctively avoided all thought of her predicament. She surrendered to her instincts, waiting for a flash of inspiration.

Kayakalali cried sharply: *"Kuame! Ayamanduli!"* Miss Eccles glanced at the doorway. The man with the leopard's head crept into the hut and knelt with folded arms beside Miss Eccles. A crowd of natives was rapidly gathering outside the hut. Miss Eccles could see them staring: the cripples and the lepers, the rachetic ones.

The leopard man began to chant. The stricken ones replied to the chant. *"Lambula bunda,"* moaned the leopard man, and the crowd moaned back, *"Bunda lambula!"*

The chieftain beckoned to Kayakalali, who squatted beside him, holding a rag. He took a knife from his belt and gently seized Miss Eccles's hand. He held it firmly to the floor and nodded silently to Kayakalali. Miss Eccles scarcely had time to scream; she had no strength to resist. With eerie skill and rapidity the man carved through her bones and in less than three seconds he had severed her left forefinger.

She uttered a low, squawking cry, like a gull's. Kayakalali seized the rag and tied it swiftly around her wrist. The leopard man got up, holding the finger in front of him, and stepped with an air of triumph into the ululating crowd.

Half crazy with pain and terror, Miss Eccles watched the chieftain as he moved among the lepers, holding the finger to their wounds as though it were a miraculous ointment: to eyes, to arms, to feet, to suppurating bubos and swollen testicles, and each patient in turn chanted a prayer and crept back to the palm grove.

Miss Eccles, writhing in the darkness, was still capable of a spiritual effort. She stared at the blackened ceiling, stunned with pain but still alert, and looked for an answer to this incomprehensible cruelty. She felt her personality ebbing away from her, leaking out of her, like the blood from her finger. She was no longer Penelope Eccles: she was a fragment of ancient savagery. She had been sucked into the bottomless quagmires of prehistory.

She lost consciousness. When she came to again the night had fallen. She could hear the lepers growling their endless prayers down in the palm grove. A faint glow of moonlight seeped in through the doorway and shone on Kayakalali, who was lying by the oven with her mouth wide open. It shone on the blackened gourds, on the bowl of water and the painted ewer, it gleamed on the dangling slippers and the dress which was pinned to the wall.

She drew herself slowly and laboriously to her knees. Her ankles were bound with rope but she managed, inch by inch, half kneeling and half slithering, to move across the room. She drew herself to her feet with a spasmlike effort and stood panting by the doorway, leaning heavily against the wall. She caught the scent of her dress hanging directly beside her. The hem of the skirt brushed lightly against her cheek. She craned her neck and tore at the dress with her teeth. It fell to the floor, and with it the knife from which it had hung. Now she knelt on the ground, gripped the knife with her teeth, and started to saw at the rope with a kind of trancelike expertise, as though she had for years been practicing to do precisely this.

Once the rope on her wrists was cut it was easy enough to free her ankles. She tossed the rope into the embers and slid her dress over her head. The pain in her hand had vanished. She felt fresh, clear-headed, vigorous. She stood by Kayakalali and regarded her calmly.

At this moment Kayakalali opened her eyes as though some one had called to her. She stared fixedly at Miss Eccles, jaws agape, without seeming to recognize her. Miss Eccles leaned down and thrust the knife into her mouth and jabbed it deeper and deeper into the woman's throat. Kayakalali, still staring, flung her arms out sideways, gurgled hoarsely, and lay motionless as the blood gushed over her cheek.

Miss Eccles slid through the doorway, quick and lithe as a stoat. All was still. The village was sleeping. The lepers in the grove had stopped their chanting. The moon was high and a cool white light hung over the piazza. She darted around the hut into the shoulder-high grasses, and went scampering through the ferns into the blackness of the forest.

The land sloped downward. The trees grew denser. A fragrant coolness rose up from the earth. Her whole body was filled with a sense of supernatural lightness. She was running barefooted, but the ground was soft and yielding. A triumphant zest welled up in her; she felt she could soar like a swallow over the topmost boughs of the forest. And everything that had happened, the filth and the terror and mutilation, all were illumined by a cold white light, without depth, without significance, and everything, the entire past, took on this shadowless intensity, as though flashed on a screen by some powerful artificial light. She wondered vaguely: "What really happened? What did they do to me? Was there a reason?"

The moss grew deep and soggy. She was standing by the edge of a stream. The light of the moon danced in the swirling ripples. A delicious smell of mint rose up from the water. She lay down beside the stream and dipped her hand in the water, which was startlingly cold, as though fresh from the mountains. Bit by bit she peeled the pig dung from her flesh and washed it clean. She lifted her hand and stared at the cavity between her fingers. There was a black bulbous sheen where the forefinger had been, and the flesh around the wound looked queerly ugly and swollen. She reached into the stream and trailed her hand in the icy water. A feeling of peace and seclusion spread through her.

"It's all over," she thought wearily, sniffing the fresh mossy fragrance. "It was all just a silly accident. Just a ludicrous *faux pas*." The moon had gone away but the stars shone through the foliage. She felt lulled and assuaged by the web of leaves and the bright cold water.

The air had turned into a dense milky gray when she woke up again. Her body was stiff with pain; her dress was soaking wet. "Good God, how idiotic. I've been sleeping in a swamp," she thought. "You've gone completely out of your mind, Penelope Eccles!"

She tried to get up but felt curiously limp. No strength or resilience was left in her body. She leaned over the stream and started to drink, but then spat with disgust when she saw that the water was filled with larvae. "Take it easy," she thought, biting her lips with desperation. "Wait for the sun to come out. Just relax. It can't be far."

There was a faint, leafy rustling. The birds were waking up. A breeze passed through the branches: a twig snapped sharply. She turned her head and saw Bundule leaning over her silently, a great snowy smile shining on his black dew-soaked face. He knelt down and picked her up in his arms, very gently.

PART VI

The Rocks

1

There was only one entry in the little "community" notebook. Miss Eccles had written: "Third day. All is well. Have captured quite a splendid little *Delias schönbergi.*"

Billy Baxter took the pencil, ripped a page from the notebook, and settled down thoughtfully in the shade of a banana palm.

DEAR MOTHER,

There has been a shipreck. Everything went up in flames. Poor Sally dropped in the water and must have got drownded. It was terible, everybody screeming. Some people jumped in a lifeboat and they pulled me into the boat and floted all the way to the beach. Mrs. Dommingo is on the beach. She is the richest widdow in the world. That's what Ibrahim said and she shoed me her jewlery. But she gives me the creeps. The Baron is a wierdie. He does funny daily exersizes and is crazy about chess. The Professor is a bookworm. He read me a poem about Sersy. Sersy was an ogress who turned all the sailors into pigs. The Waggonsellers were Americans. They went off in the hills with Senzo. Senzo was a chereful little Jap. He kept gigling at everything. Miss Eckles chased butterflies and we wonder did they eat her. Ibrahim was my friend. He padled to the rock. He was scared of Mrs. Dommingo. She said he was a theif. But I'm sure that he didn't steal that jewle. Somebody played a dirty trick and I bet it was the Baron. I have made a sort of boat. It is smaller than Ibrahim's. I will padle to the rock and live on the rock with Ibrahim. Ibrahim said there will be a ship which will take us to Australia. I wonder what it's like in Australia. Can Ibrahim stay with us in Sydney? It wasn't half bad here until Ibrahim went to the rock. Ibrahim cooked all the fish for us. Once he cooked us a rabbit. Once he cooked a little pig but that was the day he got scared. Ibrahim is darker than Scipio but lighter than Wilmetta. He is stronger than Bob Wheatley and equally bright as Rufus Mayhew. I wish I were older, maybe sixteen or seventeen. I am going to the rock to live there with Ibrahim.

He put down the pencil and gazed at the sea. Then deftly, discreetly, he tore the letter into shreds.

Mrs. Domingo came walking along the shore, all aglitter.

"You've been writing?" she said, pausing to smile at Billy Baxter.

"A letter," said Billy.

"Very sweet," said Mrs. Domingo. She lowered her head slightly. "To whom, may I ask?"

"To my mother," said Billy.

"Good for you," said Mrs. Domingo. "Family loyalty, that's what counts." She glanced suspiciously at the flakes of paper. "Tore it up, did you, child? That was silly, I must say. I trust there was nothing unsuitable in it. Tell me, is your mother a religious woman?"

Billy blushed. "Not so very."

"Well, I'm sure she raised you properly. Mind you, Billy, I am a genuinely broad-minded woman. I have no prejudices, none whatever. Race, religion, and all the rest—I assure you, it matters not a jot or a tittle to me. All the same, I think your feeling about that nigger was a bit unhealthy. I watched you two together. There was nothing sneaky, was there? Please don't fidget. I'm sure there wasn't, but I can't help feeling a responsibility. Ibrahim was terribly oversexed and that's the root of the situation. Anything will do for a boy like that— fish, fowl, or what have you. I'd hate to see you slipping into these morbid modern tendencies. He's gone, who knows where. You look like the last rose of summer. Don't brood. Get plenty of exercise! Have you learned to do the backstroke? Here's your chance to form a lasting bond with nature as the Lord intended it!"

She moved in mellow undulations toward the shawl-draped latrine; Billy rose and sauntered gloomily back to the shade of the marquee.

He stroked the parrot's wing. "What are you thinking

about, Elijah? You've got thoughts, don't you, boy? Tell me something. I'd like to know. Why do women keep poking their noses into other people's business? Why has that lousy wall-eyed bitch got such a hatred for poor old Ibrahim? I'll be damned if I'll ever tell her that he's hiding on that rock. The last rose of summer. What the hell was she driving at? Does she think I'm a goddamn fairy? I should have told her to go screw herself. I'll bet there's something nasty going on with that creep of a Baron. What about it, Elijah? You could tell me a thing or two. You look wise. You've been hearing things. How about it, Elijah?"

Elijah blinked his eyes, ruffled his wings, and screamed, "Elijah!"

"Where were you born, do you know, Elijah? I was born in Baton Rouge. In a big lonely house with morning-glories over the porch. I was born at six A.M. on the first of June. That's pretty good, isn't it? I bet you don't even know how old you are, Elijah! What do you think about it all? Why are we born? What's the point of it? How did you happen to be you, sitting there on top of the hammock? How did I happen to be me? Billy Baxter, from Baton Rouge? Why wasn't I born a fish or a bird or a nigger like Ibrahim? Did you ever go flying in those hills over there? Are there niggers in those hills, like Mrs. Domingo keeps on saying? Did they catch that poor Miss Eccles? Did they chop her to bits? Never mind. Don't bother to tell me. I don't want to hear about it, Elijah. You've got your secrets. I've got mine. We've got sense, don't we, Elijah?"

2

The heat grew wild and piercing. The air was utterly windless. The sea heaved uneasily, as though it had turned into boiling metal. It was impossible to walk barefoot in the sand in the heat of noon. The only spot which was tolerable was down by the cove, in the shade of the grotto.

Mrs. Domingo spread her mat on the brink of the cove. She dipped her hands in the sea and scattered the drops over her forehead. Her dress hung from her body in scaly golden tendrils; she looked like some frantic, forsaken old mermaid.

Professor Shishnik climbed up the rock with his monkey on his shoulder. He paused on the ledge and peered furtively at Mrs. Domingo. She now proceeded, with strange intentness, to splash the water over her thighs and up at her breasts and under her armpits. Her hair hung disheveled, her eyes glistened feverishly. She stared at the water with an anguished concentration.

The Professor watched her with awe. He felt curiously touched. There was something almost majestic in this desperate gesticulating woman. And strangely enough, instead of feeling pity or embarrassment, he felt a tremor in his heart which was close to adoration.

He called softly, "Mrs. Domingo! May I crawl down and join you?"

She turned quickly and straightened her dress. "Please do! We'll have a little chat, my dear."

The Professor climbed down and sat beside her in the shade.

"You look surprised about something, Professor. Has anything happened? Why are you smiling?"

"Nothing has happened, Mrs. Domingo. I feel happy, that is all."

"Very interesting. And what in the world are you happy about, may I ask?"

"That's just it," said the Professor. He glanced at his monkey and grinned sheepishly. "No reason whatsoever. I am full of bliss. Just being alive!"

"Amazing," said Mrs. Domingo. "I thought of you as an

intellectual. And here you are, far away from the centers of
culture and pleased as punch about it. I wish I had your
powers of adaptation, I must say."

"You have adjusted yourself very gracefully to this primitive existence."

"Well, it's sweet of you to say so. There was really no
alternative."

"We all have a little bushman lurking in our souls," said
the Professor.

"Luckily we do. Up to a point. Still, we can't go on
indefinitely. Waiting and waiting. Heaven help us. We can't
wait like this forever!"

"Waiting is better than being destroyed, don't you think,
Mrs. Domingo?"

"Bless you, child. Do I sound ungrateful? When I think of
all those others! I won't dwell on Penelope. A martyr to
science is the way I look at it. And as for those stuck-up
Wagensellers, they've made their bed, let them lie on it. It's
a hothouse situation, with that sexy Japanese boy. I have no
objection to pederasts, but I draw the line at tarts. I feel
miserable about Ibrahim, but what the hell could I do? It's my
digestion that's beginning to worry me, quite frankly, Professor. Let's face it, those coconuts are fearfully gaseous. And
now this murderous heat. Do forgive me for rambling on like
this."

"I find you very stimulating, Mrs. Domingo," murmured
Shishnik.

"Please, Professor. Isn't it time that you dropped this
formality? Call me Lily. I'll call you Boris. May I tell you
something, Boris? Time is short. I'm growing old! I've only got
a few short years still left to me. Here we are, trapped in
limbo, and who knows what's going on? Maybe a war has
broken out! Maybe that Hitler man has done it! For all we
know there's a bomb falling on Paris this very minute. Or

else it's just as usual. It's midnight there, I guess. People are hurrying out of the theater, waving their arms, looking for taxis. I don't possess your spiritual resources, my dear Boris, and there it is. Glittering gowns, champagne popping! I can't help it! It's my world!"

"Please be patient, my dear Lily. It is only a question of days. The ship will surely come. You will soon be back in the bosom of humanity. Piccadilly Circus, Place Vendôme. Do the names hold an enchantment? Personally, Lily, I am far from certain that I wish to go back."

Mrs. Domingo crossed her arms and stared intently at the Professor. "Yes, I thought so. Now I'm sure of it. You don't want to go back. I keep wondering, somehow or other. Is it possible that you're running away from something sinister, Boris? There are times when I almost feel that you've committed some awful crime."

Shishnik smiled. "You are right, Lily. I *have* committed an awful crime."

Mrs. Domingo touched her necklace and lowered her voice. "Murder, Boris?"

"Worse, Lily."

"What's worse than murder?"

"I am guilty of betrayal."

"Ah, you're smiling. You're just teasing me," said Mrs. Domingo with a leer. "But I know better. You've got secrets. Well, be secretive if you wish. I won't pry. But I have inklings. Have you noticed something psychic in me? Those shadows I see at night, those funny far-off voices. I mean it. There is something queer about this goddamn island. Maybe it's the vegetation. It's been changing our characters in the most amazing manner. Take Hugo. There is something very bizarre about Hugo."

"Not surprising," said the Professor.

"I feel worried," said Mrs. Domingo. "There are evil

influences at work here. Don't laugh, please. I am far from
superstitious, but I know we're being watched. There's a
tingling in my spine whenever I know I'm being watched."

"We are always being watched, Lily. By birds, by fish, by
insects. They watch us all day long. Look at Yuri. He is
watching us too. There is no malice in this watchfulness. I find
it rather comforting."

"There you go, teasing me again. Listen, Boris, I warn
you. I don't know what you think of Hugo, but I've noticed
the way he looks at you. There are intricacies in that man.
God knows what he's up to. I'm just warning you."

"We all," said Shishnik gently, "have our bouts of irritability."

Mrs. Domingo shook her head. "You're such a child. So
terribly innocent."

3

Now the trees grew vast and tangled. They were entering
the real rain forest. The electric blue of the lasiandra flowers
shone in the gloom. Once they saw a bright-eyed creature
squatting on a bough high overhead: a tree kangaroo with
amber fur and a pinkish snout.

They followed Tony's compass since the hills were now
invisible. Something vaguely like a path led through the vine-
knitted wilderness. Zenzo pointed to the ground: a human
footprint, unmistakably. Once or twice they heard sly, brittle
crackling nearby. And gradually they began to sense that
invisible eyes were constantly watching them, that noiseless
creatures were stealthily following them on a hidden path
parallel to their own.

"It's a jungle thing," said Tony. "A kind of aural mirage."

"Still, that footprint," ventured Laura. "That was more than a mirage."

"Exactly," said Tony. "The hills are obviously inhabited. But if they saw us they'd come and look at us. They've got nothing to be scared of, do they?"

"Maybe they *think* they have," said Laura.

"We look pretty innocuous," said Tony.

"That's the trouble, I guess," said Laura.

"Hush. Stop chattering," said Tony.

And then the trees grew sparse again. They were standing on the edge of a cliff. Way below the land sloped gently toward a slow-moving river and then rose toward the actual mountains, range after blue-shadowed range of them, with a row of foaming clouds hiding the topmost summits.

"Well," said Tony, peering at the cliff, which seemed to run the length of the valley, "I think we're almost there. Look. People." He pointed. Yes: it was obvious. Some miles eastward, clustering like shells along the river, stood a row of little huts, and from one of the huts smoke was rising.

"Rather steep, isn't it?" said Laura. She stared down at the sun-baked precipice.

"I've seen worse," said Tony placidly as he strolled along the brink.

He beckoned to Zenzo. There was a drop of thirty feet or so, and then a smooth gravelly slope which ended in a barrier of bushes. Zenzo opened his sack and started to untangle the rope and then Tony tied it firmly around the trunk of an umbrella pine. He tugged. The rope held firm. He guided it carefully into the chasm.

"There. I think that'll hold," he muttered. He looked at Zenzo. "Who'll go first?"

"I'll go first, please, Mr. Wagasala," said Zenzo, fondling the rope. He measured the drop and gripped the rope and slid down easily. When he got to the bottom he started to slip in the rolling gravel, but he grabbed at a bush and looked up at them, grinning.

"Ready, Laura? Want me to help you?"

"Oh, I'll manage. Hold it, Zenzo!"

Tony gripped her under the armpits and eased her over the edge. Then she climbed, inch by inch, down to the ground where Zenzo was waiting. Her hands started to bleed but it wasn't serious: merely irritating. Now Tony lifted the rope and tied on a sack and let it down again. The second sack followed. And now Tony himself climbed down. They tugged at the rope, all three of them, but the knot refused to give. So they left the rope dangling and scrambled down to the edge of the forest.

They followed a kind of ledge which hugged the bottom of the cliff. The ledge dipped abruptly and the cliff curved sharply inward. They heard the sound of rushing water. The shadows closed about them. They were standing in a maze of enormous wet ferns. Little rainbows were dancing in the spray of a fan-shaped waterfall. A small oval pool shone at the bottom of the waterfall and here, among the ferns, they dropped their sacks and settled for a rest.

"Well, that's that," said Tony smugly. "Goes to show we'll manage somehow."

"Your marvelous ingenuity. And courage, too," said Laura.

"I just try not to be a gloom bird, that's all," said Tony edgily.

"You're a hero," said Laura, wiping the dust from her arms.

"It's not easy, you know, Laura. Being needled perpetually."

"Oh, Jesus. Must I spend my whole life groveling in front of you?"

"Just don't be a virago. Don't be shrewish, that's all I'm asking."

"Could it be that we need a realist in the family, once in a while?"

"Ah, that female practicality! What a blessing! We would perish without it!"

"The plain fact," said Laura softly, gradually losing control of herself, "is that we've started on an idiotic journey and God knows where it's going to end. And why? I'll tell you why! Just because you've got to prove something! You've got to show the rest of the world that you're a genius, a superman! Oh, what crap! My dear boy, there's nobody in the world that gives a damn. We all know what you're really like. Quarterback at Yale, Skull and Bones, captain of the squash team, Psi Upsilon. Oh, it's all so utterly ridiculous, so parochial, such papier mâché. God Almighty, Anthony Wagenseller, must you be a sophomore all your life? You ought to go back to the locker room. That's where you belong. With those stinking jockstraps."

Tony's jaw trembled slightly. He stared fixedly at the waterfall and said in thin, measured tones: "Yes. I see. That's how it is. All these years you've resented me. You've hated my guts. You've been seething with rage. Penis envy, I think they call it. Well, my girl, let me tell you something. Since you've suffered the horrible misfortune of being my wife, I assure you here and now that you can leave me whenever you want. You're free, you're free for good, you can go straight back to Milwaukee and you're welcome to every little clitoris you can find there."

Laura's face grew strangely pale. Her mouth started to shake. "I always knew you were infantile. I didn't know you were a cheap vulgarian."

Tony caught his breath sharply, then he screamed at her

savagely: "God help me, Laura, you bitch, I've listened enough! I'm sick to death of you!"

A dragonfly shot past them, copper-bright in the sunlight. Through the fern-smelling stillness sounded the laughter of falling water. The three wanderers sat in the shade and stared silently at the waterfall.

And then faintly out of the valley rose the sound of the drums. It was so muted and yet so powerful that it sounded like a distant earthquake. The drumbeats finally died but their echo wandered on, prowling deeper and deeper toward some hidden destination.

They waited. All was still again except for the gurgling, tittering waterfall. "I wonder," said Tony finally, "whether it has some special significance?"

"Something sinister, I'm sure," said Laura. "God knows what goes on in those bushes."

"Maybe it's a kind of ceremony. A circumcision or something," said Tony.

"Well, the sound is anything but cheery, I must say," said Laura dryly.

They got up and bathed their faces and arms in the cooling water. Then they picked up their sacks and headed wearily for the river.

4

"Look!" said Laura, pointing through the saplings. They were standing below the cliff. In the side of the cliff, half hidden by the vines, they saw a cave. The sunlight fell on the blunt, brutish figure that guarded the entrance. It was carved out of limestone, half reptile, half human, with a moss-spotted membrum that trailed on the ground like a giant root.

"Looks like a temple," said Tony. He stepped through the vines and peered at the idol. He laid his palm on the snout and stared quizzically at a bulging eye.

"No touch!" cried Zenzo, agitated.

"Dangerous?" said Tony, grinning bleakly.

"Devil of Love!" whispered Zenzo.

"How do you know?" said Tony skeptically.

"We have devil in Hokkaido. Live in wood all alone. Have sex like big elephant and face like bad toad. When ladies in Hokkaido very empty and sad they come and pray to Devil to have baby and be happy!"

"Nasty, isn't he?" said Tony. "How could anyone pray to this horrible monster?"

"That's just it," said Laura quietly. "People pray to him because he's horrible."

They built their evening fire in front of the cave and spread their blankets. This time there was little for dinner: some wizened bananas that Zenzo had picked by the waterfall, followed by the tin of candied marrons and a last sip of brandy. But Zenzo was right. Something amiable was hovering in the air. A bestial bonhomie oozed out of the toad-faced devil.

"Not so bad," remarked Tony. "That's five days we've been en route. No disasters so far. No wild beasts. No poisonous serpents."

"Yes," said Laura. "Highly creditable."

"Very O.K.," said Zenzo, nodding.

"We'll be hitting that river tomorrow. Tomorrow night we'll reach the coast. I feel it in my bones. We're almost there," said Tony cheerfully.

"Still, we mustn't be careless. Those drums, you know," said Laura.

"I think," said Tony pontifically, "that we can cope with the drums, Mrs. Wagenseller."

They sat silently and watched the glow fading away from the embers and the ember-lit monster slipping back into the darkness. Laura folded her bony arms and leaned back against the tree trunk. Her face in the fading firelight looked queerly shriveled and wrinkled, as though she were ready to burst into tears. It suddenly struck Tony that she was a woman he had never seen before, an absolute stranger, prim, parched, and a bit pathetic.

Zenzo turned his head slowly and caught Tony's eye. A big teasing smile spread over his face. His lips moved conspiratorially, as though he were whispering something to Tony. His eyes shone brilliantly red, like a pair of enormous rubies.

Suddenly Laura said, "Listen!" There was a scrounging, groveling noise.

"One of those pigs, I guess," said Tony. They could hear it nuzzling in the leaves and then, suddenly alarmed, lunging off through the underbrush.

"Come," said Tony, lifting his gun. He tapped Zenzo on the shoulder. They stepped through the bushes toward the pond at the foot of the cliff. Through the stench of stale mud they caught a whiff of animal droppings. They crouched by the water and peered through the reeds. There was a sucking of hoofs in the quagmire, followed by an irritable snort. An ugly black shape suddenly sprang across the reeds. Tony could see it clear and brusque against the gleam of the water. He fired. The shot echoed. There was a spluttering and a splashing and the beast shot through the reeds and rocketed off into the jungle.

"Son of a bitch," growled Tony viciously. "Missed the dirty old bastard."

He jumped to his feet and raced past the pond, sinking into the mud up to his ankles and snatching frantically at the cattails. The jungle grew thicker. He paused and listened. Not a sound. He glanced around grimly. The bushes looked impenetrable. He dug his way back, looking for the way he had come. The swamp sucked at his heels; it stank like a corpse. Something struck him across the knee, thick and blunt, like a baseball bat. He snarled with the pain and grabbed wildly at a fallen trunk. He took a deep breath; his eyes were blurred with tears. He knelt on the ground, groped for a dry patch to sit on, then stretched out his leg into the black, gurgling mud. He sat silent for several minutes, trying to nurse his bleeding knee. He heard a sound in the distance like a high, feline squeal. He listened intently. Then he howled, "For Christ's sake, Zenzo! Where are you?"

No answer. The sound of his voice came echoing back, wet and garbled, and all of a sudden he grew horribly frightened. His throat gulped uncontrollably and his hands started shaking. He crouched lower, sniffing at the reeds, running his fingers through the mud, and shrieked wildly, "Zenzo! Zenzo! God Almighty, where are you, Zenzo?"

Several minutes passed by, maybe five, maybe twenty. A night bird came fluttering, dipping low in search of a moth. He moaned softly, "Oh Jesus. What a fool. What a goddamn idiot. . . ."

Something stirred in the reeds behind him. A voice said softly, "Mr. Wagasala!"

"Oh Jesus. Dear Jesus," muttered Tony. "Help me, Zenzo."

Zenzo knelt in the mud beside him. "You hurt bad, Mr. Wagasala?"

"Nothing serious," said Tony quietly. Then he whispered, "Just a bruise, I guess."

Zenzo peered at the bleeding knee and touched it very gently. His teeth shone in the darkness as he looked up at Tony. "You O.K.," he said soothingly, running his thumb along the calf. "Mr. Wagasala! We very unlucky! That pig make lovely roast!"

Tony reached out his hand and touched Zenzo on the cheek. Then he drew his head nearer and kissed him on the lips.

Zenzo looked at him mockingly and said, "You feel good now, Mr. Wagasala?" And he burst into a fit of shrill, triumphant laughter.

5

The light seeped through the leaves as Tony walked toward the pond with his gun. He heard Laura setting the pot on the burning logs, preparing the tea. He caught sight of last night's footprints, his and Zenzo's, in a patch of mud, and he followed the edge of the pond toward a clearing beyond the trees. He saw Zenzo standing on a rock in the dry, dead sunlight, staring into the distance.

"Do you see anything, Zenzo?"

Zenzo pointed into the valley silently.

Tony climbed to the top of the rock and stood close beside Zenzo. He caught the smell of Zenzo's body, warm and familiar, like cider. He placed his hand on Zenzo's shiny black head in a surge of tenderness and Zenzo looked up at him with a sly, coquettish smile.

Far below, in the heart of the thicket, a ribbon of wind crept through the foliage. Then Tony saw that it wasn't the wind, it was a movement under the trees, serpentine, purposeful, like the shade of a prowling beast. A disk of metal flashed in the light; there was a sheen of wet, dark bodies.

Zenzo nodded his head solemnly. "They coming, Tonee," he whispered.

In the instant before replying Tony heard a sharp little whistle: something long and swift and black slid through the brightness close beside him. He looked at Zenzo quickly, and the boy looked back at him with amazement. The look changed as he stood there into another, stranger expression: probing, desperate, profound, tender and terrifyingly intimate. Without a word he sank to the ground and clutched at the withered grass, while the spear swayed in his side and the blood started pouring.

6

Mrs. Domingo sat motionless in the shade of the marquee. Or almost motionless: her forefinger moved slowly across the sand. Her eyes were fixed on the dusky vignette at the end of the promontory: one single palm, symmetrical as a fountain, poised on the edge of the sea; and over the palm the ledge of rocks, now turning red in the evening light; and on the ledge the naked Baron, sitting quietly with his fishing pole.

Mrs. Domingo had likewise abandoned herself to nudity. All that was left of her costume was a tiny apron tied to her waist. And her jewelry, of course, which she now wore in its entirety: brooches dangling from a dozen necklaces, earrings hitched to innumerable bracelets. Her breasts, brown and leathery, hung low like a squaw's. Her multicolored hair covered her shoulders like a shawl.

Professor Shishnik came up with his arms full of flowers, which he lovingly deposited at the feet of Mrs. Domingo. He too was nearly naked: he looked like a shaggy, disreputable Buddha. His scarlet kimono was reduced to a flimsy little *cache-sexe*.

"Beautiful, are they not?" he said. "I have never seen this

color of orchid. It reminds me of the camellias I used to see up in Sintra."

"Sintra! You conjure up such beautiful memories, dear Boris!"

The Professor cocked his head and regarded her thoughtfully. "You look splendid today, my Lily. I have never seen you look so regal."

"I am the empress of this isle, that is certain," said Mrs. Domingo. "Think up a name for me, Boris. Some mysterious tribal name, please."

"Shall we call you Queen Matagawalake? Matagawalake is a Polynesian word. To the people out in the ocean it means 'knowledge of all things.' I bow to you, Lily. You have the wisdom of the sea in you."

"Wouldn't it be lovely, Boris, dear, if we could build a brave new world out here? If I only had the time, and several hundred slaves, I'd sit down and start planning a spectacular new paradise. Just think! Pavilions and palaces built of iridescent corals, the husks of dried coconuts, the spikes of sea urchins! Oh, Boris, could I stand it? Even with my wisdom, could I stand it? This silence! It's too much. Noise, noise— that's what I want. Bands playing, cheers from the grandstand, horns tooting, sirens screaming—that's Lily Domingo for you! She needs clamor, she needs frenzy. Because she's scared, that's the reason. She doesn't even know what scares her. There's one little thing I'll tell you, though. The thought of it haunts me. I've seen Hugo running his thumb along the edge of his knife. I know what it means. Don't laugh at me, please. He's planning to kill me, Boris. You're not going to allow it, are you? I'm serious. I know Hugo. I've insulted him mortally." She stretched out her arms and rattled her bracelets. Her eyes glistened strangely. "Oh, Boris, my poor Boris, with your funny little monkey. All things will be forgiven us. And even miserable, pompous Hugo. All that was wrong with him *au fond* was this asinine hankering after power. And me? Poor little Lily? She wanted romance, pure and simple. I keep thinking about the past. Just a glittering mosaic, that's all it is, patched together out of thousands of random memories. I was lovely once, Boris. I gave wonderful parties. My parties were famous all up and down the coast. I invited the *crème de la crème*. But it's odd, I can't remember a single one of them. The older I grow the deeper my mind prowls into the past. My first love was an evil little boy named Charlie Prentice. Oh, Charlie! What a devil! What a beast! What an Apollo! We went boating in June, the weeping willows tickled my shoulder, the dragonflies went zooming, Charlie was sweating at the oars. Oh, I see it all so clearly, every microscopical particle. We nuzzled our way through the cattails and all of a sudden there we were. We lay down in the bottom of the boat. I still can smell the tar and the bullrushes!" She thrust her head forward. Her voice started to shake. "Tell me, Boris. Why is the world such a heart-rending place? I look back on it all and realize that no one has ever loved me. Why has nobody in the world ever bothered to fall in love with me? Now it's over. It's too late. I've broken free. I've cast off the chains. I can laugh. See! I'm laughing! Ha-ha! It's good-by to Lily Domingo! From now on it's Queen Magacky, or whatever the hell her name is. Give me that bone there. It's my scepter. I shall make you a duke. The Duke of Oblivion! How's that? Does it sound impressive enough? No more memories of Charlie Prentice! No more dreams of Monte Carlo! All is cast to the winds, parched, puckered, and shriveled. I am filled with a strange new power. Queen Whatsis, Sorceress of Borneo, Whore of the Sea, Mother of Cannibals! My body is decomposing and I'm hideous as Hades, but my heart is suddenly bursting into hundreds of little blossoms! Bow your head, Duke, darling. I am on the brink of my biggest triumph—just one more tiny effort, one more miserable slope to climb. The Garden of Eden—look, darling, it's just around the corner. You think I've gone crazy? You're right. I'm as mad as a loon. Once I was exquisite. I smelled of roses. Now I am ugly and sick and stinking. But I feel myself moving toward the Regions of Brightness. I'm floating among the clouds, something is shining in the distance. There's a glow falling on everything, only a faint little sheen, but it's there! Look—it's there! I feel tranquil, Boris, tranquil. King of the Sun, or whatever you are! Bringer of Vision, Angel of Light! Forgive me my follies! Forgive me the treachery in Como! Forgive me that lie in Grindelwald and that scene in the Alhambra! I feel cleansed. I feel purified. Look at me, Boris. Am I beautiful?"

The Professor pressed his lips to her arm. "You are lovely, Lily. Lovely."

7

Beyond the hills in the west it seemed that the jungle was on fire, but a cold, leaden light covered the water in the east. It grew dimmer as Billy watched it. Two minutes passed. Two stars were shining. He stroked the parrot on the back of the head and whispered, "Bye-bye, Elijah! Be good! Maybe I'll be seeing you again one of these days!" He got up and strolled casually across the dunes and then around in a semicircle toward the grove of bamboos. Suddenly he ducked behind a bush, then went racing along the inlet. He slipped off his pants and headed for the root-encircled swamp. He glanced back. The fire was dying. He could see the Baron's silhouette as he picked up the chessboard and carried it into the hut. He jumped into the water and started tugging at the log. It was nothing like Ibrahim's, of course; hardly a canoe; not even a boat. Merely an arrow-shaped fragment of a dead eucalyptus which he dragged to the shore that morning while the rest were still asleep.

It went nuzzling into the slime, tipping sideways when he mounted it. Then it started to seesaw when it struck a hidden root. Finally he managed to guide it into the smooth open water, which now was almost black, with a wisp of gray on the horizon.

"An hour, maybe," he thought. The skiff was clumsy and hard to steer. It went zigzagging around the hillock and headed uneasily for the rock. The beach came into view. The dunes looked pale and empty. Then night fell abruptly and in less than a minute all grew dark and even Ibrahim's rock was scarcely visible in the distance. The paddle was only a stalk of bamboo which was flattened at the end. It was miserably inefficient, but little by little he caught the knack of it. The vessel slid seaward with gathering speed until it seemed to be gliding along on its own power. The sea grew immense. The line of the beach grew faint as a cobweb. The rock was only a fleck of deeper darkness in the sea. The smell of the ocean came welling out of the depths. It enveloped him with a loving yet menacing intimacy. He saw streaks of phosphorescence dancing in the thin, uncertain wake, and then he noticed hundreds of glistening pinpoints under the water: these were luminous animalcules, little light-bearing insects that wove patterns in the water like a swarm of fireflies.

And now he felt a chill of alarm spread through his body. He felt awed, thrilled, mystified by the black complexity of the ocean, which suddenly was so terribly close to him, so throbbing and multitudinous. He was engulfed in a strange new loneliness. He was no longer Billy Baxter. He had turned into a little water sprite, a lonely wisp of wonder floating silently and invisibly on the million-marveled sea.

The rock looked very near now. The moon oozed out of

the sea. He could see the roll of the breakers gleaming on the coral reef to the right of him. "Five more minutes," he thought. He dug briskly with his paddle. And then abruptly a hidden force struck the skiff with a crazy violence, flung the prow into the air, and shuttled Billy into the water. He sank, then shot up again and swam quickly toward the skiff, which lay ten feet away, upside down, rocking gently. Then he felt it: the thrust of a terrible vitality close beside him, a huge uncanny shudder that went spiraling through the water. He felt rather than saw the giant shadow swooping under him, then circling into the distance with lightning rapidity. There was only the slightest quiver on the surface of the sea but he felt the shafts of coolness shoot out of the deep, the splinters of bestial energy that pierced through the torpor. He clung to the bobbing log, struggling clumsily to set it right again. Then he saw the water swelling into a long, vicious sleekness as the beast arrowed back again, heading straight for the skiff. Billy clutched at the log and struck out with both legs. He could feel the sea throbbing with a kind of wild demonic playfulness as the killer swerved off and swung once more in a great parabola. A blunt, bull-like head broke the water for an instant; two tiny eyes caught the light of the moon. It dipped; then it struck. He screamed, "Ibrahim!" Ibrahim!" All he felt was an ice-cold tug, sleek as steel, swift as an illusion, and the warm massive stillness rolled back over the sea again.

8

Ibrahim dove into the water with the knife between his teeth. He prowled among the crannies, loosening the purple-spiked sea urchins, and he trapped a large crab which he pierced with the tip of his blade. He tossed them on the rock and scrambled up past the boulders. He dropped the crab in the shade and squatted in the sun to split the sea urchins. He scraped out the rich glossy flesh, the color of indigo, and licked at it gingerly. But the flavor of it sickened him.

He was fearfully thirsty. He climbed to the top of the cliff, where a disk of greenish rain water lay cupped in a hollow. He stooped down to drink. The water was warm and bitter, with a queer mucilaginous flavor, like urine. Then he saw that it was seething with tiny white worms. He spat with disgust and scratched at his armpits dejectedly. But the taste of the water made his thirst still more violent. He leaned down, closed his eyes, and lapped furiously at the evil water.

He lay in the shade a while. He felt listless, enfeebled. As he glanced across the rock he had a curious sensation. The place had expanded mysteriously. It was no longer a barren rock. It had swollen into an enormous, many-valleyed continent. The cracks in the stone looked like the beds of dried-up torrents. The pebble-ringed nooks looked like great lunar craters. The sense of proportion had turned suddenly upside down. The ocean beside him looked like a quiet little pool, and the mountains in the distance looked like knolls in a sunlit meadow. The days he had spent on the rock turned into hot, uncountable years and the rest of the world, Africa, Asia, was no bigger than a snapshot.

An undulating pain was beginning to spread through his limbs. First his forehead started to ache; then his bones; then his belly. A feverish heat licked at his testicles, like the fire of an insect bite. He dove into the water to cool the intolerable spread of the itching. He swam violently around the rock; gradually the itching subsided. He crawled out again and slumped on the sand and fell asleep.

He slept for several hours. He was dreaming of Africa: he dreamed of the snow-capped Atlas and the slopes that flowed into the desert. He was wandering across the sand and came to a small deserted mosque. He was struck with amazement at the splendor of the mosque. Great jewels lay embedded in the dirty white stucco—carnelians as big as melons, huge slabs of lapis lazuli. He reached out and tried to pluck a sapphire from the wall. It crumbled under his touch and dissolved in gray dust. Dark clouds welled out of the horizon; there was a rumbling of far-off thunder. A figure dressed in white was running frantically across the desert and then vanished abruptly as the rain started to pour. He stepped into the mosque. It was littered with pebbles; the columns were veiled with spider webs; bats went loping under the arches.

Then suddenly out of the shadows he heard a voice crying "Ibrahim!"

He woke up. The light of the moon covered the rock like a sheet of ice. Something stirred in the nearby waters: a log was bobbing in the sea swell.

A voice screamed out of the darkness: "Ibrahim! Oh, Ibrahim!"

He leapt over the boulders and stood for an instant on the edge of the jetty. Then he howled, "I'm coming, Billy!" and hurled himself into the sea.

9

The night had grown cooler in the grayish limbo before dawn. Ibrahim knelt over the boy and kept massaging his shivering body. After a while Billy's moans subsided into a long steady sobbing and Ibrahim said softly, "Try to be brave, Billy boy!"

He took off his turban, folded it neatly into a cushion, and tucked it under Billy's damp head with elaborate solicitude. Then he ran his palm tenderly over the boy's sweating brow.

He whispered: "Don't be scared, Billy. Just try and be

brave now. That ship will be coming. That ship will carry you home."

Billy stared through his tears and whimpered, "Don't leave me, please, Ibrahim!"

Ibrahim leaned over Billy and looked at him imploringly. "Do you know what we're going to do, Billy? Just listen. I'll tell you. We're going to start a fine little farm in Australia. We're going to raise thousands of beautiful white sheep. And we're going to sell those sheep for thousands and thousands of dollars. And then you know what? We're going to sail to Morocco. You've never been in Morocco? Oh, just wait till you see it, Billy! Up in the mountains the shiny snow, down in the valleys the big red flowers. And the camels! The horses! The music! The dancing! Oh, Billy, there's no horses like the horses of Africa. There's no music like that sad, lonely music of Africa. I'll buy you a lovely little cottage, that's what I'll do. Down by Outak-el-Had, which lies in the shade between the mountains. I'll show you the big sacred mosque in Bou-Denib, and the dancers in Oudja, and the foals in Aïn-Sefra. Black as coal, blacker than night, those little foals in Aïn-Sefra. There's a pool by the gateway where the donkeys come to drink. The girls walk in the morning with their jugs on their heads. And the songs, Billy, the songs! They sing them in the morning and the evening. Nothing in the whole world is sadder than those evening songs in Aïn-Sefra. . . ."

His voice grew high as a girl's as he sang into the night. He sang an old song that his sister Fatima used to sing to him.

> Three little stars shone over the mountain,
> Three little camels stood by the wall,
> Three little bells rang out of the darkness,
> When we came to Oued-Zem. . . .

He kept singing until the moon finally dipped behind the rock. Then he breathed a great sigh and looked at the boy with desolate eyes. An ugly green flush had crept over his body. The shreds that hung from his thigh had finally stopped bleeding, but a plum-colored sheen was beginning to spread over the abdomen. He lay without moving and kept staring at Ibrahim, and the terror in his eyes faded into a lusterless passivity.

10

The birds wheeled over the rock, slower and slower, lower and lower. Their shadows passed over the sea and darkened the brilliance of the corals. The first arrived at noon. It came soaring out of nowhere. Ibrahim could hear the sound of its wings, brittle and dry, like rustling branches. He looked up and saw the feverish, patient glint in its eyes. Out of the great empty blue the second bird then descended. It went circling like the first, but more intently, more aggressively. It slid down over the sea, almost scraping the water, then swooped quickly away again with a gross, heaving cowardice. It grazed the top of the rock, nearly landing but not quite daring. Toward noon came the third. It swung down over Ibrahim, so low that he could see the greenish freckles on its claws. He hurled a big stone at the horrible fowl. It swerved away indifferently and went on circling. When they dipped he caught the stink of their fetid bodies.

The heat grew tense, viscous. He crouched in the shade and stared at the sea. There was no wind and even the sea, which had seethed with vitality, now lay leaden and expressionless, as though it too were beginning to rot. His tongue seemed to swell until it filled his whole mouth. His stomach was gripped with a spasm of nausea. He vomited into the sea. The birds swooped inquisitively. He lay back in the shade, which was nearly as hot as the jellied sunlight, and fixed his eyes intently on the palm of his hand, as though looking for a key which would guide him through the chaos.

The wings of the vultures drew their shadows over the pebbles. He looked up and saw that one of them had settled on the summit. It folded its wings as though they were a pair of umbrellas and stared at him with a probing, surgeonlike scrutiny. The second sank down. It craned its pimpled neck and for a moment spread out its majestical wings. And then the third clutched at the stone with a clumsy incertitude, regained its balance, opened its beak, thrust out it head, and leered at Ibrahim.

A fit of fury shook Ibrahim. He screamed, "Away! Away, goddamn you!" He picked up his pole and hurled it savagely at the glaring gargoyles. They went flopping into the sky with a kind of grisly disdainfulness, wheeled about for a minute or two, then gradually settled on the rock again.

He caught the odor of the corpse, which trickled faintly across the heat. He turned and looked at the body with an agonized finality: the torso veined with salt, the black stumpy leg, and the thin, boyish face, now stiff and hollow but to Ibrahim still lovable. His grief shot to the surface, reviving his sanity for an instant; great sobs shook his body and he flung his arms around the corpse. He wailed, "Oh, my Billy! My beautiful Billy!"

The birds sat in a row, dusky, impenetrable, like antique mourners.

A great weariness swept over Ibrahim. The water lapped with a dull incessance. He lay back and folded his elbow over his eyes and fell asleep.

A light, feathery touch against his back woke him up. It was dusk. The light was wilting over the sleek oily water. He turned sharply. The vultures were crouching on the stone close beside him. They lifted their heads and glared at him balefully. Then they lowered their beaks and went on hacking.

He sprang to his feet and screamed with a blind, crazy rage. But the birds refused to budge. They stared back at him threateningly. They spread their enormous wings and flicked their tongues like great reptiles.

He leapt over the stones and climbed to the top of the cliff. Night fell as he stood there. The distant beach sank into darkness. Something suddenly started to tug at his mind with a desperate urgency. There was something that had to be done. But what? What could it be? He stared at the hills. But the hills gave no clue. He looked up at the stars. They were brilliant as diamonds. Then he knew. His whole body started to tremble with expectancy.

He stood at the edge of the cliff and shook his fist at the stars. Then he raced down to the jetty, pulled the boat into the sea, and started to paddle toward the furry peninsula.

PART VII

The Flames

1

They kept moving through the underbrush, trying to keep to the shadows. Finally they reached the end of the woods and entered a flat dead prairie. They moved in a cautious semicircle, veering away from the yellowish river, and now the smoke rose behind them and once again they entered the pine woods. Tony dropped his sack on the ground. The other sack had been left behind. Laura leaned against a trunk and wiped the sweat from her eyelids.

"We shouldn't have left him like that."

"Poor little fellow. What could we do?"

"We couldn't do anything. But we shouldn't have left him just lying there, I'm telling you."

They drank from the water jug; the water smelled of slime but Tony's thirst was so violent that he could hardly control himself. He passed the jug to Laura and muttered, "Just try not to think about it. Keep plodding. Keep hoping. We've got to reach that goddamn coast."

They walked on, following the river, maybe a mile to the south of the river, and once again it seemed that it was an old, untrodden path they were instinctively following. Once they passed some charred remnants of what might have been a group of huts, and once they saw two posts painted with strange, half-faded markings.

Now the land descended gradually, the heat spread its tentacles. Through the trees they caught a glimpse of the enormous valley widening below them and the pinnacles beyond, which now rose at a different angle. There was a salty whiff in the air, a faint suggestion of the sea, but the sea, if it was the sea, remained elusive, invisible. Two small coconut palms stood on a kind of sandy promontory, and they drank the tepid milk and gnawed at the white grainy flesh. Tony glanced at Laura silently. He was shocked by her appearance: terribly haggard, queerly old, with bloodshot eyes and sunken cheeks and something odd in her posture, as though she were slightly hunchbacked. Her dress was stained and tattered. Streaks of blood crisscrossed her calves. Her hair hung in loose, witchlike strands over her shoulders. He picked up the sack and they started downhill again, toward what looked like a large treeless meadow below them.

It was late afternoon now. When they finally reached the meadow they saw that it wasn't a meadow, it was a soft, weedy marshland which deteriorated into a swamp covered with smooth, oval lily pads.

"Well?" said Laura. Her jaw shook as she looked at Tony with ghostly eyes.

"We'll manage," said Tony, glancing at a mound in the distance. "Two hundred yards. Can't be more. That's terra firma on the other side there."

There was no alternative, at any rate. There was nothing but the hills they had crossed behind them, the tangle of mangroves on the left, and the towering cliffs on the right. Beyond the swamp rose the palm-studded shore of the river. Tony rolled his pants to his knees and took Laura by the hand. They started wading very cautiously into the edge of the swamp. It was filled with shiny plants which looked like jack-in-the-pulpits. The water rose to their knees, the air grew blue with mosquitoes, and patches of pointed reeds rose here and there, like upraised daggers. Suddenly Laura lost her balance and clutched wildly at Tony. She sank in the mire up to her neck, spitting and vomiting.

"I can't," she groaned. "I can't. Oh, Christ Almighty, Tony. I can't."

Tony dropped his sack in the mud and gripped her under

the arms. She was sobbing hysterically. Balls of slime clung to her body. He crouched and lifted her awkwardly on to his shoulders, legs astride. Then he plodded on again, dragging the wet gray sack behind him, grinding his teeth with exhaustion, feverish with hundreds of insect bites.

And then he struck a buried log, lunged sideward clumsily, and sank in the mud. The slime swept over his face, filling his mouth and blinding his eyes. He clutched wildly at Laura, who was floundering beside him, and with a half-crazy effort forced himself to his knees, thrust her legs back over his shoulders and went staggering on again.

And then suddenly, in his desperation, he saw something amazing. A flock of herons rose from the clustering patch of reeds directly in front of him: blue and white, hundreds of birds, all rising simultaneously, catching the last blaze of sunlight on their low-flying wings and filling the air with their multitudinous flapping.

For some mysterious reason the sight of the herons gave him strength. He halted and wiped the filth from his face and lumbered on again. Laura's arms were clamped so tightly around his neck that she almost choked him. Her legs dangled limply, her head was bobbing helplessly, and he started to feel that he was carrying a cadaver. And something curious now happened to him: as he was struggling on brainlessly with the last infinitesimal fragments of his strength, another kind of strength rose up from some emotional reservoir. A rush of passionate tenderness, stronger than anything he had known, welled up in him; he was galvanized with love for the bony burden he was carrying. The water rose to his waist; it covered his chest; it rose to his shoulders. He moved forward inch by inch, groping cautiously with his feet. Dusk fell. The birds had gone. And then, too numb to feel relief, he felt the ground slowly rising and the mud turn into sand. The swamp came to an end in a hedge of clattering cattails. Laura slid from his shoulders and they lay motionless on the sand. The stars peeped through the darkness. They said nothing, and fell asleep.

2

Ibrahim slid from the edge of his boat and started to wade into the shallows. The water was startlingly warm; much warmer than out by the rock. He stepped on the shore and glanced about uneasily. The place looked unfamiliar. It had changed in some eerie fashion. The sand looked paler than before, the palms looked taller and darker. The light of the moon covered the beach like a mask, disguising its contours, hiding its natural expression. He climbed up the dune and moved cautiously toward the palms. Now he saw the sheen of the inlet on the other side of the palms. It lay still, smooth as glass. Not a leaf was stirring. Even the wispy little bamboos higher up were absolutely motionless. The sand felt pleasantly warm, soft as wool under his heels. He crept closer. Now he was standing fifty yards from the hut. He could see the grass hammock which was slung between two palms. Someone was lying in the hammock. A rancid odor hung in the air. It suddenly struck him with horror that the shape in the hammock was a corpse. Then it stirred, groaning slightly. Ibrahim ducked behind a trunk. It was only the Professor, he realized. He could hear him snoring rhythmically.

A pale, groping figure stepped out of the hut. Sweat burst from Ibrahim's temples. He was shivering with excitement. The silhouettte moved toward the hammock, paused for a moment, leaned over the sleeper, and then went sauntering quietly through the coconut palms. The jewels shook in the moonlight. He could hear the jingling of bracelets. She headed for the dunes, passing within ten yards of Ibrahim. She glanced around casually, and then moved toward the edge of the sea.

Ibrahim darted through the trees and headed for a nook between the dunes. He could see with strange exactitude every line of the woman's body—the trembling of her buttocks, the swaying hair, the dangling amulets. She stopped by the water and lifted her arms over her head. Again she looked back, this time swiftly, as though listening. Then she knelt in the sand and started to sprinkle her thighs with water.

Ibrahim tightened his fist. He glanced down and looked for the knife. Then he realized that it still lay gripped between his teeth. An electrical rush of delight swept through his body. He felt freed as though by a miracle from some strangulating nightmare. All the nausea and frenzy fled from his soul like a cloud of bats. He wanted to sing in a surge of triumph: he felt a world-embracing tenderness. He closed his eyes for an instant and whispered, "No God there is but Allah!" Then he climbed over the dune and wandered slowly toward Mrs. Domingo.

He paused for a moment some twenty feet behind her. Her head was lowered intently; she was dabbling in the sea like a sorceress. She kept muttering, "Day of Glory! I'm the Empress of the Ocean! All is forgiven! . . ."

Ibrahim leapt through the darkness like an arrow shot from a bow. Mrs. Domingo turned abruptly and stared at the night with bloodshot eyes. Her mouth fell wide open in a half-throttled scream; she clawed at the empty air as the knife went ripping into her belly. Then she slumped and fell forward in the ankle-deep sea while her hair spread over the water like a great black chrysanthemum.

Ibrahim crouched by the corpse and started to tear at the

rings and necklaces. One by one he ripped off the bracelets and slipped them over his arms. His fingers were clicking with emeralds, the diamonds flashed on his neck. He tore off the tiara and hurled it fiercely into the sea. Then he got up, lifted his arms in a fit of exulation, and started to dance along the edge of the beach. He paused now and again and stared at the glitter on his flesh. He rippled his arms blissfully and shook his hips like a belly dancer.

He stopped by the rocks and looked back somewhat wistfully. Then he stepped into the sea, rather gingerly at first, then more and more eagerly. He dove into the blackness and lay splashing ecstatically, watching the foam leap through the air in great silver bubbles.

Slowly he floated into the warm, stealthy vastness of the South Pacific. He turned over on his back and smiled at the stars which smiled back at him, and dropped their tiny gleam on the clusters of diamonds and emeralds. On he floated. Time passed. But time no longer meant anything. He knew that he was floating into the loving arms of eternity.

3

The sun was just rising when Professor Shishnik opened his eyes. A heavy mist rose up from the inlet; the air was humid, acidulous. He crawled ponderously out of the hammock and peered into the hut.

"Lily?" he murmured.

No answer. The hut was deserted. A twinge of uneasiness gripped at his chest. He looked hurriedly through the palms, then followed the zigzag of footprints toward the dunes. Mrs Domingo was lying in the distance on the shiny wet sand. He squealed, "Lily!" Still no answer. He went scuttling over the dunes, panting heavily, sick at heart, and sank with a moan beside the body.

After the first appalling glance he avoided looking at Mrs. Domingo. He sat absolutely motionless, staring fixedly at the sea. Once he touched her arm lightly but instantly recoiled into immobility. He thought nothing, or nothing definable; he was lost in a cloud of memories. It was as though, since the corpse now was drained of human meaning, he were hurrying into the past in his desperate search for Mrs. Domingo. Whatever had happened—and oddly enough, he hardly cared how it had happened—all that was left of the event was a gesture of fate, impersonal, meaningless.

He stared at the sea so intently that his eyes started to ache. The horizon grew blurred. The present melted into the past. The Professor's mind, so gentle and tentative, could not cope with ferocity. He noticed a small dark object floating in the distance beyond the rocks. His heart froze with hope. Was it a boat moving toward them? Then he realized that it was only a fragment of dust caught on his eyeball. There was no boat. There was nothing; only a big, brightening emptiness. He picked up a shell and peered at it with curiosity. It was a fat, fleshy pink dappled with black hieroglyphics. He was struck with the exquisite precision, the occult symmetry of the little shell. It seemed to triumph in its delicacy over that flat and killing emptiness.

The air grew suddenly hot. Professor Shishnik scrambled to his feet. He went plodding over the dunes back to the coconut palms. He paused beside the hammock and wiped the sweat from his cheeks. Then he strolled toward the inlet and started to look for the Baron.

4

They carried the corpse into the shade of the hut and placed it on the octagonal mat in the middle. They sat down on each side as though by silent agreement, the Professor on the left and the Baron on the right. Neither of them looked at the body, with its mouth wide open in a noiseless scream and its stiff, bloody fingers still clawing at the air. Nor did they look at each other. They sat quietly in the semidarkness, glancing vaguely at the ceiling and swatting listlessly at the flies.

Finally the Baron cleared his throat. "Well, Professor. What do you think?"

The Professor looked startled. "Think? Yes? Is there something to think about?"

The Baron said softly: "Don't you have an opinion?"

"Oh," said Shishnik. He nodded rapidly. Then he clasped his hands together and looked at the Baron. "Opinion. Yes. Exactly. We must have a funeral. That is my opinion. She once told me, apropos of nothing, that she detested the thought of burial. She preferred cremation. She menioned that in Venice, when she was sick with amoebic dysentery, she gave instructions that her ashes were to be dropped in the Grand Canal. I am not sure that the Venetian authorities would have approved of such a ceremony. Still, she leaned toward cremation. We must burn Lily's body."

The Baron lowered his head and stared intently at his fingernails. "I don't think you have grasped the point, quite. What I meant was the following. Have you formed any opinion on the manner of her death, Professor Shishnik?"

The little monkey had been tied to the palm tree outside.

He had fallen asleep but now he suddenly woke up and started to scold, tugging angrily at the rope.

Shishnik blinked and scowled a little. He looked at the Baron and quickly away again. "She was stabbed to the heart, poor Lily. Is that what you meant?"

There was a queer little pause. The Baron glared at the Professor and the latter, suddenly embarrassed, fumbled nervously with his beard.

The Baron bared his teeth. "There is no question that she was stabbed. I think we can assume that it was a knife rather than a hatchet. I looked about for a knife but I failed to find one. All of the jewelry was removed from her body except for a pair of sapphire earrings. I found a bracelet, incidentally. Did I mention this to you? Some fifty yards from the body, half buried in the sand. We must be rational, objective. We must weigh each aspect separately. It is clear that the motive was robbery. Unless, of course, the appearance of robbery was intended to conceal some other and more sinister motive. It may even have been robbery *plus* one or more additional motives. Very well. Now the footprints. What would the footprints seem to indicate? They clearly indicate that Lily walked from her hut across the dunes and then in a reasonably straight line toward the spot where you found her. What was she doing? What was she up to? Was she looking for somebody? And if so, whom?"

Shishnik turned around quickly, as though to see if someone was listening. Then he peered at the Baron with a sudden glint of slyness.

"Looking for someone. Yes. Quite. Do continue, please, Baron."

Flies were gathering in the little hut. They started to settle on the corpse, which was spotted with stains of sand-encrusted blood. A breeze had come up, wafting the sea smell into the hut, where it mingled with the musky, wolflike odor of Mrs. Domingo.

"There are numerous possibilities, if you pause to think," said the Baron solemnly. "We must form a hypothesis about this second set of footprints. They come creeping out of the ocean, so far as I can determine, and follow the dunes toward a biggish tree not far from the hut. Here they turn at a very sharp angle, swerve about in a parabola, and head in a line for that very spot which I mentioned previously. They seem to skirmish around a bit and then to skirt the edge of the water. They form some curious patterns—little scallops and zigzags. Finally they creep into the sea again some twenty yards from the rocks. Now, we have no proof at all about the relative timing of these various footprints. Lily's footprints could have either preceded or followed those other footprints. If we learned the identity of those footprints it might throw some light on the matter. Maybe Lily heard a noise. I can hardly believe it was a deliberate rendezvous. She may have heard somebody crawling or shuffling in the darkness. She was restless at night. Sometimes she thought she was hearing burglars. One night in Calcutta she swore that a burglar was in the room. Forgive me for mentioning this. I am merely groping for light on the matter. In any case, Lily got up from her mat and walked out of the hut. We shall never know why. You were lying in your hammock all this while, I take it? You sleep soundly, I have noticed. Lily told me that you snore. This detail might seem irrelevant, but we must leave no stone unturned. Where were we? Ah, yes. The identity of the footprints. Do you have any theories?"

Professor Shishnik was staring at the Baron with a gentle bewilderment. "Identity? What do you mean? Must footprints always have a definite identity?"

The Baron looked vexed. It was very hot in the hut. Sweat was flowing down his cheeks and dripping from his silky black mustache. "Well, *these* footprints certainly had an identity. They weren't just figments of our fancy. I think we can say that the owner of those footprints was the very individual who stabbed poor Lily. Note, I say *individual*. I have jumped at no conclusions. I have studied these footprints carefully. They are considerably smaller than mine and a trifle narrower than yours. There is an abnormally big gap between the big toe and the other toes. Who are the candidates, Professor? We can go through the list. One of our group may have mysteriously returned to the peninsula. Billy Baxter I exclude. The footprints are too large. I thought fleetingly of Miss Eccles. Nothing is impossible, you must remember. It wouldn't be the first time that the jungle has transformed a harmless female into a homicidal maniac. I exclude the Wagensellers and their friend. They had no intention of coming back here. That leaves Ibrahim. Ibrahim strikes me as a clear-cut possibility, since we have no final proof that he has actually perished."

"Oh, yes. Ibrahim," said the Professor. His voice shook slightly. "He seemed so gentle."

"Lily claimed that she had seen a shape on top of that rock once or twice. She went so far as to suggest that this shape might be Ibrahim. What do you think about it, Professor?"

"I do not remember," said the Professor, "ever seeing such a shape. Our poor Lily was given to a variety of optical misconceptions."

"Our list is almost at an end. Three possibilities are still left to us," said the Baron.

"Three. Ahem," said Professor Shishnik. He raised three fingers and nodded owlishly.

"First. A savage from the jungle. Perhaps you were wondering why I failed to mention this. It seems more plausible, all in all, than any of these other speculations. A savage would be more likely to arrive from the inlet than the sea, but this same paradox would also apply to the rest of our candidates.

Somehow this notion of a murderous savage suddenly popping out of nowhere—well, I leave it to you, Professor. It seems grossly improbable."

The Professor had slumped over and was leaning against a pole. He held his hand pressed to his chest. Drops were rolling down his cheeks, but whether they were tears or drops of sweat was hard to tell. The Baron frowned impatiently, straightened his back, and went on rapidly.

"Second possibility. Have you ever considered that there may be other survivors of the *Cassandra?* It seemed unlikely at the time. Still, we have no way of knowing. It's quite possible that some of the passengers may have floated in their lifebelts to some other relatively habitable spot on the coast. Lily's monumental jewels were no secret on board the ship. If there *were* such survivors, it seems quite likely that someone unscrupulous, on learning of Lily's presence here, might decide to take advantage of it!"

The Baron had been speaking with great care and deliberation. The more absurd each theory became, the more persuasive his tone. Only the muscles of his face gave a hint of hysteria. His jaw started to twitch. There was a tic in his left eyelid. He took a deep breath and carefully stroked his mustache.

Then he went on. "Are you listening, Professor? You may feel this is academic. There is nothing we can do which will bring her back to life. But as civilized human beings we have certain obligations. Whatever happens, we must be calm. We must be lucid, analytical. We must not let ourselves be sucked into an emotional whirlpool. I hope you understand. I have no wish to seem frigid. This is a crisis. We must face it with all possible circumspection."

He pursed his lips, slapped at a fly, and thrust his head forward a little.

"Very well. What was I saying? Oh. The final conjecture.

I am excluding under the circumstances the possibility of suicide. I never detected in Lily any suicidal tendencies, and these wounds do not strike me as being self-inflicted. We come to our last hypothesis. I hope you are still following me. I have made every effort to be clear and mathematical. Let us face it, Professor. None of these theories seems convincing. Some of them less than others, maybe, but they all seem a little mythical. What remains? The myth itself. We are in the presence of the supernatural. In moments like this we must thrust aside the pedantries of science. I made a study of spiritual phenomena while I was living in Vienna. In a single year, in the city of Vienna, fifty-one murders remained unsolved. The victims were found bludgeoned, shot, strangled, stabbed, decapitated. But the murderer was never found. No murderer could be found. Why not? I shall tell you. The answer is astonishingly simple. In our castle near Klagenfurt we had a rather mischievous poltergeist. He threw an inkwell one evening at my Aunt Mathilda, ruining her dress. There is no question that ghosts exist. The evidence of the centuries is overwhelming. In these primitive eastern regions the powers of darkness are even greater. Many volumes have been written about it. In 1873 Dr. Von Seydwitz, the noted explorer, was strangled on the island of Lombok by a flying phantom in the presence of witnesses. Ghosts exist. I repeat it. And curiously enough, though invisible for the most part, ghosts leave footprints behind them. They can also wield weapons. Well, Professor, there you are. I have nothing more to say. Please reflect on my humble suggestions. We must form an opinion. Our lives depend on it."

5

Miss Eccles sat in the corner of her hut with half-closed eyes. She was watching a chameleon crawling slowly across the ceiling. The voices of the children playing leapfrog in the piazza mingled with the buzzing of a hornet which was circling around the oven.

A brisk young woman named Kandyale had replaced the surly Kayakalali. She tapped Miss Eccles on the shoulder and pointed to the shadow which darkened the doorway.

"Djungalali," she whispered.

"Yes. I see," said Miss Eccles.

Herr Krauss sat down by the oven with an air of reproachfulness. "Good evening, Miss Eccles. I have come to pay my respects."

"I am not interested in your respects, thank you kindly," said Miss Eccles.

"I hope sincerely," said Herr Krauss, "that you do not bear me a grudge, Miss Eccles. Please remember, I am merely an agent. I merely try to facilitate matters. Without my efforts, certain things might have happened a bit more crudely." He glanced sidelong at Miss Eccles, as though waiting for her reaction. He took off his glasses, wiped them absently, and put them on again. He peered at his fingers, suddenly embarrassed, and cleared his throat.

"I don't intend," he went on rapidly, trying to hide his agitation, "to discuss this little matter of Kayakalali. I've maintained strict impartiality. Not that they care especially, mind you. Kayakalali was a filthy old shrew and they all detested her. All the same, morally speaking, I don't feel that your case is impregnable."

Miss Eccles drew her palm over her forehead and nodded.

"You are perfectly right, Herr Krauss. I have nothing to complain of. Nothing at all."

Since her flight and recapture Miss Eccles had been treated with surprising deference. She was still a prisoner in the hut, which now was guarded by two garrulous warriors, but she was treated with considerably more politeness than before. The food was much better: chicken and pork instead of stale cassava bread, grapefruits and bananas instead of half-rotten yams. She was allowed to wear her dress and even her slippers. Arrangements were made for her bodily needs. Three more fingers had been chopped from her hand, one each day, by the man with the leopard skin, but it was done without malice, with an almost apologetic air. Her hand was a bloody stump but a dark green salve, surprisingly effective, was rubbed on her wounds to relieve the pain.

Her new servant, Kandyale, was a bit of a scatterbrain but she treated Miss Eccles with what looked like affection. The villagers were growing used to her. One of the boys, Mandamabwale, aware of her interest in insects, brought her some frayed little moths wrapped in a palm leaf. She gave up speculating about the future; she applied her energies to her morale and said to herself periodically, "Take it easy, Pen," or "Chin up, Eccles."

"If you could only," Herr Krauss continued with a pleading look in his eyes, "if you could only grasp the essence, penetrate into the heart of things, Miss Eccles. These people are far from cruel. They merely do what they feel is necessary. You are not an ordinary woman and yours is not an ordinary fate. Born for suffering, you were. Born for the sublimity of sacrifice! After all, life is filth, life is cruelty, life is horror. Is this wrong? Who can answer? Since it is so, it must be intended to be so. You are suffering? We were made to suffer. You are afraid? We were made for fear. Man is filth, cruelty, terror, understand that, Miss Eccles, but in this very filth and cruelty he is not only pitiable but pure. He is a part of the permeating splendor. You must grasp that, Miss Eccles!" He paused, stared at her fiercely, and went on in his thin dry voice: "This life of yours, what has it been? Pirouettes in a vacuum! Nothing more! You know it as well as I do. Just a swishing at butterflies. No, Miss Eccles, you must be reasonable. What you are abandoning wasn't life; it was merely a pretense of life. It was just an aimless fluttering about with no climax in sight, no culmination."

"Must we look for culminations?" said Miss Eccles rather aridly.

"We all look for a culmination, day after day, year in, year out. A few achieve it. Most of us don't. You are one of the happy few. It is clear that you are destined for a culmination, my good Miss Eccles." Herr Krauss got up wearily. He looked depleted, a little blurred. "The chieftain, whose name is Kyule, has asked me to bring you a message. You are leaving tomorrow morning for the Mountain of the Illustrious Rain Bird. No strangers, no white people, have ever been allowed to visit the Rain Bird. I have been asked by Kyule to inform you of the splendor of the occasion. It is only proper, says Kyule, that you should be aware of the privilege and the grandeur."

A wistful look of envy passed over his skull-like face for a moment. Then he said in a parrotlike tone, "Good-by, Miss Eccles, and bon voyage. I can only say that I rejoice with you in your exceptional opportunity!"

After he left, the girl Kandyale brought her the customary jug of kava. Miss Eccles had come to hanker for her thrice-daily kava, which warmed her thinning body and washed away the pain and anxiety. She sipped at the jug, then folded her arms and gazed at the doorway.

She immediately recognized the tall, lithe silhouette of Bundule as he entered the hut. She smiled at him and nodded as he knelt down beside her. A sudden trembling swept through her body, her eyes grew blinded with tears, and her breath came in spasms as she whispered "Bundule! My Bundule!"

The young savage leaned over and pressed his face between her breasts. She felt the warmth of his lips and the pounding of his heart against her ribs and then the pressure of the phallus and the quick, hot jet of seed on her belly. He rose silently and went tiptoeing out of the hut, and Miss Eccles lay back on her mat and abandoned herself to her dreams.

She found herself climbing a black stony hill. On top of the hill was a squat, round tower. She knocked at the door of the tower, tense and exultant, trembling with eagerness. A head appeared at the window. "Whom do you want?" said a high-pitched voice, which belonged to a fat little man who was dressed like an abbot. She was at a loss for an answer, and cried out desperately, "This is my home! I've been walking for days! Let me in! Let me in!" The door opened slowly and she entered a vaulted anteroom from which a winding stairway led down into the darkness. She climbed down the stairs and came to a cavernlike pit which was filled with filth and blood, dismembered arms and bleeding torsos. In a corner, barely visible, squatted a large black gorilla.

"Well, you've come," said the gorilla.

"It's not I, it's somebody else!"

"What do you mean, somebody else? It's *you* I'm looking at. Why are you lying?"

"I've changed," cried Miss Eccles, clutching her throat. "I'm another person."

"Stuff and nonsense," said the gorilla, and he lumbered slowly toward her.

Miss Eccles, with a violent effort, tore herself out of her nightmare. She woke up. Kandyale was crouching by the oven, stirring a pot. Somewhere or other a bird was singing in a high, brassy tone. Miss Eccles knew that her dream was a kind of vision, induced by the kava, but she sensed that these visions were also a part of a deeper reality. "It is true," she reflected. "My whole texture has changed. I have crawled out of a cocoon. I am spreading my wings. I am turning into a butterfly. It won't last long, but does it matter? What matters is the metamorphosis. What matters is the glorious burst of a new identity. . . ."

6

The river was still covered with a layer of mist when they reached the shore, but even through the mist they could see its slow-flowing immensity.

"God," said Laura. "It's almost as wide as the Mississippi, isn't it, darling?"

"Or the Nile," said Tony, scowling. "Reminds me of the Nile a bit, somehow."

Their voices were dry and broken, like little chips of celluloid. Each of them was trying forlornly to comfort the other, Laura realized. They staggered down to the edge of the river and crouched on the sand. Laura leaned over feebly and caught sight of her face in the water. "A gnome," she thought indifferently. "I've shriveled into a hideous little gnome." She dipped her hands in the river and washed the mud from her arms. Then she splashed the water listlessly over her thin, scabby legs.

She turned and looked at Tony: big red patches on his cheeks, lips slackened in an idiot grin, features twisted into a clownlike anguish. His skin was the color of a coconut. He was shivering with cold. She placed her hand on his forearm. "There. The worst of it's over, darling."

The sun rose and the mist grew luminous. The shore was

littered with lunatic driftwood and large bearded rocks which gave the place an air of absurdity.

It vaguely occurred to her that she might have died already without being aware of it, that decades had passed and she was floating in the fogs of limbo. A sand flea bit her ankle; she knew she was still alive. But the notion persisted that many years had silently elapsed and that she was drifting, ugly and gnomelike, through the chaos of purgatory.

Tony clutched at a rock, crawled forward, rose to his feet. "Come," he said. "No use waiting. We've got to try. We've got to find something."

He tugged weakly at Laura's arm, then lifted her gently. He looked into her eyes for an instant: an unseeing and slightly crazy look, yet she felt that for the first time in his life he was really aware of her. She tried to smile. "Perfectly right. No use waiting. Let's get going."

They followed the shore. There were no trees, not even palms, only tufts of yellowish thistle and occasional bamboos. The sun rose swiftly higher; the light grew ferocious. She felt her arms itching crazily, as though bitten by thousands of mosquitoes. The sweat on her thighs felt like slow-dripping poison and the pain in her eyeballs grew so sharp that it nearly blinded her. Her legs moved like sticks, stiff, anaesthetized, ready to crack. "What does it matter?" she thought suddenly. "Life. Death. It's nearly the same. What's so wonderful about being alive? Sleep, peace—that's what's wonderful. . . ."

Tony came to a halt abruptly. "There! Listen! Do you hear it?" A low vibration, like the purring of an enormous cat, stirred the air. Laura looked at the sky. Very faintly, through swollen lids, she saw a silver wasp high above, heading directly for the sun.

"O God," she cried hoarsely. "Can they see us? Do you think they can see us?"

The plane moved slowly on through the appalling blueness of the sky. Tony beat his arms frantically and screamed, "They've got to! Christ, they've got to!"

But the plane swam past the sun and over the hills toward the snow-capped mountains. For one more minute the throb of its motors hung in the air, then died away.

"Well, that's that," said Tony quietly. "Come. Relax. We'll rest awhile."

They headed for a clump of skeletal bushes and crouched, lame and panting, in the feathery shade.

"Yes," thought Laura. "At last. This is really and truly it. This is what it's like, that last exit, not really caring and almost hoping, but then clutching like a maniac at the falling curtain. One last glorious frenzy. . . . Poor old Tony. Poor little Tony." She lay absolutely still, breathing slowly, counting her heartbeats, calmly nursing the last microscopical shred of energy still left in her. "Thirty-five," she muttered vacuously. "Thirty-six. Thirty-seven." She grasped at that moment how close she had come to utter negation, how much this land of putrescence had become a part of her soul, and how finally something new, too late, unfortunately, had sprung from the misery. Truth, was it? Or merely wisdom? Was it love? Or merely acceptance? She felt poised in midair like a spider on its web. Ready to dart but still waiting, still watching, expectant.

7

It was midafternoon. Something woke her out of her sleep. Tony lay on his side with his face pressed into the sand. She wondered: "Is he dead?" But then she saw that he was breathing. She laid her palm gently on his red, burning forehead.

Then she heard it. It wasn't the throbbing of a plane this time, she realized. She peered through the bamboo stalks. The air was brilliantly clear. Something dark moved over the water as the noise of the motor grew more powerful. Slowly the boat crawled through the sunlight, half hidden by the bushes, like a shiny blue beetle crawling on a pane of yellow glass.

"Come," she said. "Wake up, darling." Tony opened his bloodshot eyes. She looked at him placidly. "It's all right. It's all over." Suddenly her lips began to quiver and she screamed at him wildly, "Oh, for God's sake, do you hear me? They've come, they've come, I'm telling you!"

8

The Professor washed the corpse and tied the hair in a big black knot. Then he lowered the eyelids and closed the gaping jaws. He tucked a white orchid in each of her hands and scattered pink magnolia blossoms over her breast. Finally he squatted next to the body and folded his arms with a great sigh. Through the doorway he saw the Baron building a fire below the dunes. The heat of the day had passed, the fierce oppression had gone from the air. A cool evening breeze was beginning to ruffle the sea.

He bent down and stroked the dead woman's forehead very lightly. The face looked quite peaceful in repose, almost happy. He peeped through the door to see whether the Baron was looking and then quickly, almost guiltily, kissed the corpse on the lips.

Then he crouched in a corner and stared fixedly at the ground. His body started to shake; his face grew queerly twisted. A hoarse little whine rose from the bottom of his throat.

The Baron entered the hut. "Come," he said. "The fire is ready."

They picked up the corpse, the Baron at the shoulders and Shishnik at the legs, and carried it down the dunes toward the bright, crackling fire. Two big logs lay side by side in the middle of the fire and they silently placed the dead body on top of them. They looked quickly away as the flames snapped at the corpse, licking deftly at the golden apron, bursting in a crown from the head of hair.

And at that moment a blaze of light shot up from the hills beyond the jungle, turning the long wisps of cloud into a swarm of fiery sea serpents. It seemed to Shishnik that the sun and the mountains and the whole wild universe had burst into a paean of mourning for the death of Mrs. Domingo.

"Our poor Lily," said the Baron. "She had her flaws but she was generous."

"She was brave, and quite clever. Yes, and beautiful," said the Professor.

"Here we are. And all we can utter is stupid platitudes," said the Baron.

"If I knew how to pray, I would pray," murmured Shishnik.

Night fell. The flames shot up, scattering their brilliance over the water. The Baron said "Good night" and wandered back over the dunes. The Professor stayed by the fire, tossing twigs on the flames. Finally he mustered up the courage to look down at the blackened corpse. It was no longer recognizable as the body of a woman. Only the teeth, exposed in a snarl, were still left to remind Professor Shishnik of the one great passion in his lonely existence.

9

The Baron stared at the brilliant moon and then scrawled hurriedly in his diary:

The day has finally arrived. The Furies are on their way. I can hear the flapping of their wings in the distance. But the verdict still hangs in the balance. What will it be? Black or white? Omnipotence or madness? Illumination or chaos?

10

The flames finally died. Professor Shishnik rose to his feet. The moon hung over the sea. It must be midnight, he decided. He glanced guiltily at the crumbling ashes, vaguely troubled by something or other. He had a feeling that there was something that still needed to be done. He thought of snatching a handful of ashes out of the embers. But he gave up the notion and went lumbering toward the grove.

The Baron was sitting motionless in the doorway of the hut. He stared blankly at Shishnik without seeming to recognize him. The light of the moon shone on his naked body—the skeleton-thin legs, the dark and jutting ribs. Shishnik was struck all of a sudden by the saintlike beauty of the Baron's face—the sharp ascetic features, with the skin stretched over the bones, the delicately flaring nostrils and the Dürer-like mouth, and above all the eyes, with their gleam of mystical intensity, as though a candle were burning behind the tiny black pupils.

"It is late," said Shishnik gently. "You are tired. You should sleep."

The Baron looked startled and then suddenly agitated. "Sleep, you say? How can I sleep? With this terror hanging over me! Day after day, night after night!" His arms were trembling, his voice grew feverish. He dug his fists in the sand and shouted, "Do you realize what is happening? Oh, believe me, my good Shishnik, this isn't just an ordinary island! I have long suspected it. Now I am sure. Our very souls are threatened, I tell you! By the Powers of Darkness, nothing less! Do you know the things I've seen? Giant lizards crawling through the slime! Bushes spreading their claws! I've heard them whispering and muttering, I've smelled their stinking breath! They are closing in on us, Shishnik, they are lusting for vengeance, I tell you! Oh, I've struggled! I've fought! I've been plodding through this heat, chopping wood, carrying water, doing my daily acrobatics! But these powers are stronger than we. Those dunes out there—just look at them, Shishnik! They are turning into dinosaurs! Do you know what is going to happen? One by one they've been dragged away, black and white, young and old. Finally last night it was poor Lily. Who is left? Just you and me! Listen to me, Shishnik! The time has come! We are the last of the sacrificial victims! It was us that they were saving for the last bloody massacre!"

"Please calm yourself," said the Professor. "It has been a sad and trying day for you."

"Calm, you say?" shrieked the Baron. "All my life I've tried to be calm! I've looked for the true reality—oh, so patiently and systematically! I've tried to strip off the veils and lay my eyes on the shivering nakedness! I've tried to pierce into the core, the real enigma of humanity! And what do I find? Treachery! Servility! Bestial appetites and bloody murder! Please don't ask me to be calm! Only an idiot could be calm!"

At this point the little monkey, who was tied to a palm, woke up from his sleep. Something or other—the Baron's voice, maybe—struck him with sudden terror. He let out a high warbling scream, like that of a hysterical woman.

The Baron's arms grew rigid; he gritted his teeth. Then he sprang to his feet and howled, *"Ekelhaftes Vieh!"* He ran into the grove, ripped the cord from the palm, and while Shishnik stood dazed with horror, he seized the monkey with both hands, wrenched it violently by the neck, and hurled the body behind the rock.

He turned and stared at Shishnik with a blind, brainless look. Then he stalked through the grove down toward the water, stiff as a mantis.

11

On the edge of the sea a feeble glow still rose from the ashes. Higher up an ugly moon was dropping shadows over the dunes. The palms rose tall and blue, every leaf distinctly visible. The Baron groaned faintly. His whole body was soaked in sweat. He turned sharply, heading for the water. It was then that he saw Shishnik.

At first it was only a fleck on the edge of the dunes, no bigger than a weasel. It spread, it dilated. It resembled a tapir, and then a rhinoceros. He could see the little eyes shining brutishly in the distance. Yes. At last. He understood. What an idiot he had been! Shishnik was far from being the plodding mediocrity he had supposed, the wide-eyed intellectual patiently following his instructions. He grasped it in a flash. He had noticed the clues, he had sensed the danger—oh, that Dostoevskian innocence, so beautifully fradulent! He had let himself be trapped. He had misconstrued that look of bewilderment. All his theories about Shishnik—voyeur, gerontophile, narcotics agent, spy, frustrated sodomite—had been childishly naïve, grotesquely beside the point. All the while, with infinite care, under this guise of soft-eyed scholarship, reading his *Odyssey*, studying his shells, sketching plants, picking flowers, Shishnik had been planning this whole baroque hierarchy of murders. Powers of Darkness! It was nothing of the sort. It was merely the explosion of a homicidal maniac.

Everything fell into place. The horrible puzzle was solved. All those curious disappearances—they had their own macabre logic. And Lily! Those footprints! Nothing but a diabolical hoax. It was Shishnik who was the murderer. Now he was out for the final kill.

Shishnik's shadow dipped and vanished for a moment behind a dune. Then he slowly reappeared, first the head, then the torso. A hundred yards away, perhaps. Was there time? Did he have the strength?

He crawled over the ledge and peered down at the moonlit cove. Then he twisted his way into the shadowless grotto.

12

Shishnik paused on top of the ledge, then slowly climbed into the cove. He knelt by the sea and dipped his arms in the water. He was panting with exhaustion. He clutched at a stone, shivered, and vomited. His eyes were blurred with tears. He slumped on the rock and started to sob.

He was incapable of thought. He stared half blindly at the stars. The warm, tingling teardrops were rolling down his neck. His mind recoiled from the crazy atrocity of all that had happened. He instinctively refused even to speculate on how it had happened. He sniffed at the salty stones, trying to shake off the nausea. His heart beat less painfully. He looked up and searched for the Dipper.

It was then that he heard the voice. "Shishnik! Listen!

Please be reasonable! We're cut off from the rest of the world! We're far away from that lunatic struggle! It's just you and me. We are the only ones who are left. Who knows, Shishnik, maybe the bombs are already beginning to drop and the whole of Europe is locked in a suicidal agony!"

Shishnik looked about mechanically. There was nothing to be seen. He lifted his head and stared at the mouth of the grotto.

The voice lapsed into a wheedling, obsequious whimper. "Listen, Shishnik. Be sensible. I know perfectly well what you think of me. You think I'm a miserable fragment of a worn-out civilization. You're right, what's more. That's all I am. Just a rotten bundle of stale obsessions. But listen. There's still hope for us. You're the lord of this island now. You're the all-controlling master. And you need a slave. I'll be your slave, Shishnik. You can't survive all by yourself on this fiendish peninsula. I have a suggestion. Let's cooperate. Let's pitch in together and make a team. Oh, I'll admit that I was wrong. In my idiotic arrogance I regarded you as my spiritual and cultural inferior. How wrong I was! You're a genius, Shishnik! I'm barely fit to grovel at your feet. Infallibly accurate in your appraisals, unerringly keen in your intuition! I've learned to feel a genuine reverence for your mental capacities. I might even be of use to you in my role as a menial. After all, I'm no fool. I'll help to enshrine you as a formidable despot. When we're finally rescued—oh, we're bound to be rescued, Shishnik —I'll help you establish a new society which will mirror the world of your dreams. What we need is a whole new system based on the wisdom of a single authority. That authority will be you. Your word will be law. Limitless power, modulated only by the fluctuations of your marvelous insight. All the upstarts will be ruthlessly executed. If someone protests, we'll chop off his head. Your loftiest visions will be exquisitely materialized. I'll be your Sancho Panza—I beg your pardon, I mean your Talleyrand, your Metternich. I'll slave unremittingly to make you the Master of the Universe, whatever is left of it!"

Shishnik stared into the grotto. He sighed and shook his head. "It is madness," he whispered sadly. "Utter, absolute madness."

And the thought of the miserable lunatic howling into the night filled him with pity. He got up from the rock and groped his way toward the grotto.

13

Shishnik peered into the grotto. "Baron," he whispered. "Are you there?"

He heard the sound of a pebble rolling. Then a deep, half-muffled groan. Something long and dark, pantherlike, sprang forth from the blackness. Shishnik ducked rather clumsily, then went scrambling toward the rock. He felt a violent blow on his head and dropped to his knees with a sickly grunt. The hot naked body was squirming crazily on top of him, digging its knees into his groin, tightening its arms around his neck. He hurled himself sideways and struck out with his elbow. Sweat poured down his belly, thick and slippery as oil. He thrust up his legs and wrapped them powerfully around the waist. Then with sudden ferocity he sank his teeth into the gullet. There was a shuddering and a wheezing. Shishnik freed his arms in a spasm and buried his fingers in the throat of the shriveling Baron. There was a noise like crackling celluloid; the body fell in his arms. The sad, broken face pressed its lips to his breast.

Shishnik lay on his back, whimpering faintly, like a puppy. Finally he rose to his knees and crawled to the water on all fours. Very gently, almost dreamily, he washed the blood from his body, and the thick alien slime, which exuded a smell of toads.

PART VIII

The Gods

1

They started before dawn. A heavy mist filled the valley.
They were walking through the shrubs along the edge of a
grassy meadow. Miss Eccles could see the figures very faintly
through the mist—the feathers on their heads, the catlike
masks, the horns and the antlers. They were carrying her in a
litter made of bamboo twigs and raffia. Through the mist a
yellowish glare was beginning to burn, and then the air grew
suddenly hot and almost suffocating. When they came to the
end of the valley the sun came out, the mist dissolved. They
started to climb the half-dried bed of a stony torrent.

They climbed all morning long through thickets of fern
and great euphorbia trees. The snow-capped peaks of the
mountains grew more and more vivid. At noon they stopped
for a rest in a grove of flowering tree ferns, where the grass had
been trampled into the mud by numerous hoof prints. Miss
Eccles stared indifferently at her fingerless hand: the swelling
had subsided, the wounds were healing. There was no pain.

After an hour they stretched their arms and started off
into the hills again. The heat was appalling but as they
climbed the air grew fresher. The litter bearer in front of her
was shining with sweat, which emitted a piquant, faintly
limelike aroma. His buttocks kept moving with a serpentine
motion. The muscles on his back shone a brilliant deep violet.
She lay back and watched the patterns of the leaves overhead.
They spread over the path like big golden feathers.

She heard a noise in the distance which was like the
chanting of many voices, and this was answered from across
the valley by a rapid beating of drums. Groups of newcomers
stepped from the forest and joined the straggling procession.
They had come a long way. They were caked with dust and

streaming with sweat. They kept staring and pointing at a spot on the horizon: a barren, black hump silhouetted against the larger hills beyond.

The drumbeats rolled on with the sound of wandering thunder. The procession grew longer as it crawled up the mountains. There was a gleam of dark turmoil, a stench of animal expectancy. Even the light that seeped through the leaves looked somehow awed and alert. Some of the hillmen seemed to be of a different blood from the men of the valley: smaller and uglier, with scrawny bow legs and wizened little faces. Some wore cockatoo feathers, others the plumes of a bird-of-paradise. Now and then there was a man with a wig made out of an owl's head, and one wore a showering headdress made from the wings of a cassowary. Now some women were beginning to join: squat and pendulous little creatures with bags on their backs where their babies nestled on pandanus leaves. And now a new tribe stepped through the trees: they were glittering with boar grease, their foreheads were painted green and their eyes were ringed with yellow. These men wore little tufts of withered palm leaves tied to their backs, which quivered and bobbed like pony tails as they walked.

The path became stony. The trees grew stunted and ceased. They were approaching a rocky hilltop, thimble-shaped, surrounded by cliffs. The path zigzagged upward through flinty crags and deep abysses. The heat was beginning to tell. The men looked haggard and hollow-eyed and the women had fallen behind, wailing gently in unison. Miss Eccles felt the spell of the horde creeping over her. She lay motionless in her litter, struggling to retain some separate awareness, but then she grew somnolent, submerged in the tribal rhythms.

Three men stood on the peak, waiting to welcome the sweating mob. One wore a bib of cowrie shells, which kept clattering like a coat-of-mail. One wore a necklace of opossum

tails interspersed with long black feathers. The third wore
the magnificent, shimmering plumes of a lyrebird, which
curved up from a headband of crimson scarab beetles.

The pilgrims settled down for a rest in the shade of rocks.
They drank from hollow gourds and wiped their bodies with
bits of hide. The sun was about to set. The air grew ruddy,
pepper-scented, and the sight of the enveloping mountains,
tier upon tier, was spectacularly lovely. Kyule, the chieftain
from the valley, took Miss Eccles by the hand and led her to
an oval-shaped rock, where some leopard skins were spread
and two old women were crouching silently. Nearby the man
with the opossum tails was building a fire. Puffs of dull
brownish smoke were beginning to jet through the branches.

The ceremony was about to begin. The man with the
cowrie shells approached. He was a patriarchal figure, with
tangled hair down to his shoulders and eyes like an orangu-
tan's, shifty but fastidious. The two women stripped Miss
Eccles and held her firmly by the arms while he deftly, almost
tenderly, pressed the knife against her breast. He started to
whisper to her in a mild, pleading tone and then with a
piglike grunt dug at the flesh and severed the nipple. Miss
Eccles gave out a scream. But the pain subsided instantly and
she lay motionless and passive, watching with cold, indifferent
eyes. What she felt wasn't horror, nor rage nor disgust, it was a
kind of flowering amazement which lifted her out of her
misery, a sense of disembodiment, of secret supremacy. The
drumbeats started again. Night had fallen. The flames shot
skyward. The pilgrims raised their arms, rolled their eyes,
swayed ecstatically.

Now the man with the lyre feathers, the oldest of the
three, approached Miss Eccles. He limped closer; he was
carrying an elephant's tusk in his arms. Now he stood close
beside her, muttering some sort of prayer: a prayer to the
Illustrious Rain Bird, presumably. Miss Eccles, as she lay

there, noticed the veins in his thin black legs and the leaflike skin of his scrotum, the long, shriveled foreskin. He lifted the ivory phallus, which gleamed in the light of the flames, and thrust it, gently at first, then more and more feverishly into her body. Queerly enough, she felt nothing at all. She felt brittle and dry as an insect. Her arms started to vibrate, huge and white, thin as mica. She felt herself soaring higher and higher, toward the Trees of Paradise, and the earth far below grew gray and tiny, like a spinning top.

2

"Really amazing," said Mr. Amesbury as he wiped his brow thoughtfully. He was a pink, protuberant man with a fuzzy red mustache. "It's the first time that a civilized man's been in those hills, to the best of my knowledge. Oh, mind you, I'm not saying that there's anything fantastic about them. Nothing at all compared to some of the stuff I've seen around here. Over in the western part especially. Leeches as big as your fist. Still, it's, well . . . rather remarkable." He glanced at Tony benevolently, then crossed the room, took off his glasses and stared at the map which was pinned to the wall.

Outside, in the dusty street, there was a steady sound of hammering. Two boys were fitting a corrugated roof onto a shed. A whistle blew feebly down in the L-shaped harbor and then suddenly the alarm clock on the desk started to ring.

"Wretched noise," said Mr. Amesbury, flicking irritably at the clock. "Everything's hideously organized here. Can't trust a soul. Climate, naturally."

Someone knocked on the door. A pock-marked woman in a pink bandana came shuffling apprehensively into the room. She placed a tea tray on the desk and peered furtively at Laura.

Mr. Amesbury said wearily, "Milk or lemon? There. Some biscuits. It's nothing lucullan, but your stomachs need a bit of a rest, I imagine." He glanced at Laura uneasily. "You're looking better already. No doubt about it. Rather a relief to me. Quite frankly, I was pretty shocked by your appearance yesterday evening. Quite a thing you've been through, isn't it? Those people aren't as dangerous as we like to think, but all the same, it's no joke about that friend of yours, is it? I wonder what those idiots were thinking about. Scared to death of you, probably. I've been in Atawake three years now and I've never known a case of it. Downright murder, I mean. They're not quarrelsome by nature. Unpredictable, I'd call them, but definitely not violent. Over in the western part it's different. They still claim there's a tribe of headhunters. Well, be that as it may, we all keep trying to make the best of it. There's no meeting of minds. Never will be, what's more. Some say it's only the climate, but take my word, it's more than the climate. It's the blood. It's the race. It's those centuries of absolute savagery. Can't just cure it at the drop of a hat, even with the noblest of intentions. I don't want to start off on a political tangent, Mr. Wagenseller, but I'll tell you right now, it's these noble intentions that are ruining the world. Good things for all and sundry—liberty, equality, a car, and a frigidaire. That's the size of it. Lots of idealistic chatter and underneath it greed and envy. You don't care much for your tea, I see. Maybe you'd like something to drink? Wouldn't mind a bit myself. . . . Watabe! Watabe! . . . Where's that woman?"

The head in the pink bandana peered through the door rather coquettishly. "Mizza Ambasri? You call?"

"What will you have?" said Mr. Amesbury. He smiled at Laura affably. "Gin and lime? Whisky and soda? I don't have any vermouth, unfortunately."

"A whisky, I think," said Laura.

"Thanks," said Tony. "Whisky. Definitely."

"Queer thing about the *Cassandra*, wasn't it? Can't get over it, seeing you sitting here. We heard about it on the wireless the morning after it happened. Not a trace, no lifeboats, nothing. They sent some planes from somewhere or other. It might have been Port Moresby. Or maybe it was Madang. Couple of ships went poking around a bit. Rather odd that they didn't spot you. You must have drifted further than they bothered to make allowance for. These things do happen occasionally. Idiotic, but what can you do? There was a Dutch boat that vanished one fine morning in the Marquesas. The *Pieter de Hooch*, it was. Never heard from again. Gross incompetence all around, not to call it criminal negligence. Takes more than just a thing or two going cockeyed to explain it. Well, those friends of yours are probably sitting in a plane this very minute. We got in contact with the airfield at Matabawake at six A.M. There's no question about the location. Shouldn't take more than a couple of hours. Well, now that the whole thing's over I kind of envy you, frankly. You've got a story that will last you till the end of your days, Mr. Wagenseller!"

"I dare say," said Tony wanly. He peered at the ice in his tumbler. "There were things one would like to forget. It wasn't just plain, unadulterated heroism."

Laura smiled. It was like a wrinkle in a sheet of yellow parchment. "No, it wasn't. Far from it. Still, there were things one would like to remember!"

3

"What is God?" thought the Professor. "Is he just a fantasy of man, concocted as an answer to the pitiful human need for comfort? Just to brush away his anguish and hide the

enormity of death? Or is God just another word for our sense
of insoluble mystery? Just an incantation to soothe our feeling
that there is no answer to our deepest questions? Or is He
merely a convenient symbol for the mighty tyranny of the
universe, whose laws we must accept but whose intentions we
can never fathom? I have no God. I have never had one. I
have studied God in a hundred forms. The Shark-God of
Ngulu, the Hippopotamus-God of Gunungapi. If our planet
burst into bits would there still be a God, as the believers
think of him? I have talked to thousands of men, many of
them good, some of them wise. Not one of all these thousands
made me feel that he believed in God. No, no, there is no God,
there is only a desperate need for God, a need so overwhelming that it has built out of thin air, in all these years of
human misery, something that much resembles a God. My
poor Yuri! My furry darling, did you too have your little God?
If nòt, I must invent one for you. Your life must find its meaning. I lived without love of any kind, my dear little Yuri,
until I came to this miserable island. And here I found love.
Three different loves, incredibly enough. A love for a woman,
rather bizarre, I suppose. A love for a child, a bit incongruous,
no doubt. And a love for all mankind, preposterous enough
certainly, springing as it did from a surge of pity for the man
whom I killed. I don't have the courage to pray for the first. I
lack the wisdom to pray for the third. All I can do is pray for
the second. I will pray for you, Yuri."

Yuri's grave was under the shadiest of the big euphorbia
trees. The Professor leaned over and brushed the grasses from
the mound and placed a blue orchid on a stone in the middle
of it. Then he muttered:

"O Kukuli, Lord of the Winds, come to our rescue!
"O Zanzu, Monarch of Dreams, calm our frenzies and restore
our innocence!
"O Tutuli, Ruler of Demons, draw the poison out of our

blood, pick the lice from our hair, dry the boils on our body!

"O Shali, Emperor of Beasts, deliver us from scorpions and leeches, banish the wasps, ward off the ticks, warn us of poisonous mosquitoes!

"O Koemamba, King of Tenacity, protect us from hunger, shade our flesh from the heat of the sun, lift our minds from the ocean's terror and frighten away the snakes of indifference!

"O Bulu, Child of the Sun, teach us to accept terror as an inevitable part of things, to draw fortitude from suffering, to find fulfillment in struggle, and to see comfort and even triumph in the bitter blackness of death!

"And finally, O Mandakala, Prince of Everlasting Night, reconcile us to our littleness, drive away the illusions of grandeur, teach us to accept all things as momentary and guide us gently into the coming darkness!"

He plucked a ripe banana, walked to the beach, and lay down in the hammock. Everything looked intensely calm—the waves lapped ever so gently, the palm leaves overhead swayed in the shell-scented air. He peeled the yellow fruit and munched away contentedly. Nothing troubled him any longer. There were no more questions to ask. He watched a spider dangling from a thread on the edge of the hammock and thought, "How very ingenious! What a lovable little beast!" Then he folded his arms, closed his eyes, and fell asleep.

He was awakened by a low, persistent buzzing in the air. For a moment he thought that a swarm of wasps had descended. It grew louder. He looked at the sea. Far-off thunder, could it be? Then he saw the lonely plane circling high over the coral reef, like a giant vulture. It turned about in a big parabola and headed directly for the promontory.

He glanced wistfully at the dunes, with their sickled, sunny solitude. One last look: the pyramid of boulders, blunt and gray, to the south, and the grove of bamboos, as delicate as plumes, in the north. He climbed out of the hammock with a sad little sigh and wandered reluctantly toward the flat, empty beach.